CARNAGE
OF EAGLES

D0047553

CARNAGE OF EAGLES

William W. Johnstone
with J. A. Johnstone

PINNACLE BOOKS
Kensington Publishing Corp.
www.kensingtonbooks.com

PINNACLE BOOKS are published by

Kensington Publishing Corp.
119 West 40th Street
New York, NY 10018

PUBLISHER'S NOTE
Following the death of William W. Johnstone, the Johnstone family is working with a carefully selected writer to organize and complete Mr. Johnstone's outlines and many unfinished manuscripts to create additional novels in all of his series like The Last Gunfighter, Mountain Man, and Eagles, among others. This novel was inspired by Mr. Johnstone's superb storytelling.

All Kensington titles, imprints, and distributed lines are available at special quantity discounts for bulk purchases for sales promotions, premiums, fund-raising, educational, or institutional use. Special book excerpts or customized printings can also be created to fit specific needs. For details, write or phone the office of the Kensington special sales manager: Kensington Publishing Corp., 119 West 40th Street, New York, NY 10018, attn: Special Sales Department; phone 1-800-221-2647.

ISBN-13: 978-0-7860-3545-8
ISBN-10: 0-7860-3545-5

First printing: August 2012

10 9 8 7 6 5

Printed in the United States of America

PROLOGUE

HANGING TODAY
2 o'clock
Public Invited.

The town of Sorrento, Texas, was filling with people as ranchers and farmers streamed in to do their weekly shopping and, as a bonus, witness another hanging. This would be the seventh hanging this year, and it was only June. But Judge Theodore "Hang 'em High" Dawes was of the belief that it was cheaper to hang someone than to incarcerate them.

Because of Judge Dawes's propensity to issue the hanging verdict, the gallows with a hangman's noose affixed had become a permanent fixture and had been added to, painted, and constructed in such a way as to become a fixture of the town. It was even a repository for advertisements, and the merchants paid a premium to have announcements of their goods and services posted on and around the substantial construction.

He Won't Be Needing
Any More Haircuts . . .
❧
But You Will at
MODEL BARBERSHOP

Two blocks from the gallows, around which a crowd was already beginning to gather, Deputy Sharp walked back to the cell where the condemned prisoner was spending his last day.

"Here's your last meal," Sharp said. "Steak, fried taters, a mess of greens, and biscuits. If it was up to me, I wouldn't feed you nothing but bread and water, but the sheriff wanted to be nice to you."

"That's very good of the sheriff. Did you bring catsup?" the prisoner asked.

"Of course I brought catsup. You can't very well have fried taters without catsup." Sharp laughed. "And I've noticed that the prisoners that's about to get hung purt' nigh always don't eat their meal, so I wind up eatin' it for 'em. And I like catsup with taters."

The prisoner took the food, then returned to his bunk and sat down.

"I tell you the truth," Sharp said, turning his back to the cell and walking to the front window to look out onto the street. "I do believe they's more folks that has come into town to watch your hangin' than any hangin' we've ever had before. Yes, sir, this is goin' to be quite a show."

Sharp heard a gagging sound from behind him.

"What's the matter, you chokin' on somethin'?" Sharp asked, heading back toward the cell.

He saw the prisoner lying back on his bunk. His throat was covered with blood, and his arm was draped down off the bunk onto the floor. The knife, its blade smeared with blood, had fallen from his open hand.

"Sumbitch!" Sharp shouted. Unlocking the door, he ran into the cell. "What the hell did you do that for? You done spoiled ever'one's fun!"

Sharp leaned down to get a closer look at the blood-smeared throat, when all of a sudden the prisoner's hand came up from the floor, grabbed him by the collar, and jerked his head down so that it slammed hard against the table where the food tray was setting.

Deputy Sharp fell to the floor, knocked out, and the prisoner, after wiping the catsup from his neck, stepped outside the cell and locked the door. Then, rifling through the sheriff's desk, he found his pistol and holster belt. Putting it on, he left through the back door of the jail and walked to the jail livery, where he found his horse and saddle.

This Horse and Saddle To Be Sold
after the Hanging

"Hello, Lightning," Falcon said quietly. "Happy to see me?"

Saddling his horse, Falcon MacCallister rode slowly and quietly down the alley toward the end of the block. He could hear Sheriff Dewey Poindexter talking from the platform of the gallows to the gathered crowd.

"Yes, sir, folks, as long as I am your sheriff, there ain't no outlaw in the country goin' to be safe in this here county, no matter how bad they might be. And this here feller we are hangin' today, Falcon MacCallister, has prob'ly kilt more men that John Wesley Hardin."

"But I ain't never before heard nothin' bad about Falcon MacCallister," someone said. "I've read about him in books. He's a folk hero!"

"They've made a hero out a' Jesse James, too, an' he ain' nothin' but a thievin' murderin' outlaw. Don't believe ever'thing you read in books."

When Falcon was clear of town, he urged his horse into a rapid, ground-eating lope.

CHAPTER ONE

Two months earlier

Emmett Kyle, a traveling salesman from Fort Worth, had just sold an order of sewing notions to Eb Smalley, owner of Smalley's Mercantile.

"You've made some good choices, Eb," Kyle said. "Your customers are going to really love that."

Smalley laughed. "I know I've bought more than I need," he said. "You're just too good of a salesman."

"I have to be. I have a wife and two kids to feed."

"Speaking of feeding, how about dropping by the house tonight for supper? You know how Millie loves company. You can fill her in on all the gossip."

"Ha! I do pick up a lot of gossip, traveling from town to town," Kyle said. "And it comes in handy; Mrs. Smalley isn't the only one willing to trade a good supper for a little news."

"I'll see you at six tonight," Smalley said.

"Six o'clock," Kyle said as he picked up the low,

round-crowned bowler hat, smoothed the little red feather, and put it on his head. "See you then."

"He's a little dandy, isn't he?" Smalley said to his clerk, Hodge Deckert, as Kyle walked out into the street.

"Yes, sir, he is."

"But you've got to say this about him. He is one Jim Dandy of a salesman."

Across the street from Smalley's mercantile, Albert Russell, Harry Toombs, Josh Peters, and Lou Hamilton were in the Long Trail saloon. The four men were sheriff's deputies, and they had been drinking since early afternoon. The other customers in the saloon tended to stay away from them as much as possible, waiting until one or more of them would pass out drunk.

"I tell you true, the day we put on these badges is the day we found the pot of gold at the end of the rainbow," Russell said.

"Well now, I wouldn't exactly say that," Toombs said.

"Yeah? I know what you was doin' before you pinned that deputy's star. If I 'member right, you was shovelin' shit out of the stalls over at Kimberly's stable," Russell said.

"Well, but if you stop to think about it," Toombs said, "I was the one shovelin' the shit, I wasn't the one takin' it."

The other two deputies laughed. "He got you on that one, Al," Lou Hamilton said.

"Yeah, well, I know this is the best thing ever to happen to me. I've cowboyed for half a dozen ranchers, burned up in the summer, froze to death in the winter. Where else could you get a job where you can spend half the day in the saloon?"

"We ain't s'posed to be in here like this," Josh Peters said. "What we're s'posed to be doin' is patrollin' the streets to make sure there ain't nobody causin' any trouble."

"Ha! Ever'one in this town is so scared of Sheriff Poindexter there ain't nobody goin' to cause any trouble," Hamilton said. "And truth to tell, the only thing we're supposed to do is collect the taxes."

Russell stood up, and when he did, the chair fell over with a loud bang. It got the attention of everyone else in the saloon, and Russell and the other three deputies laughed.

"Didn't mean to scare ever'body," Russell said. He was a little unsteady and he leaned forward, quickly putting his hand down on the table to keep from falling.

"You all right there, Al?" Toombs asked.

"Yeah. I just maybe need me a breath of fresh air, is all."

Russell, who was the most inebriated of the four, walked unsteadily over to the batwing doors. He held a whiskey bottle in his left hand, and he turned it up to drain the rest of its contents, then, when it was empty, tossed it back over his shoulder without bothering to look around. It landed on a table where two other men were sitting.

"What the . . . ?" one of the men started to say, but the other man reached across the table quickly to stop him from getting up from his chair.

"Let it be," he said quietly.

"What do you mean, 'let it be'? He could have hit one of us in the head with that."

"You're just visiting town. Trust me, Deputy Russell isn't someone you want to mess with."

"Who does he think he is?"

"He knows who he is. He is one of Sheriff Poindexter's men."

"And that means he can do anything he wants?"

"Yes, they pretty much can, and do."

"Hey, you fellers, come over here!" Russell called from the batwing doors.

"What is it?" Toombs asked.

"Come here and look at this."

The other three men came to stand beside Russell. "Look at what?" Hamilton asked.

"Look at that funny-lookin' hat on that feller. What kind of hat would you call that?"

"That's called a bowler," Toombs said.

"A bowler?"

"It's what fancy dudes wear in the city."

"Well, what the hell is he wearin' it here for?"

"More 'n likely he come in on the stage," Hamilton suggested. "Prob'ly a salesman or something."

"Look there. He's got 'im a red feather stickin' up from the hat band," Russell said. "Ain't he the dandy, though?"

"He looks pretty dandified, all right," Toombs said.

"Maybe he wouldn't look quite so dandified iffen he didn't have that feather stickin' out of his hat." Russell pulled his pistol.

"What are you goin' to do?" Toombs asked.

"I'm goin' to undandify the little sumbitch," Russell said, slurring his words. "I'm goin' to shoot that feather offen his hat."

"You're crazy. You can't hit that feather from here."

"Five dollars says I can."

"All right, you're on."

"Maybe you ought not to try . . . ," Hamilton said, but before he could finish the sentence, the gun roared and smoke streamed from the barrel.

"Oh, shit," Russell said. "I think I hit the little sumbitch."

Smalley was still looking at Kyle when, to his horror, he heard a gunshot and saw a little mist of blood fly out from the side of his head. Kyle went down in a heap.

"Emmett!" Smalley shouted. He ran from his store out into the street and knelt down beside the salesman. His head was in a spreading pool of blood, his hat lying to one side. His eyes were open and unseeing, and he wasn't breathing.

"It was an accident!" Russell shouted, coming out into the street then, still holding a smoking pistol. "I didn't mean to shoot him!"

"Where were you? Over in the saloon?" Smalley asked.

"Yeah, but like I said, it was an accident."

"That's a good forty yards from here. How do you accidently shoot someone from forty yards away?"

"I don't know, I . . ."

"He had his gun out, showin' it to us, and it went off," Toombs explained.

"Yeah," Russell said quickly. "Yeah, that's what happened. I was showin' 'em my gun, and it just went off."

"What the hell was so interesting about your gun that you had to show it off in a way that wound up killing a man?" Smalley demanded angrily.

"Look now, damn you, don't you go gettin' all high falutin' on me," Russell said. "I told you I didn't mean to kill the feller. I was just lookin' at that little red feather and . . ."

"Good Lord, man, you didn't try to shoot that feather from way over there, did you?" Smalley asked.

"Well, I . . ."

"I told you he was showing us his gun and it went off," Toombs said.

"Yeah, that's what it was," Russell said.

By now a substantial crowd of people had gathered around the salesman's body, including Sheriff Poindexter. Sheriff Poindexter was square jawed and thick set with black hair and a drooping black mustache. But what set him apart from all other men was his left eye. There was no eyelid for his left eye, and that made it bug out, almost like it was too big for the socket. The blade that had taken off his eyelid had also taken out half of the eyebrow over that eye, leaving in its stead a puffy clump of scar tissue.

"What happened here?" Sheriff Poindexter asked.

"It was an accident, Sheriff," Russell said. "I was showin' these other fellas my gun, and it went off. I didn't mean to kill this little feller."

"Anybody know who he is?"

"His name is Emmett Kyle. He's a salesman from Fort Worth," Smalley said.

"All right, Russell, since you killed him, you are responsible for him. See to it that Nunnelee gets his body all cleaned up and sent back to Fort Worth."

"All right," Russell replied.

"He got 'ny family there?" Poindexter asked Smalley.

"He's got a wife and two kids."

"Good, that means we won't have to be out any money for his buryin'."

"Is that all you're goin' to do?" Smalley asked.

"What do you mean, 'is that all'? What do you expect me to do?"

"Investigate it. Good Lord, man, there's been a killin' here."

"Nothing to investigate," Poindexter replied. "It was an accident, pure and simple."

Smalley shook his head in disgust, then walked

back into his store. He didn't know Kyle all that well; he knew him only as a salesman. But Kyle had been working his store for the last three years, and almost always had dinner with him. Smalley had never met Kyle's family, but he thought of them now, back home in Fort Worth, content and comfortable with the thought that the husband and father would be coming back home to them.

"And Sheriff Poindexter isn't going to do a damn thing about it. No investigation, nothing," Smalley said to Harold Denham. Denham was not only Smalley's friend; he was also the owner and publisher of the *Sorrento Advocate*.

"Well, come on, Eb, you know Poindexter," Denham said. "Did you really expect him to do anything?"

"I guess not," Eb said. "But it does make me angry. I just wish there was something we could do about it."

"Right now the only thing I can do is write about it in the paper and hope I can keep the pot stirred up so that maybe, someday, the people will decide they have had enough of Poindexter."

"And don't forget Judge Dawes," Smalley said. "He not only facilitates Sheriff Poindexter, he is in league with him."

"So is Gillespie, the prosecutor."

Death in the Streets of Sorrento

Yesterday, Emmett Kyle, a salesman from Fort Worth, was shot down in the street. Mr. Kyle was well known by merchants in Sorrento and other towns as an honest man who made good on his promises, and kept his end of any bargain made. He had a wife and two children.

This fine man was cut down in the prime of life when a bullet struck him in the head. The missile was energized by a pistol that was in the hands of Deputy Albert Russell. Russell has made the totally unbelievable claim that his firearm discharged accidentally when he was showing it to Toombs, Hamilton, and Peters, who are also Sheriff's deputies. It is not surprising that the three deputies verified Russell's story. However, there were other witnesses in the saloon who tell a completely different tale.

The story as told by these witnesses is that Deputy Russell, while in a state of inebriation, attempted to shoot the feather from Mr. Kyle's hat. This was from a distance of forty yards. It would be a prodigious pistol shot from an expert when he is sober. Deputy Russell missed his mark, his bullet striking Mr. Kyle in the temple.

Unfortunately, none of these witnesses will agree to testify against the deputy, and they have given this newspaper their story, only on the promise that they remain anonymous.

How long, dear readers, I ask you, will our fair community remain under the despotic control of Judge Dawes, Prosecutor Gillespie, Sheriff Poindexter, and his evil deputies? Is it not time that we, as citizens, took some action? It is our misfortune that Texas does not have petition and recall, but we can certainly unite to elect a new judge, sheriff, and prosecuting attorney at the next election.

CHAPTER TWO

Durango, Colorado

Johnny Pollard was standing at the end of the bar of the Bull's Head saloon. Johnny was a cowboy who rode for the Twin Peaks Ranch. Today was his twenty-first birthday, and he was trying to talk Belle LaForge into giving him a free visit.

"Johnny, if I gave you a free visit for your birthday, everyone would be wanting a free visit for their birthday," Belle replied. "You can see that, can't you?"

"How about if you give me a special deal? Like maybe fifty cents off?"

"How about if she just teaches you a few tricks, cowboy?" one of the other bar girls asked. "That way, you might learn something, then the rest of us might enjoy bedding you more."

Those within the sound of the conversation laughed, and Johnny blushed.

"I'm young," Johnny said. "I'm still learnin'."

* * *

Two blocks down the street from the Bull's Head, someone saw the gunfighter, Amos Drew, ride into town. The albino wasn't hard to pick out; his hair was white, his skin was without color, and his eyes were pink. It was said that he had killed at least ten men, though some insisted that the count was as high as twenty.

Drew didn't ride into town like any ordinary visitor. He was wearing a long duster. That in itself was not unusual, because many riders wore dusters on the trail. But Drew wore his duster pulled back and hooked over his pistol, enabling him to get to it quickly, if need be. And because he was a man who lived on the edge, he was always aware that someone might try to kill him, either to avenge one of his earlier killings, or to make a name for himself as the one who killed Amos Drew. As he rode into town, his eyes swept the top-floor windows and rooflines of every building on both sides of the street, ever watchful of potential assassins.

He stopped in front of the Bull's Head, one of the wilder saloons of the town. The Bull's Head was known for bad women and even worse whiskey. Drew took off his duster and shook the dirt from it before he draped it over his saddle. Then, slapping his hands against his shirt a few times, and raising a cloud of dust by so doing, he stepped up onto the wooden porch and pushed his way in through the batwing doors.

A piano player was grinding away in the back of the saloon, and two of the saloon girls were leaning on the piano, singing, not for the customers, but for themselves. There were nearly a dozen customers in the saloon; three of them were at the bar, the other three sharing a table. One of the men at the bar was a young cowboy, and he was talking with a pretty, but rather garishly made-up young woman.

"Whiskey," Drew said.

"Yes, sir, Mr. Drew, whatever you say," the barkeep replied nervously. "Nothing is too good for Mr. Amos Drew. With hands that were shaking so badly that he got as much whiskey out of the glass as in it, he poured Drew a drink. When he picked up the glass it began shaking again, so, quickly, he put the glass down on the bar, then pushed it across.

Johnny heard the bartender address Drew, and that got his attention. "Did you hear that?" he asked Belle.

Belle had tensed up the moment Drew came into the saloon.

"That there is Amos Drew."

"Come on upstairs with me, Johnny," Belle said. "I'll give you your birthday present now."

"Just a minute," Johnny said. "I'd like to meet him."

"Johnny, stay away from him," Belle said. "Please."

She put her hand on Johnny's arm in an attempt to get him to go with her, but he paid no attention to it.

"Are you Amos Drew?" Johnny asked.

Drew made only a casual glance toward the cowboy, then, almost as if he hadn't even seen him, he took a drink of his whiskey.

"You're a famous man, Mr. Drew," the young cowboy said. "I've heard a lot about you."

Drew took another drink. "Go away. Leave your woman," he said without looking back toward the young cowboy.

Johnny got a confused look on his face. "What? What did you say?"

"It's been a while since I had me a woman. I want that one."

"Well, I—uh—that is, she ain't exactly my woman. She works here."

Frightened, the woman put her hand on the young cowboy's shoulder. "Come on, Johnny, please. Your birthday present?"

The young cowboy smiled nervously. "Well, Mr. Drew, I reckon you are goin' to have to find someone else. It seems that Belle and I have our own plans. Today is my birthday, you see."

"Find another woman to celebrate your birthday. I want this woman."

"I don't care what you want," Belle said, somehow finding the nerve to speak in a firm voice. "I'm not going with you."

"You're a whore, ain't you? You have to go with anyone who pays you," Drew said.

"I don't have to go with you, you maggot-looking son of a bitch," she said coldly.

The piano player stopped the music, and everyone in the saloon gasped at Belle's words.

The evil smile left Drew's face. "Cowboy," he said, "you had better teach your woman some manners."

Johnny laughed nervously. "Mister Drew, you obviously don't know Belle. She ain't the kind of woman you can teach anything to."

"Slap her in the face."

"What?" the young cowboy sputtered. "What do you mean 'slap her in the face'?"

"You can speak English can't you? The woman insulted me. So what I want you to do is, slap her in the face and make her apologize to me for what she said. And you might also tell her to beg me not to kill you."

"Look here! This is gettin' way out of hand! I ain't goin' to slap no woman in the face, and I ain't goin' to stand here and talk to you no more, neither. So I'm just goin' to walk away now!"

"Slap her in the face and make her apologize, cowboy. Or go for your gun," Drew said.

"Mr. Drew, the boy is right, he didn't have nothin' to do with this," the bartender said.

Without even looking at the bartender, Drew backhanded him with his left hand. The startled bartender stepped away from the bar, his nose bleeding from the blow.

"I'm sorry, I'm sorry!" Belle said. "There, I've apologized! I'm the one who spoke to you like that. Please don't hurt these men."

"It's too late now, the ball has been opened. Besides which, you ain't been slapped yet." He pointed to Drew. "This is the one I'm talking to. What do you say, cowboy? Are you going to slap that woman, like I told you to?"

"Johnny, do it," Belle pleaded. "Please do it! Can't you see that he's crazy? He'll kill you if you don't do it."

"I can't slap you, Belle."

"Please do it!" Belle said. She turned her cheek to him. "It ain't like I ain't never been slapped before."

"Better listen to your woman, Johnny," Drew said. "If you don't want me to kill you, you'd better slap her."

"The hell I will!" Johnny said. "I'll be damned if I'll let the likes of you make me slap a woman."

"Johnny, please!" Belle said. "Do it. I'll go with him."

"Not yet, missy. Not till I've dealt with your boyfriend."

Johnny held his hand out, gently pushing Belle out of the way. "Better step aside, Belle," he said. "Looks like there's goin' to be some shootin', and I don't want you to get hurt."

"Johnny, no! What are you going to do? You can't go against him! Don't you know who this is?" the bartender said.

"Yeah, I know who the son of a bitch is."

"He'll kill you!" the bartender warned.

"Better to die a man than live a coward. I ain't apologizin' to this low-assed, piss-complexioned, pig-faced son of a bitch, and I ain't beggin' him not to kill me. Ever'body has got to die sometime. Could be this is his time."

Drew's evil smile returned. "Could be," he agreed. "I'll tell you what I'll do," he said. "Just to make it fair, I'm going to let you draw first."

Outside, some children were engaged in a game of some sort, and they were laughing and shouting to each other. A stagecoach rolled into town, the driver calling and whistling to his team. How detached Johnny felt from that world now—how much he wished he was a part of it. He thought back to this morning, waking up in the bunkhouse, teasing Jimmy Bob about some foolishness, shouting to the rooftop that he was twenty-one years old. Was that just this morning? Or was that a lifetime ago?

"I'm going to count to three, cowboy," Drew said. "You can draw anytime you want, but when I get to three, you had better draw because I'm going to. One," he started.

"Johnny, Mr. Drew, you don't have to do this," the bartender said.

"Two."

"Johnny, please, don't do this!" Belle called.

Johnny suddenly made a desperate grab for his gun, but it was only halfway out of his holster when

Drew's gun boomed, filling the room with its fire
and thunder. A heavy discharge of smoke rolled up,
forming an acrid, blue-white cloud over the scene.

Johnny had not drawn his pistol far enough to
clear it, and when he was hit, the gun fell back into
the holster. Johnny staggered back against the bar,
then slid down to the sitting position. He cupped
his hand over the pumping chest wound, and blood
began to spill between his fingers.

"It's funny," he said. "When I woke up this
mornin', I sure never thought I'd be dyin' on my
birthday."

Johnny's head sagged to one side.

"You," Drew said, looking toward Belle. "I need a
woman."

"Do you think I would go upstairs with you now,
after this? After you murdered . . ."

Drew held up his finger and wagged it back and
forth. "I didn't murder him," he said. "It was a fair
fight. And if you had gone with me when I first
asked, this wouldn't have happened. What did it
gain you? Now your boy-friend is dead and you are
still going to go upstairs with me."

"The hell I am!" Belle said defiantly.

Drew had not reholstered his smoking pistol,
and he pointed it toward the bartender, then pulled
the hammer back. It made a deadly sounding
double click as it engaged the sear and rotated
the cylinder, putting a fresh load under the firing
pin. "Do you want to be the cause of another
man dying?"

"Belle, go with him, please!" the bartender pleaded.

Without saying a word, but with tears of grief, fear, and frustration streaming down her face, Belle turned and started toward the stairs that led to the second floor. The others in the saloon stared at the unfolding scene in shocked silence.

Falcon MacCallister had ridden over to Durango from nearby MacCallister Valley to bring a pair of boots to Murchison's Boots and Saddle. Tim Murchison was the best leather worker he had ever met, and it was worth the ride. He was just arriving in front of the leather shop when he heard the shot. Shots were not that uncommon, so he thought nothing about it as he dismounted and reached for his boots.

Tim came out onto the front porch of his shop and smiled.

"Falcon, good to see you."

At that moment, someone came running up the boardwalk from the Bull's Head saloon.

"There's been a murder! There's been a murder!"

"Marty, what is it?" Tim asked.

"Amos Drew just kilt Johnny Pollard. He's goin' to say that it was a fair fight, but there wan't nothin' fair about it. He pushed Johnny into drawin' on him, then he said he was goin' to kill the bartender if Belle didn't go upstairs with him. I'm goin' to get the sheriff."

"Sheriff Ferrell and his deputy are both out of town right now," Tim replied.

"Somethin' has got to be done. Drew is a crazy man. I wouldn't doubt but he'll kill the girl once he's through with her."

"I'll go have a look," Falcon said.

"Falcon, you don't have to do that," Tim said. "You don't live here; I do. And from time to time Sheriff Ferrell deputizes me, so if anyone goes it should be me."

"Are you a deputy now?"

"No, but . . ."

"Then I'll go," Falcon insisted.

"It's this way," Marty said.

Falcon tossed his boots to Tim. "I need new heels," he said.

"Falcon, you don't need to do this," Tim said again.

"And don't make them too high," Falcon called back over his shoulder as he followed Marty toward the saloon.

"Is Drew still there?" Falcon asked.

"As far as I know he is. He went upstairs with Belle."

When Falcon stepped into the saloon a minute later, he saw everyone else, the men patrons, as well as the piano player and the bargirls, standing in a semicircle, looking down at the body. The cowboy was still in the upright position, leaning against the bar. Both hands were down by his side; one of his hands was bloody, as was the front of his shirt. His eyes were open and glazed, and his mouth was half open.

"Is the man that did this still here?" Falcon asked.

"Who are you?" the bartender replied.

"Percy, this here is Falcon MacCallister. I reckon you've heard of him," Marty said.

"Yeah, you're damn right I've heard of him. And if anyone can handle Drew, why I reckon it would be him. Drew's still here. He's upstairs," the bartender said, glancing toward the head of the stairs.

From upstairs, Falcon could hear the sound of a woman's voice.

"No," she said. "Please, for God's sake, no!"

"What room?"

"Belle's room is the first one on the right at the head of the stairs, Mr. MacCallister," one of the other girls said.

"Thank you, ma'am," Falcon replied.

Falcon went up the stairs quietly, his pistol in his hand. When he reached the room he tried the door, but it was locked. He knocked on the door.

"Go away!" a man's voiced called from inside.

"I have clean towels," Falcon announced.

"We don' need no damn towels!" the same voice answered.

"It's the law. You have to have clean towels."

Falcon heard someone walking across the floor toward the door, and he stepped back with his pistol ready. When the door was open, Drew was holding a gun in his hand.

"I told you I don't want any . . ."

Falcon, who was standing to one side, reached out to grab Drew's hand. He jerked forward, toward the banister. Drew spun around to bring his pistol to bear on his attacker, but instead he lost his balance, then blundered through the banister and fell, head down, onto the piano below. The piano made a large discordant sound as Drew crashed into it. He slid from the piano on down to the floor and lay there with one leg still on the piano bench. His neck was twisted crazily to one side; his eyes were open but already growing opaque.

Falcon holstered his pistol and hurried down the stairs. Amos Drew had not moved since he fell. The bartender examined him.

"It's all right, folks," the bartender said. "The son of a bitch is dead."

The others in the saloon cheered and applauded.

CHAPTER THREE

Sorrento, Texas

Harold Denham, Dr. Gunter, and Eb Smalley were sharing a table in the Hog Heaven saloon. Denham was a small man, who was hatless and bald except for a ring of thin, gray hair. He was wearing glasses, which had the effect of making his eyes look larger than they were. Dr. Gunter was in his early sixties, very slender, with white hair and a well-trimmed white beard.

"That was quite an article you wrote, Harold," Doc Gunter said. "And knowing Albert Russell, it isn't hard to imagine that he would do something like that."

"I just wish the people who talked to me would testify in court."

"What good would it do?" Doc Gunter asked. "You know as well as I that Theodore Dawes isn't a judge who lets truth get in the way."

"Unfortunately, that's true."

"There's one of Poindexter's deputies now," Smalley said, nodding toward the front door.

The deputy that Smalley pointed out was Stan Sharp, who had just come into the Hog Heaven saloon. "All right, ladies!" he shouted. "It's that time again!"

"It hasn't been a month, Sharp," Beeson, the owner of the Hog Heaven, said.

"It ain't my call," Sharp said. "This is the doin' of the sheriff, the judge, and the prosecutor. Let's go, ladies."

There were four bar girls working the floor.

"How much is it goin' to cost us this time?" one of the woman asked. "Ten dollars, same as before?"

"How the hell do I know? I don't make up the fines. I just bring you in when it's time."

"You have to give us time to get our money," one of the others said.

"All right, get your money. Anyone upstairs?"

The four girls looked at each other, then one of them replied. "Uh, yeah, Suzi is. She is upstairs with a—uh—gentleman friend."

"Well, roust her out, and you ladies report to the courthouse. I'm goin' to round up the others."

The deputy went back outside as the four girls hurried up the stairs.

"What do you think this is all about?" a man named Travers asked. Travers was sitting at the table adjacent to Denham, Doc Gunter, and Smalley's table.

"You mean you don't know?" Denham asked.

"How long have you been here? It's been at least a month, ain't it?"

"It will be three weeks Monday since I bought the feed and seed store."

"Oh, well I guess in that case you've never been here for the roundup," Dr. Gunter suggested.

"The roundup? No, I don't reckon I have. That is, I don't know what you mean by the roundup."

"Then I shall explain it to you, my boy," Denham said. "You see, once a month every whore in town is rounded up, and the sheriff hauls them into court. The judge finds them guilty of prostitution and sentences them to thirty days in jail, or a ten-dollar fine. They of course—the whores I mean—choose to pay the fine. Then, as soon as they pay their fine, they are free to leave, free to return to their perfidious profession, prostituting, purveying pornographic pictures, pimping, providing parsimonious pleasure, pitiful policy permitted only because of the lack of any sort of justice in our county."

Doc Gunter applauded quietly. "Thirteen p's, that's a new record in alliteration for you, isn't it?"

"I do believe it is," Denham said, smiling proudly.

"Well, I don't get it," Travers said. "If the judge and the sheriff don't want whorin', why don't they just stop it?"

"Think about it, Travers. There are twenty-five whores in Sorrento. Each one of them pays a ten-dollar fine every month. Do you have any idea how much money that is?"

"Two hundred and fifty dollars," Travers replied.

"That's right. That's the money that pays the deputies. There's five deputies and they make fifty dollars apiece. Do you really think they are ready to walk away from that money?"

"No, I guess not."

"That's why they are fined, then turned loose. Dawes, Poindexter, and Gillespie aren't going to shut them down. Arrests and fines for the petit crimes provide a most lucrative income for our devious officers of the court."

"But the real money is in taxes," Doc Gunter said.

"Yes, I was told when I bought the feed store that there was a business tax that I would have to pay. I think Mr. Matthews said it was fifty dollars, but I don't figure fifty dollars a year is too much."

"A month," Harold said.

"What?"

"Your tax will be fifty dollars a month."

"A month? I'm not sure I can handle that. I haven't been here long enough yet to know what kind of business I'm going to have. I mean, it's been pretty good so far, but fifty dollars a month?"

"Don't think you are all alone," Smalley said.

After he finished his drink, Denham left the saloon, then walked down the street toward the courthouse, going in right behind the gathering of women who had been summoned.

"What are you doing here, Denham?" Deputy Sharp asked. "You got no business here."

"On the contrary, my good man. As a productive member of the Fourth Estate, I most assuredly do have business here."

"The fourth estate?"

"Let the press in, Deputy," Judge Dawes said.

Sharp stepped to one side, then made a motion with his arm. "All right," he said. "Come on in."

"Mr. Denham, you came dangerously close to slander with that article about the accidental death of Mr. Kyle," Judge Dawes said.

"Judge, I was just repeating what others said. I made no personal declaration as to the truth or fiction of those comments. I don't make judgments, I just report news."

"So you say," Dawes replied. "But some of your editorial observations have come very close to being judgments."

"It may appear so, Judge, but that is just the nature of the beast."

"My advice, Mr. Denham, would be to tone down the rhetoric of your articles, lest you get yourself into serious trouble."

"I will take your warning into consideration."

The women who were gathered varied in age from a few who were barely out of their teens and still pretty to those who had been so beaten down by their profession that their only saving grace was the idea that "all cats are gray in the dark." The young women, the prettiest, were the pick of the crop, the most desirable, and as such, they worked for Miss Adele's House of Pleasure. Next came the bar girls from the various saloons of the town, still relatively attractive but with a hard edge. Finally there were the older, homely ones at the end of their productive cycle who were now practicing their profession from small cribs in the back alleys of Sorrento.

The prostitutes here gathered showed absolutely no concern over the fact that they were all, in essence, under arrest. On the contrary, they were talking and laughing with each other as if this were a social gathering.

"Quiet!" Judge Dawes said, slapping his mallet down hard.

The women grew quiet.

"Mr. Bailiff, what have we here?"

The bailiff, who was also the sheriff, looked out over the women. "Your Honor, there comes now before this honorable court these twenty-five women. They are all being charged with the practice of prostitution, said practice being illegal in this city."

"Is the prosecutor present?"

"I am, Your Honor. Burt Gillespie."

"Very good, sir. And is there defense counsel present?" Judge Dawes asked.

"No, Your Honor," Gillespie answered.

"Ladies, have you selected one of your number to speak for you?" Judge Dawes asked.

"Yeah, I'll do it," one of the bar girls from the Hog Heaven said.

"Your Honor," Gillespie hissed.

"Your Honor," the woman said.

"And you would be?"

"I beg your pardon?"

"What is your name?"

The woman smiled. "Ask the sheriff, Your Honor. He sure knows who I am, why he . . ."

Whatever she was about to say was stifled by the loud and incessant pounding of the gavel.

"I asked you for your name, not a conversation," the judge said, interrupting her response. "Now I will ask you again. What is your name?"

"Lucy Smith."

"Smith?"

"Yeah, Your Honor, there's lots of Smiths," Lucy said, and the other women giggled.

"Very well, Miss Smith. Do you or any of the ladies desire a lawyer to speak for you?"

"No, Your Honor. If we had a lawyer the result would be the same, and we would just have to pay him, plus the fine. We don't want a lawyer."

"Very well. You have collectively, and separately, been charged with prostitution. How do you plead?"

"Yes, sir, Your Honor, we're whorin' all right. That's what we do. You know that, 'cause we come here ever' month."

"How do you plead?"

"I beg your pardon?"

One of the other women leaned over and whispered to Lucy, and she nodded.

"Oh," she said. "I thought saying that we was whorin' was all that was needed. But if you need a plead, why, we're guilty, Your Honor. Ever'one of us is."

"Thank you," Judge Dawes said. He looked toward the prosecutor. "Mr. Gillespie, are there any additional charges?"

"No, Your Honor. The only charge is the charge of prostitution."

"Thank you," Judge Dawes said. "Ladies, you have been charged, and have pled guilty to the offense of prostitution. I therefore find you guilty and sentence you to thirty days in prison, or a fine of ten dollars each. If you choose to pay the fine and walk out of here free, then you must settle with the bailiff."

Again Dawes slapped his gavel hard on the desk before him, and as he did so the ladies hurried over to the sheriff to pay their fines.

"Next case," the judge said.

"Your Honor, comes now A.J. O'Dell. O'Dell is charged with stealing a horse," Sheriff Poindexter said.

A.J. O'Dell had been sitting in the front row, without restraints of any kind, enjoying, as were others in the gallery, what everyone called "the whore show."

When his case was called, he held up his hand.

"That's me, Your Honor. I'm A.J. O'Dell."

"I am told you turned yourself in," Judge Dawes said.

"Yeah, I did. I figured this was the best way to get attention to my problem."

"How do you plead, O'Dell?"

"Can't we talk about the problem I'm havin' with Clyde Dumey first?"

"How do you plead, Mr. O'Dell?"

"Well, I did take a horse from Clyde Dumey," O'Dell said. "But you can't really say I stoled it, 'cause that horse ain't worth no more'n a hundred and fifty dollars, and the son of a bitch owes me five hundred dollars for a seed bull and six cows that he bought and never paid for."

"Then you confess to stealing Mr. Dumey's horse?"

"I tole' you judge, I didn't steal it. I took it."

"That is the same thing as stealing."

"All right, maybe it is. I stoled his horse, but like I told you, he owes me five hundred dollars. Besides which, soon as I got his attention, I give him his horse back, so you can't really say I stoled it. Now, Judge, since we're talkin' about this, what I'd like you to do is order Dumey to give me the money he owes me."

"Mr. O'Dell, you have confessed to stealing Mr. Dumey's horse. That makes you a horse thief. A horse is a man's most personal possession, and by committing the crime of separating a man from his horse, you must pay the maximum penalty prescribed by law. But before I proceed, I want it well understood by everyone in this court that you are pleading guilty to horse thievery."

"Yeah, Your Honor, I done told you, I plead guilty to takin' his horse," O'Dell said with a rather disdainful expression. "But it's like I said. I did it to get his attention. If you'll look on your record book, Judge, you'll see that I filed me a complaint against Dumey for not payin' me for that seed bull and the six heifers. That's two months ago now, it was. You ain't done nothin' about it yet, 'cause you said your docket, or somethin' like that, is full. And like I also said, I've done give him his horse back. He's got his horse, but I still ain't got my money. So what I'm hopin', now that this has all come to your attention, is that you'll make Dumey give me the money he owes me."

"I'm afraid, Mr. O'Dell, that you will no longer have need for the money."

"I won't have no need for the money? What are you talkin' about? Of course I got need for the money. I got bills to pay just like ever'one else."

"You will have no need for the money, Mr. O'Dell, because I am going to make an example of you. It is the sentence of this court that you are to be taken to the public gallows, and there, you will hang by the neck until you are dead."

"What?" O'Dell gasped. "What are you talkin' about? You're hangin' me? Look here, Judge! You can't do that! That's no more than murder!"

"Execution will be carried out at ten o'clock tomorrow morning. Return the prisoner to his cell."

"Wait!" O'Dell shouted, no longer angry and belligerent, but now frightened and pleading. "Wait, please! No, don't do this! I told you, I just borrowed his horse to make a point! Judge, I didn't steal it! I told you! He's got his horse back! I'm sorry, please, I'm . . ."

O'Dell's voice faded into the distance as the deputies dragged him away back to his cell.

CHAPTER FOUR

Durango

"No charge for these boots," Murchison said. "No, sir, no charge at all."

"I'm perfectly willing to pay for them, Tim," Falcon said. "I hate the idea of you doing all that work for nothing."

Murchison smiled. "I'm not doing it for nothing. Half the town took up a collection to give you a reward. I told them that I might be able to talk you into taking the boots, but was sure you wouldn't want anything more than that."

Falcon chuckled. "All right, tell the town thanks," Falcon said. He looked at the repaired boots Murchison gave him. "And thank you. You did a fine job, but then, you always do. Otherwise I wouldn't ride this far to get them done."

Just outside Murchison's shoe shop, there was a gathering of at least forty or fifty people standing around in front of the leather store.

When Falcon emerged, they began to applaud. Falcon was embarrassed by the applause, but he smiled, nodded, and accepted it as graciously as he could.

Behind the crowd passed the undertaker's wagon. Drew's body was on the wagon. He wasn't in a coffin, or even in a shroud. He was lying facedown in the back of the wagon with one of his arms hanging over the tail end, his fingers barely clearing the ground.

"There goes the son of a bitch toward the graveyard," someone said. He spit on the ground as the wagon passed by.

"Ponder don't even have him in a coffin," another said.

"No sense in wasting good wood. Ponder is just going to dump his dead ass in a hole and let the worms have him."

In contrast to Amos Drew's body, young Johnny Pollard had been put in a highly polished, silver-splashed, ebony coffin, and his coffin, in the back of a glass-sided hearse, was being taken down to the railroad depot. A weeping young woman was walking behind the hearse. This was Belle, the woman who had been in the room with Drew when Falcon knocked on the door.

"Mr. Forsythe owns Twin Peaks, and he paid for the coffin," Tim Murchison said. "Turns out Johnny is from Denver, so they're sending his body back to his family."

"That's a heck of a way to have to come home,"

Falcon said. He swung into the saddle, then, with a wave toward the grateful citizens of Durango, rode on out of town.

Sorrento

There were over a hundred people standing around the gallows the next morning, drawn there for various reasons from a sense of horror and pity, to curiosity, to those who experienced a morbid enjoyment over watching someone else die. A few minutes earlier, the preacher had climbed up onto the podium to try to take advantage of a larger congregation than any he ever saw on a Sunday, but he was shouted down after only a few sentences.

One entrepreneur moved through the crowd selling recently rendered cracklings and keg beer; the latter he was dispensing from a bucket. Denham told himself that as a newspaper man, he had to watch this, though he felt a sense of anger and despair over what was happening.

"Here they come!" someone shouted, and all conversation stopped as everyone turned their eyes toward the jail. There were five men walking toward the gallows: Sheriff Poindexter in front, Deputy Sharp in the back, the prisoner, O'Dell, in the middle, flanked on either side by deputies. O'Dell's hands were bound behind his back.

As the small procession came to within sight of the gallows, surrounded by well over one hundred people, those who were waiting turned and craned their necks to get a better view. Sheriff Poindexter moved back and stood closer to O'Dell. Behind them rumbled an open box wagon containing the plain wooden coffin into which O'Dell's body would be placed immediately after the hanging. The procession came right up to the edge of the crowd, where the deputy sheriffs with revolvers in hand shouted, "Make way."

When the procession reached the gallows, Sheriff Poindexter went up the steps first, followed by O'Dell, who was prodded along by two of the sheriff's deputies. The preacher followed the deputies up the steps. The hangman was already on the platform, standing calmly, unobtrusively, to one side.

As O'Dell stood there next to the dangling noose, a hush descended over the crowd. Then, one voice called out over all others.

"Clear the way, folks! Clear the way so I can get a good picture!" This was from Phillip Simmons, the photographer.

There were various exclamations from the crowd, such as: "They say all he done was steal a horse."

And, "Yes, and didn't he give it back?"

"What they hanging him for?"

"I hear it's to make a point."

"What point would that be?"

"Don't go borrowing horses, is what I'd say."

Mixed up with all this hubbub of voices, too, there were the whinnying of horses, the barking of dogs, and, from somewhere down the street, the crying of a baby.

Harold Denham thought about that, considering that the last memory to be impressed upon the brain of A.J. O'Dell would be the crying of a baby. He couldn't help but make the analogy of an entire lifetime encapsulated in but a moment . . . from a baby's cry to a man's last breath.

The Reverend Charles Landers stepped up beside the prisoner.

"Would you like me to pray with you, my son?"

"I'll be sayin' my own prayers, preacher," O'Dell said.

"Then I'll be takin' this opportunity to say a few words to the souls who are gathered here to watch your final departure from this earth."

"Yeah, you do that."

Opening his Bible, the Reverend Charles Landers read for fully ten minutes, no doubt making up for having been shouted off the gallows half an hour earlier. His reading was punctured by the shouts of Thomas Rafferty, the vendor selling the cracklings and beer.

"Cracklin's here! Cracklin's here! Get your hot cracklin's and cold beer here!"

After Pastor Landers finished with his reading, he prayed for another ten minutes, often punctuating his prayer with the remark that, "O Lord, in another minute this poor sinner will be launched into eternity. This, O Lord, is a sad and mournful occasion. Thou art about to take one from our midst."

Then he shouted out to the crowd so all would hear him: "This man, convicted of a crime, is standing on the line of time and eternity, his immortal soul to face final judgment. You would do well to mark this moment, for it is a moment that we all must face. Every man, woman, and child here present will one day face that final judgment."

"Mama!" a young, frightened voice called out. "Does that mean we are all going to hang?"

Nervous laughter greeted the boy's question.

Throughout the long, and seemingly interminable fifteen minutes, O'Dell maintained his composure, though once or twice during the prayer his knees were seen to shake.

"Looks to me like O'Dell is holdin' up pretty well."

"Yeah? Well, his knees is a wobblin' some."

"Wouldn't your knees wobble if you was about to be hung?"

When the prayer was finally over, the sheriff stepped up to the condemned man and said, "Mr. O'Dell, do you have any last words you wish to say?"

There were one or two shouts from the crowed, imploring O'Dell to make a speech. But there were many others who shouted, "Hang him and get it over with! Don't keep us standing out here in the sun all day!"

"Yeah, there's a lot I'd like to say. About how this ain't right, that there's no way I should be standing here about to hang for no more than taking a man's horse, which I give back to him."

"Get your fresh hot cracklin's here!" Rafferty shouted. *"Cracklin's and beer, cracklin's and beer!"*

O'Dell shuffled up to the edge of the deck of the gallows and looked out over the crowd.

"I—bid—farewell—I bid you all good-bye." He

paused for a moment, then swallowed and continued.

"God help any man who goes afoul of the judge and the sheriff in this town. I know you are all afeared to talk, but I ain't got nothing to be afeared of anymore. What the judge and the sheriff is doing by hanging me now is nothing but murder pure and simple, and that's the sure and certain truth of it. They've got this town and county under their thumb, same as a king of old. And this, being America, that ain't in no way right."

After he finished, he turned to the sheriff. "I thank you for letting me say my piece. I figured you would try and shut me up."

"Seein' as you are about to be hung, and are goin' to be dead in a few minutes, ain't no need for me to be trying to shut you up now," Sheriff Poindexter said.

O'Dell walked back to the rope, and the hangman, who had been standing to one side, was there waiting for him. He pointed out the exact spot where he wanted O'Dell to stand. While the hangman was adjusting the straps, O'Dell looked around, and as he recognized people he bowed to them and they shouted.

"Good-bye, A.J., good-bye."

Mingled with the good-byes came the voice of Rafferty. *"Get your hot cracklin's and cool beer, right here!"*

"I will remember you, A.J.!" a woman shouted. This came from one of the soiled doves.

"Do you want a hood?"

"No," O'Dell said. He stared directly at the judge, who was standing in the front row. "I want to be lookin' directly at the son of a bitch who is murderin' me."

The hangman fitted the noose over O'Dell's head, then the sheriff and deputies stepped away from the trap door. The hangman walked over, pulled the lever, and A.J. O'Dell dropped out of this world.

There was silence for a moment after the fall and then a babble of voices.

"Is he still kicking?"

"Is he dead?"

These questions were made necessary by the fact that O'Dell's body could only be seen from mid-chest up; the bottom two-thirds of his body was hanging below the open trap and hidden from sight by the curtain that kept the under part of the gallows from view.

The babble continued until at the end of four or five minutes some of O'Dell's friends shouted out: "All right, you sons of bitches! You've let him hang there long enough. Take him down."

Sheriff Poindexter, perhaps responding to the plea, nodded toward his deputies. "Go ahead, you can take him down, now."

The body was taken down, lifted into the wagon, and delivered to Nunnelee's funeral home. Within two hours after he was hanged, he was put into a hole and covered up.

The show was over.

* * *

Harold Denham was a newspaper man, and he duly reported the hanging. But he liked to consider himself a crusading newspaperman, so in addition to reporting the news, Harold Denham felt compelled to write an editorial as well.

A.J. O'Dell Hanged

WAS THIS HANGING NECESSARY?

In what has become all too common an occurrence, Mr. A.J. O'Dell, a rancher, became the sixth person to be hanged in Sorrento this year. Mr. O'Dell's crime, if indeed it could be called a crime, was to take possession of a horse from his neighbor, Clyde Dumey, as a means of reminding Dumey that he owed O'Dell five hundred dollars for an unpaid debt over the sale of a seed bull and six breeding heifers. Ironically, the horse that Mr. O'Dell "borrowed" was valued at no more than one hundred dollars, a sum much less than the amount owed by Dumey.

Judge Dawes, in a trial that had neither jury, nor defense attorney (it is the contention of the judge, prosecutor, and sheriff that O'Dell waived those rights), found Mr. O'Dell guilty of horse stealing. The sentence affixed was death by hanging, and that sentence was carried out, as described in another article in this newspaper.

The question must be asked, why did Mr. O'Dell waive his right to a trial by jury, and to legal representation? In the opinion of this editor, it is because Mr. O'Dell was never informed of the seriousness of the charge against him. Indeed, when confronted by the court as to whether he took the horse, he readily admitted to same, then attempted to use that opportunity to appeal to the court to see to it that the fair debt owed him was paid.

Judge Dawes dismissed without comment Mr. O'Dell's petition for redress of his grievance. Instead, he sentenced O'Dell to death by hanging.

Because this case seemed puzzling, the editor of this journal has done some investigation. It is now known that Mr. Dumey, against whom Mr. O'Dell had a claim, is Judge Dawes's brother-in-law. As Mr. O'Dell has no immediate next of kin, his claim against Dumey for moneys owed has now been dropped.

As citizens of Texas, we are but five years free from the oppressive policies of Reconstruction. But while freedom has reached our fellow Texans, we, in Sorrento, have a yoke upon our necks that is as heavy and tyrannical as anything forced upon us by Reconstruction, or by the Mexicans before we fought for, and achieved, our independence.

The merchants of our town are struggling with a draconian tax burden. The citizens of our town live in fear of the most extreme retaliation for the slightest provocation. No one dare speak their feelings in public, because freedom of speech has been denied them.

Who is responsible for these chains of repression under which our town struggles to find but one breath of free air? The guilty parties are none other than our "elected" leaders. Notice, dear reader, that I put the word elected in quotation marks. I did that to make a point—the point being that while there have been free and unrestricted elections in Texas since the end of Reconstruction, no such freedom has reached Sorrento. Judge Dawes and Sheriff Poindexter, who hold their offices by the ballot, have ensured that they will continue to occupy these offices by intimidating voters.

The sheriff's deputies watch every polling place, making certain that only those whom they know will vote the way the judge and the sheriff want have free and unfettered access.

CHAPTER FIVE

"I see you are still the crusading journalist," Doc Gunter said the day after the newspaper came out.

"Are you talking about the story about the hanging, or the editorial comment?" Denham replied.

"Both. You're taking a chance, you know."

"Not that big a chance," Denham said. "Believe me, I'm not that brave. But I figured that if the editorial appeared in the newspaper, enough people would read it that the publicity itself would provide me with some protection."

"How do you figure that?" Eb Smalley asked. Smalley owned Smalley's Mercantile, and he, Doc Gunter, and Luke Travers were at "their" table with Harold Denham in the Hog Heaven saloon.

"No, he's right," Doc Gunter said. "If a lot of people read this, then something suddenly happens to Harold, it would raise a lot of suspicions, especially since Harold was very specific about naming names."

"You two were at the hanging, weren't you?" Smalley asked.

"I had to be," Doc Gunter said. "I had to pronounce him dead."

"And I felt that I needed to be there as a newspaperman," Denham added.

"I didn't go. I didn't want to. I've seen 'em before," Travers said.

"Yes, and you can always catch the next one. It isn't as if it is a rare event in this town, is it?" Doc Gunter replied.

"Did James Earl Van Arsdale argue O'Dell's case before the jury?" Smalley asked.

"There was no jury trial," Denham said. "I was there."

"Yeah, well, the judge, sheriff, and all the deputies are making the claim that before they took O'Dell from the jail down to the courthouse, he said he didn't want a jury trial," Doc Gunter said. "I believe he thought that the most that would happen would be a fine. And I think he thought that he could enlist the court's assistance in getting back the money Dumey owed him. He didn't realize that Dumey is one of Judge Dawes's biggest supporters."

"It probably wouldn't have made that much difference if there had been a jury trial. Judge Dawes hand-picks his juries, and they all do exactly what he tells them to do," Smalley said. "Besides which, I doubt seriously that James Earl Van Arsdale has drawn a sober breath in three years."

"Van Arsdale's a good man, though. Drunk or

sober, he's a better man than Gillespie, Poindexter, or Dawes," Denham said.

"You've got that right," Doc Gunter added in agreement.

"O'Dell wasn't exactly what you call a sterling citizen," Smalley said. "I know damn well he has stolen from me a couple of times. And there's some that swear he's the one that held up the stage from Commerce City a couple of years ago. But it doesn't seem to me like he deserved to hang. Especially since he didn't really steal the horse; he just took it to hold until he got the money that was owed to him."

"I think at least three of the previous five who were hanged would not have been hanged in any other court. And even the two who probably did deserve to hang didn't exactly get what you could call a fair trial," Denham said.

Across the street from the newspaper office, upstairs over the hardware store, James Earl Van Arsdale had his office and his living quarters. At one time he had a house on the north end, in the more affluent part of town. But three years ago a fire had destroyed his house and taken the lives of his wife and infant son. The house lay in burned cinders for more than a year afterward until Van Arsdale finally succumbed to the neighbor's pressure to get it cleaned up.

He still owned the lot on which the house had

stood, but he had no plans of rebuilding. Instead, he moved a cot into his law office and that's where he lived. Van Arsdale started drinking soon after that, and his law practice, which was once very profitable because he had been a good lawyer, was now barely making enough to sustain him.

Tonight, Van Arsdale was sitting in the dark, drinking, and looking through the window, when he saw two of the sheriff's deputies stop in front of the newspaper office. They stood there for a moment, looking up and down the street, then, when they determined that they weren't being watched, they threw a brick through the front window of the newspaper office. Even from up here, and across the street, Van Arsdale could hear the crash of glass.

The two deputies, whom he recognized as Harry Toombs and Josh Peters, ran quickly away from the newspaper office, then darted up the gap that separated the apothecary from the gun store. They disappeared in the shadows, so that by the time the sound of the crashing glass brought others to the scene, they were gone.

"Who did this?" someone asked. "Did anyone see it?"

"Someone better go tell Mr. Denham."

"I'll tell him," another said. "He ain't goin' to like it, though. He ain't goin' to like it one little bit."

Back in the saloon, Denham, unaware of the attack on his office, was involved in a discussion about Dawes and Poindexter with the others at his table.

"Somebody should do something," Travers said.

"You think we haven't thought about that? Yeah, we want to do something, but the question is, what? What can we do?" Smalley asked.

"I don't know, maybe Harold's editorial will wake some people up," Doc Gunter said. "It isn't just the fact that Dawes is on a hanging spree, it's everything he does. The way they fine the whores once a month, the way they collect taxes on every business in town. And not just retail business, mind you. I'm having to pay thirty-five dollars a month just to practice medicine."

"Yeah, fifty a month for me to keep my mercantile store open," Smalley said.

"I haven't been here for a month yet, but apparently it will be costing me that much to run the feed and seed," Travers said.

"Don't think I'm exempt," Denham said. "I'm paying thirty-five dollars a month to publish my newspaper."

"Harold, you know what you should do? You should send a copy of your newspaper to the governor," Doc Gunter suggested.

"Yeah!" Smalley added enthusiastically. "If the governor read your article, he would maybe do something about it."

"The governor is an elected official just like the judge and the sheriff. He's not going to take a hand in dealing with other elected officials," Denham said.

"How about the Texas Rangers?" Doc Gunter asked. "If we could get a Texas Ranger here, could be he could straighten a few things out for us."

"Good idea," Smalley said. "I know a ranger; I'll send him a telegram."

"Better not send it from here," Denham cautioned.

"Don't worry. I won't."

"Hey!" someone shouted from the front door. "Denham! You better come quick! Someone just threw a brick through your front window!"

Denham did get up quickly, followed by Doc Gunter, Smalley, and Travers. The four men hurried down to his newspaper office. The front door was still locked, with the sign turned to read CLOSED. But there was a big, gaping hole in the front window. Denham unlocked the door, pushed it open, then stepped inside. He could see a brick on the floor, surrounded by bits and pieces of the glass that had come from his broken window.

Denham bowed his head and pinched the bridge of his nose.

"I'm sorry, Harold," Doc Gunter said.

Denham looked back toward his composing room, the press, the table, his trays, and the type drawers. Except for the shattered glass, nothing else seemed to be disturbed.

"It could have been worse," he said.

"Have you got a broom? I'll help you get this mess cleaned up," Smalley offered.

"No," Denham said, holding out his hand. "Leave it be."

"What do you mean, 'leave it be'? You've got to get it cleaned up," Smalley said.

"No, I don't. I don't want it cleaned up. Evidently someone did not like what I wrote. I intend to leave it just like it is—as a badge of honor."

"Harold, you be careful," Doc Gunter said. "I mean it. I don't put anything past Dawes or Poindexter."

"If he thinks throwing a brick through a window is going to keep me quiet, he has another thing coming," Denham said. He pointed his finger into the air, then, and as if giving a speech, bellowed out: "Preserve the freedom of the human mind and freedom of the press. Every spirit should be ready to devote itself to martyrdom; for as long as we may think as we will, and speak as we think, the condition of man will proceed in improvement."

"Those are some words," Smalley said.

"They are indeed, sir, but I cannot take credit for them," Denham replied. "Those words, sir, were uttered by Thomas Jefferson."

Van Arsdale took another swallow of his whiskey and sat in the dark loneliness of his room, looking down onto the street. He saw Harold Denham the newspaper owner come, along with Doc Gunter, Mr. Smalley, and the new man who had bought the feed and seed store from Donald Lewis.

"Who did this?" one of the other townspeople asked aloud.

"It was our noble sheriff," Van Arsdale answered quietly in the dark of his room. He held the bottle out toward the window as if in salute. "Our noble sheriff did it." And though he spoke the words aloud, he did not say them loudly enough for anyone to hear.

James Earl Van Arsdale, son of Congressman Van Arsdale of the 1st Congressional District of Virginia, graduated from William and Mary with honors. He had a bright future ahead of him, a future planned by his father.

"I may seek a seat in the Senate," the senior Van Arsdale told his son. "And when I do, you will take my seat in the House."

James Earl didn't want to run for congress. He wanted to marry Martha Jane Malcolm. Martha Jane was a beautiful girl, but Martha Jane had a flaw in her past that the senior Van Arsdale could not overlook. Indeed, the flaw in Martha Jane's past was such that not even the State of Virginia could sanction the marriage. Martha Jane's beautiful dark eyes and golden skin were the result of her grandmother. Martha Jane's grandmother was a black woman.

Determined to marry the woman he loved, James Earl Van Arsdale left Virginia and moved to Texas. Of course, Texas also had a law against miscegenation, but who, here, was to know?

The marriage had been happy, and Van Arsdale's law career had been very productive, until the night of the fire. Van Arsdale had been in Austin when the fire broke out. He knew nothing about it until he returned home, to find his house in ruins and his wife and child dead.

The cause of the fire was never determined, but it didn't matter. Van Arsdale blamed himself, not for causing the fire but for not being there when it happened. He was sure he would have been able to save them. And if he couldn't have saved Martha Jane and James Earl junior, then better he would have died with them.

He got drunk that very day and had been drunk ever since.

Now, as he sat here in the darkness, looking down on the newspaper office, he felt a begrudging respect for Harold Denham. Denham was a decent man, and a man of courage. Denham, almost single-handedly, was fighting the corrupt policies of Judge Dawes, Sheriff Poindexter, and Prosecuting Attorney Gillespie.

Van Arsdale knew what they were doing and knew that if he had as much courage as Denham, he could write a brief and submit it to the State Supreme Court.

Ah, but there was the rub.

Van Arsdale's courage was in the bottle. And, right now, that bottle was empty.

Van Arsdale went to his cabinet for a new bottle. He wondered how much of this one he would have to drink before his mind would turn everything off enough to buy him another night of relative peace. He held the bottle up and looked at it for a moment.

"And now," he said, paraphrasing a verse from Philippians, "comes the peace that passeth all understanding."

Turning the bottle up, he took several Adam's apple–bobbing swallows before staggering off to bed.

CHAPTER SIX

MacCallister Valley, Colorado

After leaving Durango, MacCallister followed the Gunnison River for a while, though with no particular destination in mind. The river snaked out across the gently undulating sagebrush-covered prairie before him, shining gold in the setting sun, sometimes white where it broke over rocks, other times shimmering a deep blue-green in the swirling eddies and trapped pools.

The ragged mountains to the east of him were dotted with aspen, pine, cottonwood, and willow. There were bare spots on the mountains in between the trees. These bare spots of rock and dirt were sometimes gray and sometimes red, but always distant and foreboding.

Just in time for supper, a rabbit hopped up in front of MacCallister and bounded down the trail ahead of him. MacCallister stopped his horse, pulled his rifle from the saddle scabbard, looped his leg around the pommel, raised the rifle to his shoulder, rested his elbow on his knee, and squeezed the trigger. He saw a puff of fur and spray of blood fly up from the rabbit. The rabbit made a headfirst somersault, then lay perfectly still.

Since he had no particular destination in mind, MacCallister stopped here and made camp under a growth of cottonwoods. He started a fire, skinned and cleaned the rabbit, then skewered it on a green willow branch and suspended it over the fire between two forked limbs. When it was golden brown he seasoned the meat with the supply of salt he always kept on hand, and began eating.

After his supper, MacCallister stirred the fire, then lay down alongside it, using his saddle as a pillow. He stared into the coals, watching, while the red sparks rode a heated column of air high up into the night sky. There, the still glowing red and orange sparks joined the jewel-like scattering of stars.

MacCallister had a full belly, a good fire, a good horse, and a nearby supply of water. He was content.

One might think, seeing MacCallister this way, that he was a man without a home, subsisting on rabbit, fish, and such as he could provide. But such a thought would be wrong, for MacCallister was truly among the most affluent in all of Colorado. Falcon MacCallister was the kind of man who was a welcome guest in the governor's mansion, a frequent visitor to New York where he stayed in the finest hotels and dined in the most elegant restaurants, yet equally comfortable, and always welcome, around the campfires of nomadic Indians. And he very much enjoyed his frequent excursions into the mountains.

It was late in the afternoon of the next day when Falcon MacCallister approached the little town. He stopped on a ridge and looked down at the town as he removed is canteen from the saddle pommel. He took a swallow, recorked the canteen, then put it back. Slapping his legs against the side of his horse, he headed Lightning down the long slope of the ridge. He was sure he had never been in this town before, and he thought he would like to check it out.

The town was typical of many others he had seen with several unpainted, wood-frame shanties and even a couple of sod buildings lining the street. Then, just as abruptly as the town started, it quit, and the prairie began again.

MacCallister knew about such towns, festering and inbred, bypassed by the railroad and just hanging on. He was sure the population couldn't be more than a hundred, if that many. He knew that in the spring the street would be a muddy mire, worked by the horses' hooves and mixed with their droppings to become a stinking, sucking, pool of ooze. In the winter it would be frozen solid, while in the summer it would bake as hard as rock. It was summer now, and the sun was yellow and hot.

The buildings were weathered and leaning, and the painted signs on front of the edifices were worn and hard to read. A wagon was backed up to the general store, and a couple of men were listlessly unloading it. They looked over at MacCallister, curious as to who he was and what brought him to town, though neither of them were ambitious enough to speak to him.

MacCallister dismounted in front of the building that had the word SALOON painted on the front, just above the door. Shadows made the saloon seem cooler, but that was illusory. It was nearly as hot inside as out, and without the benefit of a breath of air, it was even more stifling. The customers were sweating in their drinks and wiping their faces with bandannas.

As always when he entered a strange saloon, MacCallister checked the place out. To one unfamiliar with what he was doing, MacCallister's glance appeared to be little more than idle curiosity. But it was a studied surveillance. Who was armed? What type guns were they carrying? How were they wearing them? Was there anyone here he knew? More important, was there anyone here who knew him, and who might take this opportunity to settle some old score, real or imagined, for himself or a friend?

It appeared that there were only workers and cowboys here. The couple of men who were armed were young, probably wearing their guns as much for show as anything. And from the way the pistols rode on their hips, MacCallister would have bet that they had never used them for anything but target practice, and not very successfully at that.

The bartender stood behind the bar. In front of him were two glasses with whiskey remaining in them, and he poured the whiskey back into a bottle, corked it, and put the bottle on the shelf behind the bar. He wiped the glasses out with his stained apron, then set them among the unused glasses. Seeing MacCallister step up to the bar, the bartender moved down toward him.

"Beer," MacCallister said.

"Don't think I've seen you before," the bartender said.

"I don't think I've been here before."

"What brings you to town?"

"I'm not in town," Falcon said. "I'm just passing through. Thought I'd have a couple of drinks, eat some food that isn't trail-cooked, and maybe get a room for the night."

"We don't get too many of your kind in here," one of the men at the bar said.

Falcon paid for his drink, then lifted it to his lips. Taking a swallow, he wiped his mouth with the back of his hand.

"Is there a place to eat in this town?"

"The Mountain Café is just down the street. A woman named Sally Morgan runs it. The food ain't fancy, but she sets a good table," the bartender said. "She can put you up, too. She has a couple of rooms in the back that she rents. Sometimes you have to share it, but most of the time you don't."

"Hey, mister, are you deef?" someone at the bar said. "I said we don't get too many of your kind here."

The tone of the man's voice was more challenging than friendly, and Falcon turned to look at him. He was a big man with an unkempt, black beard.

"Oh?" MacCallister replied. "And just what would my kind be?"

"I'd say you are a saddle tramp," the bushy, bearded man said.

"Well now, we seem to be getting off on the wrong foot here," Falcon said. "I tell you what. Why don't I buy you a drink?" Falcon put a coin on the bar and slid it toward the bartender, who took the coin, then poured a new drink for the bearded man.

"Here you go, Pierce," the bartender said. "Compliments of the gentleman."

Pierce picked the glass up and held it toward Falcon as if offering a toast. Falcon returned the gesture, then lifted his glass to his mouth. Pierce poured his drink into the spittoon that was on the floor beside him.

"I'm pretty choosy about who I drink with," Pierce said.

"Are you? Well, I suppose I'm just more eclectic."

"Ec—what?"

"It means I'm not quite as choosy. I mean, look,

you are clearly a tick-infested sack of horse shit, but I'm willing to drink with you."

The others in the saloon, surprised to hear Falcon's response, laughed out loud.

"Mister, nobody talks about me like that," Pierce said.

"Oh, I'm sure they all do. They just don't say it where you can hear them."

Again there was laughter.

"I don't like you, mister," he said. "I don't like you at all."

"Pierce, you had better back out of this conversation while you can," one of the bar patrons said. "I've got a feelin' that this is a man who can't be buffaloed."

Pierce, his face flushed red with anger and embarrassment, charged toward MacCallister with a loud yell.

Falcon saw the glint of a silver blade flashing toward him, and he jerked to one side just in time to keep from having his belly ripped open. At almost exactly the same time, he pulled his pistol from his holster and brought it down hard, on Pierce's head. Pierce went down like a sack of potatoes.

Falcon put his pistol back in his holster, then picked up his drink.

"That's a hell of a welcoming committee you've got there," he said.

"You got it right, mister," the bartender said.

"Pierce is a horse's ass. He has the whole town buffaloed. I reckon he figured he needed to take you down, just to show everyone else that he was still the top rooster."

Falcon nodded. Finishing his drink, he put the glass down and slapped another nickel on the bar beside it. "That was a pretty good beer. I think I'll have another."

The bartender pushed the nickel back. "This one is on me." He drew another beer from the keg behind him.

"Thanks."

"I think I'll give Pierce a drink on me as well." The bartender filled another mug with beer, then, leaning over the bar, poured the beer down on Pierce's face.

Pierce came to, spitting and swearing. When he sat up, he saw the bartender holding an empty glass.

"Why you . . . ," he said, getting to his feet angrily. "I'm going to . . . ,"

"Leave," the bartender said.

"What?" Pierce asked.

"I was just finishing your sentence for you. You were about to say that you were going to leave."

"I wasn't about to say no such thing," Pierce sputtered.

"Yeah, you were," the bartender said. He reached under the bar, then pulled out a double-barrel shotgun. "I want you to leave, right now."

"What kind of saloon is this, where you think you can just throw anyone out that you want to?"

"Oh, I'm not throwing anyone out. The only one I am throwing out is you."

"Listen, what about the rest of you?" Pierce asked the others in the saloon. "This man is a stranger. Are you people takin' his side over one of your own?"

"You ain't one of our own, Pierce, and you never have been," the bartender said.

"All right, all right, I'm a'goin'," Pierce said. He looked at each one of the remaining bar customers. "But I plan to remember who was here, and who didn't stand beside me. And when I come back, there's going to be a settling of accounts."

"Is that a threat, Pierce?" one of the saloon patrons asked.

"You damn right it is a threat."

"Well, this isn't a threat, Pierce, this is a promise. If you come back, we'll kill you," the saloon patron said. He spoke quietly and calmly. And it was that, the matter-of-fact delivery, that made the words so chilling.

Pierce pointed at the speaker. "You think you are man enough to kill me?" he asked.

"He didn't say 'I,' Pierce. He said 'we,'" one of the other patrons said. "If you come back, we will kill you."

The anger and defiance on Pierce's face was replaced by a flicker of fear. He stood there for a moment longer, blinking, trying unsuccessfully to regain a little of his self-respect. Finally, he ran his hand through his beard, then turned toward Falcon.

"You," he said. "You're the cause of this. What's your name, mister?"

"MacCallister. Falcon MacCallister."

"Falcon Mac . . . you? You are Falcon Mac-Callister?" There was an expression of awe and fear in Pierce's voice.

"Yes."

"I . . . uh . . . I didn't know."

Pierce moved toward the door with the bartender behind him. Everyone but Falcon went to the door as well, and they watched as Pierce climbed onto his horse.

"I didn't know," he said again.

CHAPTER SEVEN

Sorrento

Lucy Smith lay in bed staring up at the ceiling. Sheriff Poindexter was lying in bed beside her, still breathing hard from the exertion of a few moments earlier. Lucy had chosen this profession because she thought it would be an easy way to make a lot of money.

There was nothing easy about it. It did have its moments, such as when she helped some young man through his first experience. But more often than not, she found herself dealing with men who were angry with their alcohol-induced impotence, men who sometimes struck out at her in their anger.

Poindexter had never hit her, but because he frightened her, it took all she had just to be able to force herself to be with him. She breathed a sigh of relief that she managed to do so once more. Then she got up from the bed and walked over to the chest of drawers, where she poured water into the large, porcelain basin. In the mirror above the chest, she saw Sheriff Poindexter staring at her, so she picked up the basin and went behind the dressing screen.

"What for did you go behind that screen?" Sheriff Poindexter asked.

"I don't like performing my ablutions before an audience," she answered.

"Say what?"

There was a sound of rippling water as she dipped the washcloth into the basin. "It means I need a little privacy."

"You're a whore," Sheriff Poindexter said. "There ain't nothin' a whore does that's private. Whatever it is that you're a' doin', do it out here so I can watch."

There was another rippling sound of water, but Lucy Smith did not come out from behind the screen.

"I said, come out from behind that screen!" Sheriff Poindexter walked over to the folding screen, picked it up, and threw it.

Lucy let out a little scream of fear, then cringed, frightened that he was about to hit her.

"What are you duckin' for?" Sheriff Poindexter demanded. "I ain't plannin' on hittin' you. Not as long as you do what I say. All I'm goin' to do is watch. Now, go on with what you were doin'."

Lucy, now sobbing silently in fear and embarrassment, dipped the cloth in the water and continued to clean herself. There was a loud knock on the door.

"Lucy, is everything all right in there?" a man's voice called.

"This is Sheriff Poindexter," Poindexter called back. "I've got ever'thing under control."

"Lucy?"

"I told you I got ever'thing under control. Now you just go on about your business; leave me to mine!"

"I want to hear her voice," the man outside the door insisted.

Sheriff Poindexter pulled on his pants, strapped on his pistol belt, and then walked over to jerk open the door. Beeson, who was not only the bartender, but the owner of the Hog Heaven saloon, was standing on the other side.

"Sheriff, what's goin' on here? Why did I hear Lucy call out?"

"Beeson, you're just the man I'm wanting to see," Poindexter said. "I've just discovered that you're runnin' a whorehouse here," he said. "A whorehouse mind you, in clear violation of the law. You're under arrest."

"Under arrest? What do you mean? You're the one that came up here to Lucy's room."

"It was just part of my investigating," Sheriff Poindexter said. "I suspected you were runnin' a whorehouse, and now I know for sure that you are. So, you can pay me the fine now, five dollars for each one of your whores, or you can come down to the courthouse and pay ten dollars for each of your whores. Which is it goin' to be?"

"First, I want to see that Lucy is all right."

Poindexter pulled his pistol, pointed it at Beeson's head, and pulled the hammer back. "I told you, you were under arrest. I could shoot you for resisting arrest."

"No, don't, please!" Lucy shouted. "Mr. Beeson, it's all right! I'm fine."

"I heard you call out," Beeson said.

"It's all right, really," Lucy said. "I . . . I knocked over the dressing screen by accident, that's all."

"All right, if you are sure," Beeson said. "I'll just go back down to the bar."

"Not yet," Sheriff Poindexter said.

"What do you mean, 'not yet'?"

"There is the little matter of twenty-five dollars that you owe me, five dollars for each whore you have workin' here."

"You aren't serious about that, are you? You know that I pay a fine once a month so I can do business, just as all the girls do."

"Yes, well, this is a special fine. Now what is it to be? The fine, or I take you to jail? Or do I shoot you for resisting arrest?"

"I'll . . . I'll have to get the money from downstairs," Beeson said.

"You do that."

Lucy started to get dressed.

"What are you doin'?" Sheriff Poindexter asked.

"I'm getting dressed."

"What for?"

"Because I'm finished with my toilette."

"You are? You mean that's all there was to it?"

"Yes."

"Hell, what was you so private about? You didn't do nothin' but splash a little water onto yourself."

"Sheriff, would you like me to bathe you?" Lucy asked. She smiled seductively at him, hoping in such a way to defuse his anger.

"No. Why the hell would I want that? I took me a bath not no more than a couple weeks ago."

"Some men seem to like it," Lucy suggested.

"Seems to me that only a girly man would like something like that. No thanks, I'll be doin' my own washin'."

Poindexter went downstairs, still tucking his shirttail in as he was on the steps. He walked over to the bar.

"You got that money ready for me yet?"

"Sheriff, this ain't in no way right, and you know it," Beeson said.

"It's right 'cause I say it's right," Poindexter said.

With a sigh of frustration and anger, Beeson gave Poindexter two bills: a twenty and a five.

Ranger Corey Davidson had been with the Texas Rangers since before the war, returning to serve with the Rangers once they were reconstituted after Reconstruction. He was one of the Rangers around whom myths had developed—once he bested four armed men, killing three of them and taking the fourth prisoner.

Today he was in a cantina in the small border town of Los Carrilous. He was looking for a man named Paco Bustamante. Bustamante had robbed a small country store, taking the fifteen-year-old daughter of the store owner hostage. The nude body of the young girl had been found later that same day.

Davidson was the only gringo in the cantina, but that didn't elicit too much attention. Gringos were frequent visitors to the cantina, sometimes because they had developed a taste for tequila, but more often their tastes were somewhat more ribald and ran toward the dark-eyed *putas* who worked the cantina.

Davidson held up his badge.

"I am a Texas Ranger," he said loudly. "I am looking for Paco Bustamante."

No one responded, though Davidson saw a few of them glance nervously toward the back of the room. Davidson followed the glance and saw a Mexican against the wall was dumping the bargirl from his lap. She screamed in surprise and fright as the Mexican came up with a pistol in his hand.

Davidson brought his own gun up, even as the Mexican's gun burst the firing-cap. The Mexican's bullet hit the deck of cards some of the patrons had been playing with, sending them scattering. By now everyone in the place had dived for cover, leaving only

Davidson and Bustamante standing. But Bustamante didn't stand for long, because Davidson fired before the Mexican could pull the trigger a second time.

Bustamante staggered forward, then crashed through a nearby table. Glasses and bottles tumbled and tequila spilled. The gun smoke drifted slowly up to the ceiling, then spread out in a wide, nostril-burning cloud. Davidson looked around the room quickly to see if anyone else might represent danger, but he saw only the faces of the customers, and they showed fear, awe, and surprise.

When Davidson returned to Austin, he had a telegram waiting for him. The telegram was from Eb Smalley, a man who had served in his regiment during the war. The telegram asked him to please come to Sorrento to look into conditions there. Because Davidson considered the telegram to be a personal, rather than an official, request, he did not notify his superiors of his intention; therefore, his visit would be in a nonofficial capacity.

When Davidson reached Sorrento, he rode directly to Smalley's store, dismounted, then went inside. Smalley, who was with a customer, saw Ranger Davidson come in.

"Mr. Deckert, would you take care of Mr. Evans, please?" Smalley said to his clerk. "I see an old friend."

"Yes, sir, Mr. Smalley," Hodge Deckert said as, smiling, he moved in to tend to the customer's needs.

Smalley wiped his hands and advanced toward Ranger Davidson; then, with a huge smile, he extended his hand.

"Colonel Davidson, sir, how good it is to see you."

"Hello, Major Smalley. I got your telegram. Would you like to tell me what's going on in this town?"

"I'll tell you what is going on in this town," Smalley said. "Judge Dawes, Prosecutor Gillespie, Sheriff Poindexter, and his deputies have turned this town into hell. The judge is using the hangman's rope as a means of legal murder, and they are bleeding the town dry with illegal taxes and fines."

"Have you got any proof of this? I mean, I believe you, Eb, but when you are dealing with officials like a judge, sheriff, and prosecuting attorney, you are going to have to have some sort of backup."

"Come with me to see Harold Denham. He's the newspaper editor, and he has been keeping a really close record."

On their way to the newspaper, Smalley stopped by Doc Gunter's office, inviting him to join them.

"I have to admit," Ranger Davidson said half an hour later, after he had examined all the material Denham had collected, "that this is pretty damning. And you say O'Dell didn't get a trial by jury?"

"The judge, prosecutor, and sheriff all claim that he said he didn't want one. But, Ranger Davidson, I was in the court when they brought him in. He had no idea that the trial could end in such a way. In fact, I believe he welcomed the trial because he thought he would be able to get support from the court on recovering the money that was owed him," Denham said.

"This article suggests that Judge Dawes is a brother-in-law to the man who owed O'Dell money."

"I'm doing more than suggesting it. I'm coming right out and saying it."

"Do you have any proof of that?"

"Let me show you something," Denham said. He opened a drawer from one of the cabinets in his composing room, then took out two pieces of stiff card material that were tied with a strip of cloth. Undoing the cloth, he removed the top card, disclosing a photograph of a document.

"What is this?" Ranger Davidson asked.

"This, Ranger Davidson, is proof that Dumey is Judge Dawes's brother-in-law. It is a photograph of the wedding license. You see here that the woman's maiden name is Lila Dawes. And you see here that the judge was not only the issuing authority, but is also listed as 'brother to the female applicant.'"

"Judge Dawes should have recused himself from the O'Dell case," Ranger Davidson said.

"Yes, that's what I think as well."

"You did well to send for me, Eb."

"So, what are you going to do? How are you going to handle it?"

"The judge can only be removed by the state supreme court ethics committee, or by impeachment."

"What about the sheriff? I've shown you a list of his violations as well."

"Ah, now that I can do something about," Ranger Davidson said. "I can arrest him. That will do two things. It will take away Judge Dawes's 'army' so to speak, and, in the ensuing trial, we will be able to turn up enough evidence to use against the judge in impeachment."

"Are you going to arrest the sheriff?" Denham asked.

"Yes."

"I don't know if you ought to do that."

"What do you mean? I thought that was what you wanted."

"Yes, I do want it. But the sheriff has at least two deputies around him all the time. I don't know if it would be all that good of an idea for you to go up against him all by yourself. Shouldn't you get some help?"

"I'm all the help I'll need," Ranger Davidson said confidently.

Davidson stood up, loosened his pistol in the holster, then left the newspaper office. "I take it he will be in the sheriff's office?"

"You will find him in one of the saloons. More

than likely it will be the Long Trail saloon; that's the one he frequents the most," Denham said.

"Are you saying the sheriff spends all his time in a saloon?"

"Yeah, and why not?" Smalley added. "He drinks free, he eats free, and anytime he wants one of the girls, why, she is free as well."

"That's using his badge for personal gain," Ranger Davidson said. "That's all I need to arrest him."

Ranger Davidson left the newspaper office and started toward the Long Trail.

"I wish he would get some help before he does something like this," Denham said.

"He was a ranger before the war, and I served in the war with him," Smalley said. "He is one of the bravest, if not the bravest, men I have ever known."

"I don't question his courage," Denham said. "But I do question his wisdom."

A game of checkers was being played by two gray-bearded men in front of Travers's Feed and Seed Store, watched over by half a dozen kibitzers. Luke Travers was standing at the front door looking out onto the street when he saw someone walking from the newspaper office toward the Long Trail saloon. He recognized the badge that is unique to the Texas Rangers.

"Boys, that there is a Texas Ranger," he said.

"What's a Texas Ranger doin' in Sorrento?"

"I think Mr. Smalley sent for him," Travers said.

"To deal with the sheriff?"

"That's my understanding."

"Good. I hope they lock the son of a bitch up and throw the key away."

"Crown me," one of the players said.

The shopkeeper who was running the dry goods store came through his front door and began vigorously sweeping the wooden porch. His broom did little but raise the dust to swirl about, then fall back down again. He brushed a sleeping dog off the porch, but even before he went back inside, the dog reclaimed his position, curled around comfortably, and, within a moment, was asleep again. Like Luke Travers, the shopkeeper recognized the badge as a Texas Ranger badge, and he stayed out on his front porch watching until the ranger reached the saloon.

When Ranger Davidson reached the saloon, he stood out front for a moment.

In a nearby building, a curtain was pulled to one side and a curious onlooker came to the window.

Somewhere down the street a dog started barking.

A fly buzzed past Davidson's ear, did a few circles, then descended quickly to a freshly deposited horse apple and was joined almost immediately by a dozen others.

Ranger Davidson pushed through the batwing doors, then stepped to one side so that a wall was

at his back. At the bar, with a glass of beer in front
of him, stood a big man with a deformed eye.
Davidson would have recognized him from his
description, even if he hadn't been wearing a sheriff's badge.

"Well, if it ain't a Texas Ranger," Poindexter said.
"Welcome to my town, Ranger. Step up to the bar
and have a drink. The bartender don't charge
nothin' for lawmen. Do you, bartender?"

Ranger Davidson made no movement toward
the bar.

"Well, maybe you ain't a drinkin' man," Poindexter said. "That's all right. Look around at the girls.
See one that you find pleasin'? Take her. The girls,
they don't charge the lawmen nothin', neither."

Davidson remained in place.

"Well, if you don't want a drink, and you don't
want a whore, what are you doin' in here? What do
you want?" Poindexter asked.

"I'm putting you under arrest," Ranger Davidson said.

"What?" Poindexter replied in surprise. Then he
laughed. "You're funnin' with me, ain't you, Ranger?"

"This is no joke, Poindexter. You are under arrest
for malfeasance in office."

"Mal . . . mal . . . what? What is that?"

"It's enough to get you twenty years," Davidson
said. "Like I said, Poindexter, you are under arrest.
Take off your badge, and drop your gun belt."

"You got that a little backwards, ain't you,
Ranger? I'm the sheriff here. You are in my town

and my county. I'm putting you under arrest for threatening an officer of the law."

Poindexter turned to face Ranger Davidson. "Now, you drop your gun belt."

"Poindexter, my authority comes from the State of Texas. Are you saying that county authority supersedes state authority?"

"Look over here, Ranger!" Deputy Sharp called. When Davidson looked toward him, he saw Sharp was standing near the piano, holding a double-barrel shotgun pointed directly at him.

"If you so much as touch your gun, I'll blow your head off."

Poindexter drew his pistol and pointed it at Davidson. "Well now, Mr. Texas Ranger, you seem to have gotten yourself into quite a little bind here. There are two guns pointed at you."

"That doesn't change anything," Davidson said. "You are still under arrest."

"Draw, Ranger!" Poindexter shouted. And even as Poindexter yelled, he pulled the trigger. Sharp pulled both triggers at nearly the same time.

When Davidson heard Poindexter shout, he realized that he had no choice but to draw his own gun. He was fast, fast enough to get a shot off even as both Poindexter and Sharp fired at him. Davidson was hit by Poindexter's bullet and a double load of buckshot from the shotgun Sharp was holding. The shots slammed Davidson backward, crashing through the batwing doors and falling flat on his back on the boardwalk in front of the saloon. His chest looked like raw meat from the wounds, and blood gushed out to soak the boards around him.

There was a moment of silence, then one of the patrons nearest the door ventured a peek over the top of the batwings. He turned and shouted back to the others.

"He's dead, folks. He's deader than a doornail."

"Bartender," Poindexter said.

"Yes, Sheriff?"

"I'll be havin' another drink now."

"Dead?" Smalley said when someone brought him the news. "Davidson is dead?"

"Yes, sir."

Smalley ran his hand through his hair. "I would've thought he could handle Poindexter."

"He probably could have handled Poindexter if it had just been him. But Sharp was there, too, and Sharp got the drop on him with a double-barreled Greener. Then Poindexter pulled his gun, and the next thing you know he was yellin' at the ranger to draw. Well, of course by then there weren't naught the ranger could do but try and draw his own gun. Even then, he managed to get it out of his holster before both Poindexter and Sharp unloaded on him. He didn't have a chance."

CHAPTER EIGHT

"What do you mean, you're trying me for murder?" Poindexter asked Prosecutor Gillespie.

"It's for your own protection," Gillespie replied.

"I don't see how me bein' tried for murder could be for my own protection."

"That's because you don't understand the law," Gillespie said. "If you are tried and found innocent, no other judge can ever try you again for that same crime. It's called double jeopardy."

Poindexter smiled, though it was difficult to see because of his deformed face. "Well I'll be damned. That's the way it works, huh?"

"Yes."

"What about Sharp? He shot him, too. Fact is, with that double load of buckshot, why it's more 'n likely that he's the one that actual kilt the ranger."

"If you are found innocent by way of justifiable homicide, then there will be no need to charge Sharp."

Poindexter was silent for a moment, then he

nodded. "All right," he said. "Let's get it done." He took his pistol belt off, lay it on his desk, then walked back to let himself into one of the jail cells. He lay down on the bunk and crossed his hands behind his head. "Until the trial starts, I'll just be my own prisoner." He laughed. "I'm goin' to take me a little nap now. You can wake me up when it's time for supper."

"I'll wake you up long before then," Gillespie said. "I plan to have the trial today."

The trial began less than two hours after the shooting had occurred. Because of the sensational aspect of a shooting between two lawmen, the court-house was full, despite the short notice.

They fidgeted about as they watched the jury pool take their seats.

"There's nobody new on the jury," Denham said to Smalley.

"It's how Dawes packs the court," Smalley replied.

Burt Gillespie, with a few questions, narrowed the jury down to twelve men.

"Your honor, the jury is empaneled," Gillespie said.

"Very good. We are going to need someone to represent the defendant."

"Your Honor, if it please the court . . . I would like to make the petition that I be temporarily excused from the position of prosecutor, so that I might defend Sheriff Poindexter."

"Hmm," Judge Dawes mused, stroking his chin. "All right," he finally said. "But that means I will have to appoint a new prosecutor."

"Yes, Your Honor."

"Very well," Judge Dawes replied. "Deputy Sharp, please locate James Earl Van Arsdale, and tell him he has been appointed as prosecutor for this case."

"James Earl Van Arsdale? Hell, Judge, he's a drunk!" Deputy Sharp said.

There was a smattering of nervous laughter from the gallery.

"He is also the only other lawyer in town. Locate him, please, and bring him here, to the courthouse."

The deputy smiled broadly, looked over at the sheriff, then back toward Judge Dawes. "Yes, sir."

"Van Arsdale?" Denham said to Doc Gunter. "James Earl Van Arsdale? Is the judge serious?"

"Think about it, Harold," Smalley said. "If you want to make certain the case turns out the way you want, what better way to ensure it than to pack the jury, then select a drunk to act as a prosecutor?"

"I doubt that Van Arsdale has even heard about the shooting," Doc Gunter replied.

The gallery fidgeted as they waited for Van Arsdale to arrive so he could assume the duties of prosecution attorney. During that time, Gillespie and his client spoke quietly at the defense table as they prepared their case.

A few minutes later Deputy Sharp returned to the courtroom with James Earl Van Arsdale in tow. Van Arsdale looked at the crowd in the courtroom, and it was obvious by the vacant look in his eyes and the expression on his face that he had no idea what was going on.

"Mr. Van Arsdale, approach the bench, please," Judge Dawes directed.

Hesitantly, cautiously, Van Arsdale did as instructed.

"Mr. Van Arsdale, raise your right hand."

When Van Arsdale didn't respond quickly enough, the deputy raised his hand for him.

"Do you, James Earl Van Arsdale, solemnly swear you will faithfully and impartially discharge and perform all the duties incumbent upon you as prosecuting attorney under the Constitution and laws of the United States and of the State of Texas, So help you God?"

"What? I'm to be the prosecutor?"

"Counselor, the only answer I will accept is yes, or no," Judge Dawes said sternly.

"No, Your Honor, I'm not prepared to be a prosecutor."

"Let me put it this way, Mr. Van Arsdale. You will either accept this assignment, or you will spend thirty days in jail for contempt of court. And I will personally see to it that you are disbarred. Now, what is your answer? Are you willing to serve as prosecuting attorney for the case at hand?"

"What is the case?"

"Sheriff Poindexter is on trial for the murder of a Texas Ranger."

Shocked by the comment, Van Arsdale looked over at Poindexter. Poindexter smirked at him.

"What will it be, Counselor?" Judge Dawes asked. "Jail and disbarment? Or you'll act as prosecutor?"

"I'll prosecute," Van Arsdale said.

"I thought you might see it my way. Now, raise your hand."

This time Van Arsdale raised his right hand without assistance.

"Do you, James Earl Van Arsdale, solemnly swear you will faithfully and impartially discharge and perform all the duties incumbent upon you as prosecuting attorney under the Constitution and laws of the United States and of the State of Texas, So help you God?"

Van Arsdale hesitated for a moment before he answered. "Yes," he said, mumbling the word very quietly.

"Would you repeat that please, Mr. Van Arsdale? You must say the word loudly enough that all here may bear witness."

"Yes," Van Arsdale said loudly and distinctly.

"Very good. You will act as prosecution attorney in the case of *Texas versus Sheriff Poindexter*. You may make your case."

"Your Honor, may I have some time to prepare for this case?"

"How much time do you need?"

"A week. A few days at least."

"I will give you fifteen minutes."

"Fifteen minutes? Your Honor, that's impossible!"

"Your fifteen minutes has already started," Judge Dawes said.

"Your Honor, you are asking me to prosecute the sheriff for murder, but I know nothing about this case!"

"Very well, Mr. Van Arsdale. I will increase your preparation time to one half hour in order that you may become acquainted with the case. You may retire to the jury deliberation room. I now ask that anyone who has information pertinent to the case that they think may help the prosecutor, to meet with him in the jury deliberation room."

"And, Judge, perhaps some coffee?"

"Deputy Sharp, get the prosecutor some coffee," Judge Dawes ordered.

"Yes, sir."

Harold Denham, Doc Gunter, and Eb Smalley were the only three people from the gallery who went into the deliberation room to meet with Van Arsdale. Van Arsdale was sitting at the far end of the table drinking cup after cup of coffee. He was going through a bad case of the shakes.

"Would someone please tell me what happened?" Van Arsdale asked.

"Corey Davidson went down to the Long Trail saloon to arrest Poindexter," Smalley said. "Poindexter and Deputy Sharp shot him."

"Corey Davidson. Do you mean Texas Ranger Corey Davidson?"

"Yes."

"I am only prosecuting Sheriff Poindexter. But you say both Poindexter and Deputy Sharp shot him?"

"Yes," Denham answered. "I think the idea is to try only Poindexter and if he is found not guilty, there will be no charges against Sharp."

"Did any of you actually see it happen?"

"None of us saw it, but we have heard accounts of it from those who did see it," Denham replied. "Apparently both Poindexter and Sharp had their guns pointed at him when Poindexter invited him to draw."

"You two can handle this," Doc Gunter said. "I had better get back out there and hold our seats."

"How do you know that the sheriff and Sharp already had their guns out?"

"That's what some have told us," Smalley suggested. "They are afraid to testify, but I would be willing to testify as to what they told me."

Van Arsdale waved that aside. "That would be hearsay and wouldn't be admissible. Why was Davidson trying to arrest Poindexter?"

"Mal something or the other," Smalley said. "I don't remember the word."

"Malfeasance," Denham said.

"Malfeasance, good. Yes, we can go with that," Van Arsdale said.

Deputy Sharp stepped into the deliberation room then. "Judge Dawes says you've been in here long enough. He's about to call court into session."

"Deputy, I need more time," Van Arsdale said.

"You ain't goin' to get no more time."

"Just a few minutes more."

"Let's go," Deputy Sharp ordered.

The jury was still sitting in the jury box when Denham and the others returned.

"Your Honor, I ask for a continuance until tomorrow. I need time to study this case."

"Request denied," Judge Dawes said.

Van Arsdale looked over at the jury. "Your Honor, there are only twelve men here. Am I to be given the right of *voir dire*?" Van Arsdale asked.

"*Voir dire* has already been completed. Make your case, Mr. Prosecutor," Judge Dawes ordered.

Van Arsdale walked over to the prosecutor's table and stood there for a moment. He looked out toward Denham, Smalley, and Doc Gunter, all of whom had taken their seat in the gallery. Doc Gunter made a motion as if drinking, then pointed to the table, whereon set a glass of water.

Van Arsdale shook his head no.

Gunter repeated the motion.

"Mr. Van Arsdale, the court is waiting," Judge Dawes said.

Again Gunter, and this time Denham and Smalley as well, made the motion.

Wondering why all three were so insistent that he drink the water, Van Arsdale picked the glass up. As soon as he brought it close enough, he realized that it wasn't water, it was tequila. With shaking hands he brought the glass to his lips. Once he had a drink, the shakes eased, and his mind cleared up somewhat.

"The case is a simple one to make, Your Honor. Corey Davidson, a well-known, highly respected, and honored Texas Ranger, attempted to place Sheriff Poindexter under arrest. Instead of acquiescing to the arrest as any ordinary citizen should and would do, Poindexter reacted in the most hostile way one can imagine. He pulled his pistol and shot Texas Ranger Corey Davidson. Poindexter was resisting arrest, and in so doing, killed Ranger Davidson. That is a clear case of felony murder."

Gillespie responded with a fifteen-minute-long impassioned defense plea. Davidson had come into the saloon looking for trouble, and when Sheriff Poindexter, in performance of his duty, attempted to place Davidson under arrest, Davidson drew his pistol and fired.

"Sheriff Poindexter was surprised by this unexpected response from someone who is supposed to be an officer of the law. He saw someone drawing on him, someone who had the reputation of being as quick as thought with a gun.

"I ask you, gentlemen of the jury. What would you have done? What would anyone have done? Naturally, when you are placed in a life-or-death situation, you are going to do whatever you must in order to save your own life.

"Sheriff Poindexter did just that. He drew his pistol and, fortunately, was able to get his gun out before Davidson. As the drawing and shooting in such an event is one continuous motion, there was no opportunity for him to order Davidson to drop his gun. There was but one option open to him if he would save his life, and that was to shoot Davidson.

"Sheriff Poindexter is aware of the sterling record that Davidson had put up as a Texas Ranger, and in truth, was surprised by Mr. Davidson's reaction. He feels bad about having killed this hero of Texas, but contends, and with justification, that he had no choice."

"Witnesses, Mr. Prosecutor?" Judge Dawes asked after Gillespie sat down.

"Your Honor, I call Deputy Sharp to the stand."

"Very well, the court calls Deputy Sharp to the stand."

"What do you want me for?" Sharp asked. "I thought we was goin' to try the sheriff, and once you found him not guilty, there wouldn't be no charges against me."

"There are no charges; you are being called as a witness."

Sharp looked over toward Gillespie, who nodded, then he walked to the front of the court.

"State your full name, please."

"Stanley Millard Sharp."

"Millard?" Deputy Josh Peters called out with a loud guffawing laugh. "Your name is Millard?"

"I was named after a president; what is wrong with that?" Sharp retorted.

Judge Dawes slammed his gavel on the bench. "Order," he called.

The courtroom quieted.

"Now, Deputy Sharp, do you swear to tell the truth, nothing but the truth, and the whole truth, so help you God?"

"Yeah."

"Say I do."

"I do."

"Your witness, Counselor."

Van Arsdale stared at Sharp, holding the stare for a long moment without saying a word. It began to have an effect on Sharp, who started fidgeting in the witness chair.

"What you starin' at me for?"

"Objection, Your Honor."

"What are you objecting to, Mr. Gillespie?" Van Arsdale said. "I haven't said anything yet."

"He's badgering the witness."

"How the hell can you call that badgering?" Denham blurted out.

Again, Dawes struck the bench with his gavel. "The next person who speaks will be found in contempt. Objection sustained. Counselor, you called this witness, now either ask him a question, or dismiss him."

"Very well, Your Honor. Deputy Sharp, when you shot Ranger Davidson, were you using buck and ball, or double-aught shot?"

"Hell, I was usin' buck 'n . . ."

"Deputy, don't answer that question! Your Honor,

I object!" Gillespie shouted loudly. "The deputy isn't on trial!"

"Sustained."

"Deputy, were you present when Ranger Davidson was killed?"

Sharp looked over at Gillespie, who nodded.

"Yeah, I was there."

"Tell the court what you saw."

"I saw Sheriff Poindexter try 'n' arrest Davidson, only Davidson went for his gun."

"Prior to that, did Ranger Davidson attempt to arrest Sheriff Poindexter?"

"I don't know."

"Were you close enough to see and hear what was going on?"

"Yes."

"Did you shoot at the same time as Sheriff Poindexter? Or was it a bit later?"

"It was about . . ."

"Don't answer that, Deputy. Objection, Your Honor."

"Sustained. Counselor, you have been warned before about this kind of question."

"Your Honor, I'm just trying to ascertain Deputy Sharp's participation in the incident, so the jury will be able to give some weight to his testimony."

"Do not question him again about his alleged participation."

"I have no further questions of this witness."

"Defense?" Judge Dawes asked.

"No questions."

"Your Honor, with your indulgence," Van Arsdale said. "Since I was not assigned this case until forty-five minutes ago, indeed, was even unaware of it, I have no other witnesses, and request permission to poll the gallery."

"Mr. Van Arsdale, the entire town was aware of this shooting incident. How is it that you were not?"

"Your Honor, I'm a drunk," Van Arsdale said. "Sometimes I'm barely aware that the sun is out."

There was more laughter from the gallery.

"Very well, you may poll the gallery for witnesses," Judge Dawes said.

Van Arsdale picked up the glass to take another drink but hesitated just as it reached his mouth and put it back down, without so much as tasting it. He faced the gallery.

"I ask anyone who saw this shooting take place to please volunteer now, to be a witness."

Deputies Russell and Peters stood. Van Arsdale saw Denham, Smalley, Travers, and Doc Gunter shaking their heads no, and he understood that these witnesses would not be helpful to his case.

Then Eb Smalley stood.

"Did you see the shooting, Mr. Smalley?" Van Arsdale asked.

"No, sir. But I can testify as to why Ranger Davidson was in Sorrento."

"Your Honor, prosecution calls Eb Smalley as a witness," Van Arsdale said.

Smalley came to the front and was sworn in.

"Mr. Smalley, I believe you stated you could testify as to why Ranger Davidson was in Sorrento."

"Yes."

"Please tell us."

"Objection, Your Honor. The reason Davidson was here has no relevancy to this case."

"Your Honor, Ranger Davidson did not spontaneously appear in the Long Trail saloon this morning. He was here for a purpose, and I believe Mr. Smalley can shed light on that."

"Objection overruled; you may examine the witness."

"Mr. Smalley, did you know Ranger Davidson?"

"I knew him very well. I was a company commander in his regiment during the war."

"What kind of man was he?"

"He was one of the finest men I ever knew. He was a Texas Ranger before the war, he was a very well-respected regimental commander during the war, and he rejoined the Texas Rangers again, as soon as they were reconstituted after the war."

"I believe you said you could shed some light on why he was in Sorrento today."

"He was here because I asked him to come."

"Why did you ask him to come?"

"I believe Sheriff Poindexter is guilty of malfeasance of duty, and I . . ."

"Objection, Your Honor. Sheriff Poindexter is being tried for murder, not for malfeasance," Gillespie interrupted.

"Sustained."

"Your Honor, this goes to the heart of why Ranger Davidson was here. It also provides a possible reason for the confrontation between Ranger Davidson and Sheriff Poindexter."

"The objection is sustained, Mr. Van Arsdale."

"Exception."

"Exception noted. Please continue."

"Continue where? You are gutting my case."

Judge Dawes slammed his gavel down hard. "Careful, Counselor, you are bordering on contempt."

"My apologies, Your Honor." Van Arsdale continued his examination. "Do you think Ranger Davidson went down to the Long Trail with the intention of killing Sheriff Poindexter?"

"No, I do not. I think he went down there to arrest him."

"Objection, Your Honor, hearsay."

"Sustained."

Van Arsdale shrugged his shoulders. "No further questions."

"Cross, Mr. Gillespie?" Judge Dawes asked.

"Not needed, Your Honor. This witness did no harm to my client."

"Call your next witness, Mr. Van Arsdale."

"Why?"

"Careful, Mr. Van Arsdale," Judge Dawes said sternly.

"I have no further witnesses, Your Honor. Prosecution rests its case."

Gillespie recalled Deputy Sharp, who testified

that Sheriff Poindexter had attempted to arrest Davidson for threatening a law officer.

"Davidson, he just got real mad and drew his gun on the sheriff. Sheriff Poindexter had no choice but to draw his own self, and what he done was, he beat Davidson to the draw."

"Thank you. Your witness, Counselor," Gillespie said.

"Deputy Sharp, why are you the only witness?"

"I don't know."

"Wasn't anyone else there? Other customers? The bartender? Any of the women?"

"I think they was all so scared that they didn't see nothin'."

"Or is it they all saw something but are too scared to testify?"

"Objection. Argumentive."

"Withdrawn." Van Arsdale returned to his seat.

"Closing, Mr. Van Arsdale?"

Van Arsdale didn't even stand. "I believe that Ranger Davidson attempted to arrest the sheriff and the sheriff killed the ranger while resisting arrest. The fact that Poindexter was resisting arrest renders the claim of self-defense invalid. Poindexter killed Davidson while he was resisting arrest. That constitutes felony murder, and I ask the jury to return that verdict." That was the full extent of his closing argument.

"Mr. Gillespie?" the judge said.

Taking a cue from Van Arsdale, Gillespie didn't stand, either. Nor did he speak more than one sentence.

"There was only one witness to the shooting, and his testimony makes it clear that this was a justifiable homicide."

It took the jury five minutes to render a not guilty verdict, and, with that verdict, all of Poindexter's deputies, and those who had allied themselves with him, rushed to congratulate him.

"Drinks are on me at the Long Trail!" Poindexter called out, and with enthusiastic shouts, his followers rushed from the courthouse to the saloon.

James Earl Van Arsdale remained at the prosecutor's table, long after everyone else had vacated the courthouse. He was still there, half an hour later, when Harold Denham went back into the courthouse.

"I thought you might be here," Denham said. Denham noticed that the glass of tequila was still full.

"I was a joke," Van Arsdale said. "Poindexter just got away with murder because of me."

"It wasn't because of you, James Earl. This whole thing was fixed from the beginning."

"Including getting a drunk to prosecute," James Earl added.

"Don't be so hard on yourself. The finest prosecutor in the state could not have overcome a stacked jury and a crooked judge."

"This incident has done one thing for me," Van Arsdale said. "It has provided an epiphany. From this day forward, I will never drink again."

CHAPTER NINE

When Falcon finally returned to MacCallister, he rode in on Kate MacCallister Boulevard. The Katy, as the locals called it, was the main street in town. Kate MacCallister had been Falcon's mother. And in the middle of town, in a square, was a statue of James Ian MacCallister, the town's namesake and Falcon's father.

Falcon rode by the City Pig restaurant where someone called out to him, then he passed Sikes Hardware until he reached the post office. Because he had been gone for the last two weeks, he knew he would have mail piling up, so that would be his first order of business.

Sheriff Cody came walking up the boardwalk toward him.

"Hello, Falcon. I heard about your little fracas over in Durango a couple of weeks ago."

"I figured you would have," Falcon said as he tied off Lightning.

"You figured right. News does get around," Sheriff Cody said. "By the way, I don't know if you know it, but there was a pretty large reward for Drew. Twenty-five hundred dollars. I'll be happy to file for it, if you want."

"Yes," Falcon said. "Do file for it. And when you get the money, give it all to the orphanage."

Sheriff Cody smiled. "Ha! I figured you would do something like that. I'll be glad to take care of that for you."

Falcon didn't really need the money. He owned mineral rights to working gold and silver mines, and he was drawing more money from those enterprises than the men who were actually working the mines. In addition, he had a very productive and profitable cattle ranch. As a result of his being independently comfortable, he often donated any unexpected money to charitable causes, be it the orphanage, various widows' funds, or anything else that might catch his fancy.

Falcon went into the post office.

"Hello, Falcon," the postmaster greeted warmly. "It's good to see you in town for a change. You are gone so often."

"Hi, Will. What have you got for me?"

"You got a letter from some newspaper in Texas. Or so the printed copy on the envelope says."

"You reading my mail, are you, Will?" Falcon teased.

"Not reading your mail, just the envelopes. And I have to, that's my job," Will replied.

Falcon chuckled. "I was just teasing." He tore open the envelope, then pulled out the letter and began to read.

Dear Falcon

I do hope you remember me. I am Harold Denham and I was editor and publisher of the Higbee Journal, when the town of Higbee was still in existence. I learned then that you are a man of honor, courage, and integrity. Such a man is badly needed in Sorrento. I have been publishing a newspaper, the Sorrento Advocate, since I arrived here. When I arrived the town was vibrant, with fair minded and industrious people, anxious to help the community grow.

But in the last 3 years things have changed drastically. We have a judge and sheriff who have taken over the town. Anyone who attempts to run against them is discouraged to the point of physical danger. Extremely heavy local taxes have been assessed, and our local judge, Judge Theodore Dawes, is known as "Hang 'em High" Dawes, not without good reason.

There have been to date, six hangings this year. It may well be that one or two of the victims deserved to be hanged, though the justification of all the hangings has been questionable and no doubt the sentence, if not the verdict, would have been overturned on appeal. But no appeal is allowed. The judge, with a handpicked jury, tries the defendants, often in less than an hour. The

jury finds the defendant guilty, and the judge
sentences the defendant to hang, the entire process
taking less than one 24-hour period.

Sheriff Dewey Poindexter is Judge Dawes's right-
hand man and enforcer. Those who are in the judge's
or the sheriff's favor are exempt from normal behavior.
The town is terrorized, and neither merchant nor
citizen can expect any support from the legal system.
Vandalism, assaults on our citizens, public
drunkenness, obscene behavior, all such activity as
would normally be dampened by an honest and
aggressive legal system are allowed to flourish here.

A recent incident will illustrate the sad state
of affairs in our town. A concerned local citizen
wrote to a friend of his, who was a Texas Ranger.
He invited the ranger, a genuine Texas hero by the
name of Corey Davidson, to come to Sorrento to
investigate malfeasance on the part of our sheriff.
Sheriff Poindexter shot and killed Ranger
Davidson. Judge Dawes then held a trial,
charging Poindexter with murder. Though it was
reported to me by witnesses that it was indeed cold-
blooded murder, those witnesses were too frightened
to testify, and the result was exactly as Judge
Dawes, Prosecutor Gillespie, and Sheriff
Poindexter expected. The sheriff was found not
guilty, thus immunizing him against any future
charge of murder.

I have no way of persuading you to come, other
than to appeal to your sense of honor, justice, and
fair play. Should you decide to help us, you may

*find me at the Sorrento Advocate, 311 Front Street,
Sorrento, Texas.*

With Respect, I remain:

> *Your Obedient Servant,*
> *Harold Denham*

Letter in hand, Falcon walked down to the sheriff's office, where he saw Sheriff Cody looking through reward posters.

"I haven't found the Drew poster yet," Cody said. "But I know I've seen paper on him."

"Thank you, Amos, but I'm not here to check on that," Falcon said. "I want you to see what you can find out about a judge Theodore Dawes and Sheriff Dewey Poindexter."

"Hmm, I don't think I've ever heard of either one of them," Sheriff Cody said.

"I wouldn't really expect you to. They are both down in Texas. Sorrento, Texas."

"All right, I've got some sheriff friends down in Texas. I suppose I could send a few telegrams and see what turns up," Cody promised.

It was nearly noon, so Falcon walked back down to the City Pig. He was greeted warmly by the customers when he stepped inside, and Kathy Johnson, the pretty waitress, escorted him back to "his" table. He ordered ham, rice, and gravy.

As Kathy walked away with his order, Swayne Byrd, a neighboring rancher, came over to Falcon's table.

"Miss Kathy, if you would please, put Falcon's dinner on my tab."

"Thank you, Swayne," Falcon said.

"No, sir, thank you. Johnny Pollard worked for me. I went to Durango and made arrangements to put his body on a train and send it back to his folks for buryin'. He was a good kid. From a little town in Southeast Missouri, he was."

"I wish I had been there in time to have prevented it," Falcon said.

Swayne nodded. "Some things are just bound to happen," he said. "Well, I'll leave you in peace with your dinner. I just wanted to thank you for what you done."

Kathy brought Falcon's meal just as Swayne left the restaurant and, with a large and pretty smile, put it on the table before him.

Falcon had just finished his meal when Sheriff Cody came in, clutching three pieces of paper in his hand. He walked over and sat across the table from Falcon.

"I've heard from three different people," Cody said. "And they all say the same thing. Not one of them has anything good to say about either Dawes or Poindexter."

Cody slid the telegrams across the table.

DAWES AND POINDEXTER ARE AS CORRUPT AS THEY COME. I DON'T KNOW HOW THEY HAVE AVOIDED PRISON THIS FAR.

The second was as damning as the first.

I KNOW THAT THERE HAS BEEN TALK
THAT DAWES AND POINDEXTER
SHOULD BE INVESTIGATED. I EXPECT
THAT TO HAPPEN SOME TIME SOON.

The third telegram, more succinct than the first
two, was no less condemning.

HAVE ONLY GUT FEELING THAT BOTH ARE
CROOKS.

"Why did you ask about them?" Cody asked.
"Where have you heard of them?"

"I hadn't heard of them at all, until I got a letter
from a friend of mine, a newspaper editor who lives
in Sorrento. He has asked me for help."

"Help in doing what?"

"I'm not sure," Falcon said. "But he is a friend
and he has asked for help. That's all I need."

Cody smiled. "All I can say is, he is a lucky man to
have a friend like you. But then, all of us who know
you are lucky to have such a friend."

Falcon grinned across the table at Sheriff Cody.
"With syrup like that, Amos, you don't ever have to
put anything on your flapjacks, do you?"

Cody's smile grew self-conscious. "I'm sorry. I
didn't mean to embarrass you."

"Hold down the praise just a bit, will you?"

"What if I call you a bandy-legged, two-bit hustling
sidewinder, who doesn't have sense enough to get

in out of the rain and couldn't throw a ringer in horseshoes if his life depended on it?" Cody asked with a broad, teasing smile.

"Ouch! Now, that really does hurt—the part about the horseshoes I mean."

Both men were laughing as they left the restaurant.

Money had neither been offered nor implied in the letter, which was simply a plea for help. And it was that, the earnest plea from an honest man, that had made Falcon decide to respond to the request.

He arrived in Fort Worth by train late in the day, off-loaded Lightning and put him up in a stable for the night, and then went into the White Elephant saloon on Rusk Street. Pushing through the batwing doors, he stepped into the saloon, well lit now with two dozen glowing lanterns hanging in wagon wheel chandeliers from the ceiling. This saloon was in Texas, but it could have been in New Mexico, Arizona, Colorado, Kansas, or Wyoming. Falcon could have closed his eyes and described it.

There was a long bar running down the left side of the saloon, a brass foot rail at the bottom of the bar, and bronze rings every six feet or so from which hung towels for the customers. Brass spittoons were placed every ten feet, with a wide circle of floor stains around each container, indicative of the poor aim of the tobacco chewers.

Behind the bar was a long, narrow mirror,

fronted by a glass shelf upon which various bottles of liquors, liqueurs, and wines sat, their numbers doubled by the reflection in the mirror. Falcon was met instantly by one of the girls working the bar.

"Hello, cowboy." Her voice was low and throaty. "I don't think I've seen you in here before."

"Don't expect you would have, ma'am, seeing as this is the first time I've ever been in here."

"Ma'am? Oh, how nice. I can't remember the last time anyone called me ma'am."

It was difficult to tell her age. She could have been anywhere from the low twenties to mid-forties and had no doubt been attractive at one time, though the immoderation of her profession was taking its toll.

"Don't you be gettin' used to it, Millie." one of the other customers shouted. "Just because some fancy-talkin' sissy boy says ma'am don't change nothin'. You're still a whore."

There were two others sitting at the table with the heckler, and they laughed at the jibe.

Millie blushed. "You don't need to be calling me names, Posey."

"I'll call you any damn thing I want," Posey replied. "I'm payin' to drink in here, which means you got to entertain me."

"Miss Millie, would you care to join me for a drink?" Falcon asked.

Millie smiled, and the smile rolled away some of the dissipation. "Why, I would be glad to," she said.

"You pick out a table, cowboy, and I'll bring you a drink. What would you like?"

"I would like a beer."

Falcon chose a table and sat down, wondering if the saloon served food. He hoped that it did; he would like to just have a beer or two, then a bite to eat, before going to bed.

As Millie passed by Posey's table, he reached out and slapped her on the behind.

"Ouch!" Millie said. "That hurt, Posey!"

"That hurt, Posey," Posey repeated in falsetto, mimicking Millie's complaint.

When Millie came back by the table carrying Falcon's beer and a small glass for herself—Falcon assumed it was tea—she was smiling at him from across the room.

Because she was looking at Falcon, she didn't see Posey stick his leg out at the last minute. Posey tripped her and she fell, dropping the beer and her drink.

"You clumsy bitch! You got beer on the table!" Posey said.

As before, the other two men at the table laughed loudly at Posey's antics.

"Now, you go over there, get a towel, and come wipe off this table," Posey demanded.

Neither Posey nor either of the other two men saw Falcon get up and walk over to them. Reaching down to grab Posey's shirt from behind, Falcon gave it a jerk and literally ripped it from Posey's back.

"What the hell?" Posey shouted in shock and anger.

Falcon handed Posey the ripped-up shirt.

"Here's a rag," Falcon said. "You wipe it up."

"What? Why you son of a bitch! I'm goin' to beat the hell out of you!" Posey shouted, standing up so quickly that he turned over the chair he had been sitting on.

Posey didn't get all the way up before Falcon took him back down with a powerhouse right to the jaw.

The other two stood up then.

"Mister, I don't know who you think you are, but . . ."

That was as far as they got, because Falcon picked up the table, then turned it on its side. Using it as a train would a snow plow, he rammed the table into them, pushing it so hard and so fast against them that they were unable to do anything but retreat before it. He pushed them all the way through the batwing doors, then, tossing the table aside, took each of them down with a couple of sledgehammer blows.

With the two men lying unconscious on the porch in front of the saloon, Falcon reached down to remove their pistols. When he came back, Posey was just beginning to sit up, and seeing Falcon coming toward him, he reached for his pistol. Before he could pull it from his holster, Falcon put him out again, this time with a kick to the head.

Millie hurried over to pick up Posey's pistol, and

Falcon handed her the two he had taken from Posey's friends.

"Put these somewhere out of the way," he said.

Millie took the three revolvers over to the bar.

That done, Falcon retrieved the table he had thrown aside, then brought it back and put it in place alongside the prostrate Posey, then reset the chairs.

"Did you—did you kill him?" Millie asked, returning from having given the pistols to the bartender for safekeeping.

"I didn't kill him," Falcon said. "But more than likely he'll be eating oatmeal instead of steak for a while."

"I'll get you another beer," Millie said.

"Millie, honey, that man's beer is on me!" one of the other customers shouted. "It's been a long time since I've enjoyed anything as much as seeing Posey and those other two buzzards getting their comeuppance."

He applauded, and several of the others in the saloon applauded as well.

CHAPTER TEN

"Are you a cardplayer, mister?" the man who paid for Falcon's beer asked.

"I am."

"I'm Buck Paddock. I publish the newspaper here. This is Doc Burtz, and this is Tom Tidball," he continued, introducing the others at the table with him.

"I'm pleased to meet you gentlemen. I'm Falcon MacCallister."

Paddock reacted to the name. "You are Falcon MacCallister? Gentlemen, we have a famous man among us."

"Or infamous," Falcon replied self-deprecatingly. "Sometime's it's hard to go far enough to get away from the name."

"We have an empty seat here, sir, and we'd be honored if you'd join us," Doc Burtz said.

"I appreciate the invite," Falcon said.

Falcon joined the card game and had been playing for a few minutes when the two men

Falcon had driven outside came back in. By now Posey was up, sitting at the table, holding his hand to his jaw.

"You all right, Posey?" one of them asked.

"I—I don't know," Posey replied, his voice distorted. "What happened to me? Why the hell does my jaw hurt so?"

"You mean you don't remember?"

"I don't remember nothin'. Hey, where's my gun?"

"I don't know," one of the other two said. "We don't have our guns, neither."

"Posey, Slim, Red, I've got your guns over here, behind the bar," the bartender said.

"Well, what the hell are you doin' with 'em?" Slim asked. He walked over to the bar with his hand held out. "Give 'em to me."

"You boys come back in tomorrow, and I'll give you your guns then," the bartender replied. "You ain't gettin' 'em tonight."

"You!" Red said, pointing his finger at Falcon. "You're the one done this to us, ain't you? Well, I ain't finished with you yet!"

Red picked up a chair and started toward the card table.

"Hold it right there, Red!" the bartender shouted. "Unless you want a load of buckshot in your ass!"

The bartender had pulled the shotgun out from under the bar and was pointing it toward Red.

"Look here, Clayton, this man is a stranger and we're regulars!" Red said. "You takin' his side agin' us?"

"I'm takin' my own side," the bartender said. "I ain't goin' to see no furniture broke up in here. You three boys get on back to the ranch."

"All right, give us our guns, and we'll go."

"Like I said, when you come in tomorrow, I'll give you your guns back."

"What do you mean you'll give 'em back tomorrow? What if we run into a road agent or somethin' on the way out to the ranch? How we goin' to defend ourselves if we ain't got our guns with us?"

"Now what self-respecting road agent is going to rob three cowboys who don't have a dollar between them?" Clayton replied, and the others in the saloon laughed.

"That ain't right," Red said. "Posey, tell 'im! Tell 'im that ain't right!"

"Let's go home," Posey said. "My jaw hurts somethin' awful."

The three men started toward the door, but before they left, Red turned back toward Falcon and pointed at him again.

"You ain't heard the last of us, mister!" he shouted. "Do you hear me? You ain't heard the last of us!"

"You going to spend any time in town, Mr. Mac-Callister?" Doc Burtz asked.

"I'm just passing through," Falcon said. "I'm heading on down to Sorrento."

The other players looked at each other just for a quick beat before one of them spoke.

"You live in Sorrento, do you?"

"I've never been to Sorrento," Falcon replied. "But I have a friend who does live there. Well, more of an old acquaintance than a friend. His name is Harold Denham. He owns the newspaper there."

Buck Paddock chuckled. "He sure does," he said. "And he is a ripsnorter, too. It's a wonder Judge Dawes hasn't closed his newspaper down, when you read some of the stories Denham has printed about him."

"You mean close him down just for what he is printing? How can he do that?" Falcon asked.

"How can he do it? It's very simple," Paddock replied. "All he has to do is order Sheriff Poindexter to do it, and it's done."

"Sheriff Poindexter is Judge Dawes's man. He doesn't do anything unless Judge Dawes tells him to. And he'll do anything the judge tells him to do," Tidball said.

"Whatever happened to freedom of the press?" Falcon asked.

"Freedom of the press?" Paddock replied. "That's a good question. And I have to hand it to Denham. He is doing everything he can to keep a free press. I have to confess that he has more gumption than I do. I don't know but what I wouldn't just leave."

"Ha!" Doc Burtz said. "Mr. MacCallister, our newspaperman here was born in Wisconsin, a Yankee who believed so much in states' rights that, at the age of seventeen, he left home and went to Mississippi to join the Confederacy."

"Where, I might add," Tidball continued, "he became the youngest officer in the entire Confederate army."

"So when he says he lacks gumption and would leave, he is being disingenuous," Doc Burtz added.

Paddock chuckled. "My, my, 'disingenuous.' That's quite a word for you, Doc."

"Are you surprised? The books in medical school are written in English," Doc Burtz said.

"Yes, well, getting back to Sorrento and freedom of the press. If left up to the judge and sheriff, there would not only be no freedom of the press, you wouldn't even be able to go out on the street and start speaking ill of the judge or the sheriff. You can't say anything negative about either of them, because the judge has passed a rule against it."

"What kind of rule can prevent freedom of the press or freedom of speech?" Falcon asked.

"A rule that says such conduct promotes disorder and advocates the violent overthrow of a legally constituted government," Tidball said.

"That's ridiculous."

"Yes, indeed it is. But that is also Sorrento," Paddock said. "However, I am proud to say that my fellow crusading journalist, Harold Denham, is fighting to maintain those freedoms which every American holds so dear to their heart."

A new man stepped into the saloon then, and he

stood just to one side of the batwing doors, backed up against the wall as he studied the saloon. He was taller than average with shoulder-length black hair and deep-set dark eyes. His skin was naturally dark and deeply tanned so that he lacked only the high cheekbones to pass as an Indian.

After perusing the room for moment, he stepped up to the bar, where, without asking, he was given a beer.

"There's Marshal Courtright," Doc Burtz said.

Falcon looked up. "Courtright? Jim Courtright?"

"You've heard of him?"

"Yes, I've heard of him." Falcon stood up and turned toward the tall man at the bar. "Courtright! You low-life mangy cur! Turn around and face me like a man!" he shouted.

Courtright was known as a man who was quick on the draw and a deadly accurate shot. At Falcon's challenging words, everyone in the saloon moved quickly to get out of the way of any impending gunfire.

Courtright turned toward Falcon with an angry expression set on his face.

"So, MacCallister," he said. "You didn't learn the lesson the last time we met? I have to teach you again?"

"You couldn't teach a thirsty dog to drink," Falcon replied.

The saloon grew very quiet as the two men looked at each other, and the bartender moved to the far end of the bar. The tension was palpable, and both Falcon and Courtright held their hands just over the grips of their pistols, their fingers curling and uncurling.

"What's this all about?" Tidball asked in a voice so low as to nearly be a whisper.

"I don't know," Paddock replied, his voice as quiet as Tidball's. "But I sure don't like the looks of it."

The pregnant silence continued for several seconds more as the two men glared at each other. Then, suddenly, and unexpectedly, both men began laughing and moving quickly toward each other, shook hands, and grasped each other by the shoulder.

There was a corporate sigh of relief from everyone in the saloon.

"Falcon, you mangy old mountain lion, how are you?" Courtright asked.

"Doing well, Jim. The last time I saw you, you and your wife were doing trick shooting with a Wild West show. How is Betty, anyway?"

"Just as bossy as ever. You're looking good," Courtright replied.

"How about joining me at the table with my new friends?" Falcon invited.

Tidball hustled to bring another chair to the table, and Courtright sat down to join them.

"Now, this isn't fair," Courtright teased. "These gentlemen always let me win when I play. But with you in the game, I don't know."

Paddock laughed. "Jim Courtright, you haven't won a hand of poker since Reconstruction. But I give you credit for continuing to try."

As a new hand was dealt, the five men continued with their conversation.

"What is the story with Posey, Slim, and Red?" Courtright asked. "Someone stopped by the office and told me they were making trouble. That's why I came down here."

"They tried to make trouble," Paddock said. "But Mr. MacCallister handled them."

"Oh?"

Paddock, Tidball, and Doc Burtz took turns then, with laughter and elaborate hand gestures, describing how the three belligerent cowboys were sent home.

"You be on the lookout for them, Falcon," Courtright said. "I've had run-ins with them before. They are troublemakers."

"Thanks for the warning."

"Mr. MacCallister is going to Sorrento," Tidball said.

"Why in heaven's name would you want to go there?" Courtright asked.

"A friend has written to me for help."

"Denham," Paddock said.

"Denham? Oh, yes, the newspaper editor. Has he wound up in jail?" Courtright asked.

"Not yet, though from what these gentlemen have been telling me, he may be there now, for all that I know."

"Falcon, I advise you to be very careful around Poindexter and Dawes. They have more power than any other judge and sheriff that I know of in the entire State of Texas."

"How did they get so much power?" Falcon asked.

"That, my friend, I can't tell you, because I don't know," Courtright replied.

"Jim, maybe you could do something to help him," Tidball suggested.

"What, you mean go to Sorrento with him? I don't think the city fathers of Fort Worth would care much for that, do you?"

"I wasn't talking about that," Tidball said. "I was talking about Senator Maxey. You know him very well. Maybe he could get Mr. MacCallister appointed Deputy U.S. Marshal."

"Yes," Courtright replied. "Yes, that's not a bad idea. I'm sure it would only be a temporary appointment, but it would give you the authority you might need to deal with a sitting judge and sheriff."

"How long would it take you to do this?" Falcon asked.

"I'm not sure, a few days, a few weeks. Would you be interested?"

"Yes, I think I would be. But I don't want to wait around here for it. From the tone of Denham's letter, I need to be getting on to Sorrento as soon as I can."

"All right, you go ahead," Courtright said. "As soon as the appointment comes through, I'll send it to you by telegraph."

"May I make a suggestion?" Paddock asked.

"Sure."

"You had better work out some code to use in the telegram. From what I understand, you don't quite know who you can, and who you can't, trust in

Sorrento. If you send MacCallister a telegram saying he has been appointed a Deputy U.S. Marshal and the telegrapher is in the camp of Dawes and Poindexter, MacCallister might not even get it. And if he does get it . . . chances are Dawes and Poindexter would get it first."

"You may be right," Courtright agreed. "All right. As soon as the appointment is confirmed, I will send a telegram that says, 'the horse you want to buy is for sale,' and that will be your signal."

"Your bet, Jim," Paddock said.

Courtright looked at his hand. "Who dealt this mess?"

"I did," Doc Burtz said."

"I ought to throw you in jail for malpractice." With a groan, Courtright threw down his hand. "I'm out."

Falcon took a room in the El Paso Hotel. The El Paso advertised itself as one that could "match any hotel in San Francisco, St. Louis, or New York," and having stayed in the finest hotels in all those cities, Falcon couldn't argue with the boast.

His room was large, well lighted by gas lanterns, and comfortably furnished. Because he would have a full day of riding the next day, he decided to go to bed early. Through the open window, he could hear the sounds of the town at night: competing music from half a dozen saloons, a departing train down at the depot, the braying of a mule. Finally it all faded away as he drifted off to sleep.

CHAPTER ELEVEN

Outside, Posey, Slim, and Red were standing on the bank of the Trinity River, looking at the reflection of the moon in the dark water that flowed swiftly by. Red picked up a rock and tossed it into the river, then watched as the ripples caused the reflected moonlight to shimmer.

"I'd feel better waitin' until tomorrow when we have our guns," Red said.

"You heard what they said. He's leavin' town in the morning," Slim said.

"Besides, I don't want to kill the son of a bitch, I just want to beat the livin' hell out of him," Posey said.

"Yeah, well that didn't work out too well the last time, did it?" Red said. "He was just one man, and he handled all three of us."

"That's because he caught us by surprise," Posey replied. "You don't really think he could whip all three of us at the same time if it was a fair fight, do you?"

"I don't know," Slim said. "He handled himself pretty good."

"That's why this time, the surprise is goin' to be on our side," Posey said. "What time is it?"

"It must be after midnight," Red said. "There's a city ordinance that says the pianos in the saloons have to quit playing at midnight, and I don't hear none of 'em playin'. Do you?"

"No, I don't hear nothin', neither. Let's go."

"You're sure he's stayin' at the El Paso?" Slim asked.

"We seen him go in, didn't we?" Posey replied. "Did we see him come out?"

"No."

"Then the son of a bitch is in there."

"How are we goin' to do this?"

"This time of night, it's more'n likely that the clerk is goin' to be sound asleep. We'll just take a look at the registration book, figure out which room MacCallister is in, go up to his room, sneak in, and just start beatin' the hell out of him."

"Well, if we're goin' to do it, let's do it," Red said. "Ain't much need in just standing around like this."

"Red's right," Posey said as they started toward the three horses standing nearby, tied to the branch of a tree.

The three men mounted, then rode back into town, the clopping sound of hoofbeats echoing back from the dark and quiet buildings.

They dismounted in front of the hotel, tied their

horses off at the hitching rack, and then went inside.

The lobby was dimly lit by the gas lights that hissed quietly in the background. The three men moved silently across the carpeted floor to the check-in desk. Posey's declaration that the clerk would be asleep was correct, as he was sitting in a chair that was tipped back against the wall.

Posey turned the registration book around, ran his fingers down the list until he came to the name *MacCallister*. Then he got the room number and, reaching up, over the desk, took the spare key down from a hook of the same number.

"Let's go," he whispered, starting back across the carpeted floor to the stairway.

Falcon was awakened from a sound sleep. He wasn't sure what woke him up, whether it was a sound or something as subtle as a change in the air pressure when the door to his room opened. Or perhaps it was just a sixth sense developed over years of living on the edge. Whatever it was, he no longer questioned it. Instantly alert, he sensed danger, and very quietly he rolled out of his bed on the side away from the door, snaking his pistol from the holster at the same moment. He crawled, quickly, to the opposite side of the room, then stood up in the shadows of the corner.

From the dimly glowing gas lantern that provided illumination for the hallway, a wedge of light spilled into the room. Falcon saw three men come quietly inside. He could see them in silhouette only, but because there were three of them, he knew that they were the same people he had encountered in the saloon earlier today. Or was it yesterday? He had no idea whether it was before or after midnight.

"Let's see you fight now, you son of a bitch!" one of the three men yelled, and they leaped onto the bed.

"What the hell? Where is he?"

"Hello, boys, I thought you might come back for a visit," Falcon said. Even as he spoke, he struck a match head with his thumb, then held it to the gas lantern on the table beside him. A glowing bubble of golden light filled the room.

Startled, the three men turned toward him and would have rushed him had they not noticed that he was holding a pistol leveled toward them.

"What? What are you going to do?" Posey asked, his voice edged with fear.

"What would anybody do when they see someone breaking into their bedroom?" Falcon asked. "I'm going to shoot you, of course. All three of you."

"What? No!" Posey said. "No! Don't shoot us!"

"Give me one good reason why I shouldn't."

"I . . . we'll leave!" Posey said. "The three of us! We'll go back to the ranch, and you'll never see us again."

"And Millie?" Falcon asked.

"Millie?"

"The girl in the bar. You won't bother her anymore?"

"Why do you care? She ain't nothin' but a whore. Whores is supposed to be bothered," Red said.

"And people who break into other people's rooms are supposed to be shot," Falcon reminded them.

"All right, no, wait. All right, we won't none of us bother Millie no more," Slim said.

"Not just Millie. Don't you mistreat any woman, anywhere. Because if you do, I'll come back here and settle with you, personally."

"No, we won't. We'll treat 'em all good, I promise," Posey said.

"Get out of here," Falcon said. "Don't ever let me see any one of you again. And you," he said, pointing specifically to Posey.

"Yes?"

"Change your pants."

"Oh, damn, oh, damn, I peed in 'em," Posey said as the three men shuffled out of the hotel room. "I peed in 'em."

Falcon chuckled as he crawled back into bed. But before he got into bed this time, he moved the heavy clothespress against the door.

Somewhere in the predawn darkness, a calf bawled anxiously and its mother answered. In the distance, a coyote sent up its long, lonesome wail, while out in the pond, frogs thrummed their night song. The moon was a thin sliver of silver, but the night was alive with stars . . . from the very bright, shining lights, all the way down to those stars that weren't visible as individual bodies but whose glow added to the luminous powder that dusted the distant sky.

Around the milling shapes of shadows that made up the small herd rode three cowboys, all of them riders for the Big Star Ranch, located seven miles south of Sorrento. Known as "nighthawks," their job was to keep watch over the herd during the night.

"You know what?" one of the cowboys asked. "I think Lucy is in love with ole' Arnie here."

Arnie was seventeen, and the youngest of the three.

"Hah, Lucy's a whore. She's in love with anyone that has a dollar and a half."

"No, Cal, I'm serious. I think Lucy is in love with Arnie. What have you done, Arnie? I been tryin' to make her fall in love with me for the longest time, but here you come; you ain't been here more'n six months and she's in love with you. You must'a shown her a real good time."

"Stop your teasin', Parker," Arnie said. "You know I ain't never been with Lucy." He was quiet for a moment. "Fact is, I ain't never been with no woman at all."

"You never had a woman? Why, boy, you ain't

goin' to be a man till you have yourself a woman. How come you ain't never been with Lucy? I mean, her lovin' you so much 'n' all."

"She don't love me."

"You know what I think?" Cal said. "I think she loves 'im just 'cause he is a virgin. Whores likes to break in young virgins."

"That's it," Parker said. "Arnie, next time we go into town, you are goin' to get broke in, and Lucy is the one that's goin' to do it."

The calf's call for his mother came again, this time with more insistence. The mother's answer had a degree of anxiousness to it.

"Sounds like one of 'em's wandered off," Arnie said. "I'll go find it."

"Hell, why bother? It'll find its own way back."

"I don't mind," Arnie said, slapping his legs against the side of his horse and riding off, disappearing in the darkness.

"Did Lucy really say that about Arnie?" Cal asked.

"Sort of."

"Sort of? What is 'sort of'?"

"She asked if I thought he was a virgin."

Cal laughed. "That's a long way from sayin' she was in love with him."

"You just got to understand how whores talk, is all," Parker said.

Suddenly, from the darkness came the sound of gunshots.

"What the hell is that fool boy shootin' at?" Parker asked.

Arnie's horse appeared out of the darkness, an empty saddle on its back.

"Son of a bitch, what's happenin' here?" Cal asked.

Both men drew their guns, then rode out into the darkness in the direction they had last seen Arnie.

"Arnie! Arnie, where are you? Answer us, boy!"

Suddenly, several gunshots erupted in the night, their muzzle-flashes lighting up the herd.

"Parker! What's going on?"

"Let's get out of here!" Parker shouted.

"The herd! Somebody's stealin' the herd!"

"Better the cows than us! Let's get out of here, I say!"

"That's it, Pogue," a rider said. "We've took near two hunnert and fifty cows."

"What about the cowboys?"

"We kilt one; the other two run away."

"Let's move the cattle out of here fast," Pogue said.

There were four men in the group of rustlers, Pogue Allison, Ron Mace, Jack Andrews, and Frank Little, and they started moving the rustled cattle south, away from the main house of Big Star Ranch.

* * *

"Turn out! Turn out! Rustlers!" Parker and Cal were shouting when they galloped into the compound where the big house, bunkhouse, cookshack, and barn were located.

Dawn was just breaking, and the person awake was the cook. He came out onto the porch and began clanging on the circular piece of steel that he used to call the men to their meals.

"What the hell's wrong with Cookie?" a grumpy voice called from within the bunkhouse. "It's too damn early for breakfast."

Cal ran into the bunkhouse to shout the news while Parker knocked loudly on the back door of the Big House.

An hour later the cowboys returned, bearing the body of young Arnie Perkins. They tracked the cows to the river, but Rope's End Ranch was on the other side of the river, which made it impossible to separate the tracks of the cows they had been trailing with the cattle that were indigenous to Rope's End.

Cal and Parker, finding Arnie's newest and cleanest clothes, got them ready; then, putting the boy's body in the back of a buckboard, they drove him into town to Nunnelee's Funeral Home. David Boardman rode into town with them, then, after making arrangements for Arnie to be buried, he went to the sheriff's office.

"How many cows did you lose?" Sheriff Poindexter asked after Boardman gave him his report.

"About two hundred fifty," Boardman said.

"About two hundred and fifty? You can't give me a closer count than that?"

"Two hundred forty-seven was the last count," Boardman said. "But we've moved some in and some out, so, about two hundred and fifty is the best I can do."

"All right, that's good enough. I'll see what I can do to find out what happened to them. But once cows gets stole, the rustlers purt' near always get the beeves out of the county as quick as they can. And when they do that, I don't have any more authority over 'em."

"Yeah," Boardman said with a frustrated sigh. "Well, do what you can."

When Boardman left, Poindexter got out a piece of paper and began doing a little figuring. He had set this cattle rustling operation up, and he was due to get four dollars a head. Now, if Pogue and the others stole 248 cows from the Big Star. . . . Poindexter began figuring the numbers, and when he finished he leaned back in his chair and smiled. He would have 992 dollars coming from this operation.

CHAPTER TWELVE

The town of Sorrento, Texas, had reached its peak when it was thought that an extension of the Texas Pacific Railroad would reach the town. But when the railroad bypassed the town, Sorrento lost all of its importance and much of its population. The town was gradually beginning to recover, though, and its hearty citizens hung on, waiting with the sure and certain hope that at some time in the not too distant future, some railroad would find them.

Two young men, passing through the town, stopped in front of the Hog Heaven saloon. Swinging down from their horses, they patted their dusters down.

"Lord a' mighty, Luke, if you ain't blowin' up a dust storm all by yourself," one of the men said, laughing at his friend.

"Yeah, well you don't look like you're wearin' no Sunday go to meetin' clothes yourself," Luke replied. "What do you say, Hooter? Let's me 'n' you get us a couple of beers?"

"Sounds good to me," Hooter said.

Pushing through the batwing doors, the two men entered the saloon and stepped up to the bar. The saloon was relatively quiet, with only four men at one table and a fifth standing down at the far end of the bar. The four at the table were playing cards; the one at the end of the bar was nursing a drink. The man nursing the drink was wearing a badge.

As the boys stepped up to the bar, the man with the badge looked over at them with an unblinking stare. At least it was half an unblinking stare, because one of his eyes had no eyelid.

"What'll it be, gents?" the bartender asked.

One of the two young men continued to stare back at the man who was standing at the end of the bar. He had never seen anyone who had an eye without an eyelid before, and he found the lidless, oversized eyeball to be disquieting.

"Hooter?" Luke said. "The bartender asked what'll we have."

"Oh," Hooter replied. "Uh, two beers."

"Two beers it is," Beeson replied. He turned to draw the beers.

"And I'll have the same," Hooter added.

Beeson laughed. "You boys sound like you've got a thirst."

"Just sayin' we're thirsty don't quite get it," Luke said. "Why, I got that much dust you could grow cotton in my mouth."

"Cotton, huh? You boys must be farmers."

"We've done some farmin'. You got somethin' against farmin'?" Hooter challenged.

"No, Lord, no," Beeson replied, chuckling. "I'm an old farmer myself. Or at least my pa was, and I grew up on a farm back in Mississippi. I've picked many a pound of cotton. Chopped it, too. What brings you boys to Sorrento?"

"Truth to tell, there don't nothin' in particular bring us to Sorrento. We just got a little bit of the wanderin' fever, so we're goin' first to one place, then to the other. Sort of seein' the country, we are," Luke said.

Hooter chuckled. "So far, though, the only country we've seen is Texas."

"Well, Texas is a big state, and you couldn't go wrong just by takin' it in," Beeson said.

"How are you two paying for your wandering around?" This question came from the man with the badge.

"Now, I don't know that that is any of your business," Hooter said. "But I'll tell you 'cause maybe you can help us out."

"How am I supposed to help you?"

"Well, sir, we're pretty good cowhands. And bein' as you're wearin' a badge, I'd reckon you've got a pretty good handle on things around here. Do you know if any ranchers are hiring?"

"Cowhands, huh?" The man with the badge snorted what might have been laughter.

"Why do you laugh?" Luke asked.

"I'd be willing to bet that you ain't never punched one cow. You might be farmers, but you ain't cowboys. More than likely what you are is thieves, comin' to see what you can steal."

"Who are you callin' thieves?" Hooter asked angrily.

"I'm callin' you boys thieves."

"Who are you?"

"Maybe you didn't notice my badge."

"Yeah, I seen your badge."

"Sheriff, why don't you ease up on these boys? They haven't broken any laws," Beeson said.

"You stay out of this, Beeson."

"You got no right to go 'round accusin' people of stealin' with no cause," Hooter said.

"I've got every right. I'm the sheriff here. The name is Poindexter. Now what about them horses you rode in on?" Poindexter asked. "You got somethin' to prove you own them horses?"

"My daddy give me my horse. I raised him from a colt," Luke said.

"So what you are sayin' is, you ain't got nothin' to prove you own them horses, do you?"

"I don't need nothin'. I told you, I raised him from a colt."

"What about you?" Poindexter asked Hooter.

"Mister, I don't need to prove nothin' to you," Hooter replied.

"I told you. It ain't 'mister,' it's 'sheriff.' And yeah, you do need to prove it to me. 'Cause if you don't, I'm goin' to have to put you two boys in jail and start sendin' out telegrams to see if there's two horses that's been stoled somewhere."

"Now, wait just a minute here! That ain't no way right," Luke said. "Hell, they's always goin' to be some horses that was stole somewhere."

"Yes, and ever' time I find a couple of missin' horses, I'm goin' to have to make sure it ain't the two you boys rode in on."

"Sheriff, why are you rousting these two men like this?" Beeson asked. "These two boys haven't done a thing since they came here but buy a drink and ask if you knew where they could get on as ranch hands."

"You stay out of this, Beeson," Sheriff Poindexter said. "Unless you want to wind up in jail with them."

"Jail?" Hooter barked out loudly. "What do you mean 'jail'?" He pointed at Poindexter. "You ain't puttin' us in jail," he said. "No way, and no how. Leastwise, not without no reason, you ain't."

"I'm the sheriff. And if I say you're goin' to jail, that's all the reason I need," Poindexter said. He took another swallow of his beer. "Of course, if you two boys would be willin' to pay the search and clearance tax, you wouldn't have to go to jail."

"Search and clearance tax? I've never heard of nothin' like that. What is it?"

"If I'm goin' to start sendin' out telegrams about you two boys, you don't expect the town or the county to pay for it, do you?" Poindexter asked. "That wouldn't be right. I figure, ten dollars apiece ought to just about cover it. You boys come up with ten dollars apiece, you can ride on out of here."

"Hell, I ain't got nothin' but twelve dollars. And I'll be damned if I'm goin' to give ten dollars to you," Hooter said.

"And I ain't got but nine dollars," Luke added.

Sheriff Poindexter chuckled. "Well, that ain't no problem. You can just borrow a dollar from your friend here, and you can both pay the tax and be done with it."

"What if we don't pay you nothin'?" Hooter asked.

"Then, like I said, you'll go to jail."

"The hell I will. If you're plannin' on puttin' me in jail, then you better bring along some help, you bug-eyed bastard."

"Easy, Hooter," Luke said, reaching out for his partner. "We come up here to get work, not to get into no fight."

Hooter glared at the bug-eyed man, but the expression on the sheriff's face never changed.

"Well, I sure as hell ain't goin' to let this one-eyed son of a bitch throw us in jail for no reason a' tall," he said.

"All right, that's it," Sheriff Poindexter said. "You boys shuck out of them gun belts. You're goin' to jail. Both of you."

"The hell I am. And I ain't takin' off my gun belt, neither. You want it, you're goin' to have to take it offen me."

"Oh, I can do that, farm boy," the sheriff replied with an evil smile spreading across his face. "Trust me, I can do that."

"Cowboy, no!" Beeson warned. "Listen to me. You don't want to mess with the sheriff."

"Whoever he is, there's only one of him and two of us. I reckon we can handle the likes of him," Hooter said.

"Hooter," Luke said. "I don't like the way this is playin' out. Come on, let's just go. We'll find us another town. One that's a mite more friendly than this one has been."

Hooter stared at the sheriff for a moment longer, then, with a shrug, he turned back toward the bar. "All right," he said reluctantly. "I'll let it go this time. Maybe folks here just don't know how to be friendly."

"Maybe you boys didn't hear me," Sheriff Poindexter said. "I said you two are going to jail until I find out whether or not them horses you two are ridin' is stoled."

"And I told you them horses ain't stolen and we ain't a' goin' to jail!" Hooter said angrily. Hooter turned to face the sheriff, then hung his hand down near his pistol.

"You plannin' on drawin' on me, are you, farm boy?" Sheriff Poindexter asked.

"If it comes to that," Hooter said.

"There are two of you. Do you think that's fair?" the sheriff asked.

"Fair ain't got nothin' to do with it. You're the one started this here fracas. All we done was come in here for a beer. If we ain't welcome here, we'll just leave and that will be the end of it."

"You think so?" Sheriff Poindexter asked.

"Please, Hooter, let's just go now," Luke said.

Hooter stared in anger at the sheriff for a moment longer, then he sighed and shrugged his shoulders. "My friend is right. There's no need to carry things any further. Let's just drop it here and me 'n' him will walk out of here. This isn't worth either one of us dying over."

"Oh, it won't be *either* of us, farmer. It'll just be you," Poindexter said. He looked over at Luke. "Both of you," he added. "You came in here together; you are going to die together."

Luke shook his head. "No, it ain't goin' to be either one of us. 'Cause there ain't neither one of us going to draw on you," he said. "So if you shoot us, it's goin' to have to be in cold blood, in front of these witnesses."

"Oh, you'll draw all right. You'll draw first, and these witnesses will say that."

"They ain't goin' to be able to say it, 'cause we ain't goin' to draw on you," Luke said. He looked over at the four cardplayers who had stopped their game to watch what was going on. "I want you all to hear this. We ain't goin' to draw on the sheriff."

"Oh, I think you will," the sheriff said calmly, confidently.

"Please, Sheriff, we don't want any trouble," Luke said. "I told you. We'll be goin' now."

Sheriff Poindexter shook his head. "The only place you are going is to jail until I check on them horses."

Luke and Hooter looked at each other; then, with an imperceptible signal, they started their draw. Though the two young men were able to defend themselves in most bar fights, they were badly overmatched in this fight. They made ragged, desperate grabs for their pistols.

So bad were they that Sheriff Poindexter had the luxury of waiting for just a moment to see which of the two offered him the most competition. Deciding it was Hooter, Poindexter pulled his pistol and shot him first. Luke, shocked at seeing his friend killed right before his eyes, released his pistol and let it fall back into his holster. He was still looking at Hooter when the sheriff fired a second time, this shot so close to the first that it sounded as if it were one report.

Sheriff Poindexter stood there for a moment looking down at the two bodies on the floor. He put the smoking gun back in his holster, then picked up his drink and turned his back to the bar.

"Deputy Sharp?" he called to one of the four who had been playing cards earlier but moved aside when the confrontation started.

"Yes, sir, Sheriff?"

"Go out there and get them two horses. Take 'em down to the livery and tell Finney he is to sell 'em both and give the money to the sheriff's office. He can have ten percent."

"What if the horses is stoled?" Sharp asked.

"More'n likely they ain't," Sheriff Poindexter replied as he tossed his drink down.

"You had no call to do that, Sheriff," Beeson said. "They were just two cowboys, passin' through, mindin' their own business. You picked that fight with them; you know damn well you did."

"They didn't have to draw on me. They could a' either paid their taxes, or just gone to jail like I asked. I would a' got it straightened out about them horses in a few days. And we would a' also heard if these boys is wanted anywhere else."

"You got 'ny reason to think that they were?"

"No reason at all, 'cept they was actin' awful peculiar."

"Hell's fire, man! Who wouldn't act peculiar the way you were goadin' 'em?" the bartender asked. "You pushed them into that fight, and you know it."

Sheriff Poindexter glared at the bartender. "You wantin' to take their side in this, are you, Beeson?"

"No, no, it's not that. It's just that, it doesn't seem to me like any of this needed to happen."

Poindexter didn't answer. Instead, he put a silver dollar on the bar. "Give these boys a drink on me, and have one for yourself," he said.

"A drink, yes," one of the cardplayers said. "Damn, do I need a drink."

The three remaining cardplayers rushed to the bar. Sheriff Poindexter looked again at the two bodies lying on the floor, then, with what could only be described as contempt, left the saloon, leaving the bodies of Luke and Hooter behind.

Gene Nunnelee was the mortician in Sorrento. He was working on the remains of Mr. Clyde Barton. Mr. Barton, who had died at the age of eighty-six, had been with Andrew Jackson at the Battle of New Orleans and with Sam Houston at San Jacento. He was a rancher and leading citizen of Scott County, and Nunnelee was doing everything he could to give Mr. Barton's last remains the respect he deserved.

He looked up from his work when he heard the shots, and, coming as they did, one right on top of another, he had the idea that his services might be needed. His suspicion was borne out a minute or two later when Deputy Sharp came into the funeral parlor.

"Who's that you're workin' on?" Sharp asked.

"It's Mr. Clyde Barton."

"Oh, yeah, I heard old man Barton had kicked the bucket. Anyway, a couple of cowboys tried to go up against Sheriff Poindexter, and they lost. So it looks like you got two new customers."

"Cowboys? What ranch?" Nunnelee asked.

"There don't nobody know. They was just passin' through."

"Just passing through, and Poindexter killed

them," Nunnelee said. It was a statement, not a question.

"Yeah, that's about the size of it."

"So, they will be buried at city expense, I take it."

"Yep. Ten dollars apiece, and all you have to do is dump 'em in a hole," Sharp said with a little chuckle. He turned to leave.

"Where are they?"

"They're layin' in the floor back up there at the Hog Heaven."

Nunnelee sighed, then pulled a black sheet up over Barton's body. "I'll only be a few moments, Mr. Barton," he said quietly.

"That's dumb, talking to a dead man like that," Sharp said. "You know damn well he can't hear you."

"How do you know he can't?"

"I just know, that's all." Sharp thought for a moment, then repeated, "That's dumb."

"Think so? I've been around a lot more dead bodies than you have."

"You mean—you mean they can hear you?"

"I'd better get the buckboard hitched up," Nunnelee replied without answering Sharp's question. Sharp stayed behind for a moment as Nunnelee went outside to hitch up a horse to his buckboard. This was a different horse from the two he used to pull the black-lacquered and silver-ornamented glass-sided hearse.

Sharp spoke to the shrouded body lying on the preparation table.

"Hey, Barton. Can you hear me?" Sharp asked.

Then with a disgusted sigh, he chastised himself. "That's dumb. Of course you can't."

Sharp walked over to the table and pulled the black sheet back. Barton's eyes were open, and he appeared to be staring at the deputy.

Sharp felt a quick, gasping reaction from the unexpected sensation of being stared at by a dead man. He turned quickly and hurried out of the funeral parlor.

"A couple of customers for you, Gene," Beeson said when the undertaker stepped into the saloon.

The two young cowboys were lying on the floor, one on his back and the other on his stomach.

"Has Doc Gunter looked at them? Are we sure they are both dead?"

"You can ask him, he's right over there," Beeson said.

Seeing the undertaker, Doc Gunter came over to him.

"They're dead," he said.

"I understand they tried to go up against the sheriff."

"So I'm told; I wasn't here."

"Beeson?" Nunnelee asked. "Is that right?"

"In a manner of speaking, you might say they tried to outdraw the sheriff."

"What in the world would make them do such a thing?"

"They didn't really have much choice in the

matter," Beeson said. "It was either draw against him or stand there and let the sheriff shoot them down."

"What did they do to get the sheriff so mad at them?" Nunnelee asked.

"That's just it," Beeson said. "They didn't do a damn thing. Somehow Poindexter got it in his mind that the two horses they were riding had been stolen, and he planned to keep them in jail until he found out about it. That didn't give those two boys much of a chance."

"I don't suppose you know who they are, by any chance."

"They called themselves Hooter and Luke. That's all I know."

"I hate buryin' folks without even knowing who they are." Nunnelee looked around the saloon. It was much more crowded now, the news of the shooting haven gotten out. "Would a couple of you boys help me out here?"

Four strong young men came forth, and, with two men on each body, Hooter and Luke were carried out to the buckboard.

CHAPTER THIRTEEN

At one time, the sign on the window had read SORRENTO ADVOCATE. Harold Denham had paid Charley Keith, the local, and often drunk, sign painter, five dollars to do the job. He painted it in a beautiful three-color script, red outlined by white, outlined by blue.

But now half the window was broken out and boarded over, so that all that remained of the sign was SORRENTO AD.

Denham still didn't know who broke the window; several days earlier, he had been visiting with his friends in the Hog Heaven when he was summoned by someone to come quickly to his newspaper office. When he'd gotten there with the others, he found a brick lying in the middle of shattered glass on the floor of his office. Although he didn't know who it was, because he had no proof, he had a strong suspicion that the window was broken by one of Sheriff Poindexter's deputies. That suspicion was strengthened when Denham reported the incident to the sheriff.

"Well, what the hell do you expect, Denham?" Sheriff Poindexter had asked. "Most of the stories you print are half-truths, or outright lies. You are bound to piss off the decent citizens of this town."

Now, several days after the brick incident, he visited the sheriff again, asking if he had any clues on who had vandalized his office.

"I haven't looked in to it that much."

"So, what you are telling me, Sheriff, is that you have no intention of trying to find out who did it."

"This town has over five hunnert people," Poindexter said. "You expect me to question ever' damn one of 'em just to find out who broke your window?"

"I expect you already know who broke it."

"What is that supposed to mean?" Poindexter asked, his one lidded eye glaring in hostility.

"Why, Sheriff, I just mean that you have your fingers on the pulse of this town, and there are few people who can put anything over on you."

Poindexter stared at Denham for a long moment, as if judging his comment. He didn't know if he had just been put down by the newspaper editor or complimented by him.

"You just remember that," Poindexter said. "If someone breaks the law in my town, they are going to pay for it."

"Like the two young men you killed yesterday?"

"Exactly like the two men I killed yesterday."

"Whose names we don't even know."

"That doesn't matter. They had to have been outlaws, or they would have cooperated with me."

Denham knew that he was not the only one who wasn't comfortable with the way the judge, the sheriff, and his deputies were running things. There was a mayor and city council, but they were so intimidated by Poindexter that they were afraid to do anything to go against him. The average citizen had told Denham that they felt oppressed, and they asked him—generally quietly—to please continue to report the truth in his newspaper.

After setting the type for his lead story today, Harold Denham reread the article he had just composed. Although he had once had as many as three people working for him, they had been so intimidated by the sheriff and his deputies, all three of them had quit. Denham was now operating the newspaper alone, which meant he gathered the news, set the stories, sold the advertisements, sold subscriptions, and delivered the paper.

Having heard the story of the shooting in the Hog Heaven, Denham interviewed a few people, promising them anonymity, then wrote the story that would appear in today's newspaper. He knew it would not be a story that Poindexter approved, but he didn't care.

Even though the type was backward, Denham had been in the business for so long that he could read copy backward as easily as he could forward.

He made a quick perusal of the story he had just composed.

Two Men Hurled into Eternity

Yesterday afternoon a terrible shooting affair occurred at the Hog Heaven saloon. Two young men, their names as yet unknown except as they had referred to each other as Luke and Hooter, arrived in Sorrento, ostensibly to look for employment as cowboys.

An altercation developed between the two cowboys when they expressed resentment over an unfounded accusation made by Sheriff Poindexter that they were horse thieves. Despite the young men's believable claims that they were the rightful owners of the horses, Poindexter, without any cause for doubt, continued with his baseless accusations. It has been reported by eyewitnesses that the two cowboys attempted to walk away before the incident became even more confrontational, but Sheriff Poindexter would not allow it.

Tempers grew hotter, angry words were exchanged, and the two cowboys went for their guns. Although the witnesses are all in agreement that the cowboys drew first, all, except Deputy Sharp, insist that the cowboys were "goaded into drawing," by the sheriff who had no valid reason for their initial harassment.

These are not the first unsuspecting, if not innocent, men to fall before the too ready guns of the sheriff and his deputies. And those who are not killed by gunfire often wind up at the end of a rope as a result of Judge Dawes's perverted sense of justice.

It is the opinion of this newspaper that the citizens of our beleaguered town are being held hostage to Judge Dawes and Sheriff Poindexter, who, with their minions, have turned Sorrento into their own private fiefdom.

The two young men were buried last evening on the same day they were shot, put in rough-hewn pine boxes and laid side by side in a single, unmarked grave. This newspaper will attempt to learn their true identity so that somewhere anxious parents and family can learn the fate of their loved ones.

Even as Denham was putting his newspaper to bed, some ten miles from town the Fort Worth to Sorrento stagecoach was making its return trip. The road was straight and flat, and the six-horse team was maintaining a swift, eight-mile-per-hour lope. The wheels of the quickly moving stagecoach kicked up a billowing trail of dust to roll and swirl on the road behind them, though a goodly amount of dust also managed to find its way into the passenger compartment.

One of the women passengers began coughing. "Oh, this dust is awful. I can scarcely get my breath. Do something, Paul."

Her husband chuckled. "Tell me, Gladys, just what would you have me do?"

"You could tell the driver to slow down. Perhaps if we wouldn't go so fast, the dust wouldn't be so bad."

"I can't do that. He has a schedule to keep. And so do we."

The woman was traveling with her husband and a young boy. They were from Dallas but were relocating to Sorrento because Paul, who was a dentist, was planning to open a practice there.

There was another passenger in the coach, a pretty, eighteen-year-old girl, but because of the way she was dressed, one had to look at her twice to see that she was Indian. The dress she was wearing was one that would not be out of place in any drawing room in Dallas. She took a handkerchief from her handbag, held it under the spigot of the water barrel, and wet it. She wrung it out so that it wasn't dripping, then handed it to Gladys.

"Try this," she said. She made a motion with her hand, holding it over her nose to demonstrate.

Gladys took the damp handkerchief and did as the young woman suggested. After a few moments, she took the damp handkerchief down and smiled at the pretty young Indian girl.

"Why, thank you, dear," she said. "But how is it that you aren't bothered by it?"

The girl smiled. "Oh, but I am bothered by it. It's just that I've learned to put it out of my mind."

"You're an injun, ain't ya?" The little boy asked.

"Kenny!" the mother scolded.

The girl laughed. "That's all right," she said. She looked at the boy. "Yes, I am Comanche."

"The Comanche are the worst kind. The Comanche and the white man have been enemics," Kenny said.

"We used to be," she said. "But we are friends now. My name is Mary."

"Mary? That's a white name? Don't you have an Indian name?"

"Perhaps if I told you my whole name. It is Mary Little Horse."

"Mary, how is it that you speak English so well?" Gladys asked.

"I was back East for two years, attending school."

"Oh, how exciting for you."

"Yes, it was," Mary agreed. "And I saw many wonderful things while I was there. Once, I even got to go to Washington to see the Capitol. But I must confess that I am very glad to be coming home again."

"Yes, I suppose having been gone that long you would be more than happy to be coming back home."

* * *

Coop Winters and Travis Eberwine were waiting behind a large rock outcropping just around a sharp turn in the road. Winters was on top of the rock, looking back toward the direction from which the stagecoach would be coming.

Eberwine was standing on the ground behind the rock.

"Damn," he said. "I got too many letters in my name."

"What?" Winters asked. He continued to stare down the road.

"My name," Eberwine said. "They's too many letters in Travis. If I didn't have no more letters than you have, I could do it. Or, iffen I had been named Tom instead of Travis. But I can't do it with Travis, there's just too many letters."

Winters looked down at Eberwine. "What in the hell are you talking about?"

"Ever' time I take a piss, well, what I try 'n' do is write my name in the dirt, you see. But I can't do it. I purt' nigh always run out of pee 'bout the time I get to the 'v.'"

"We ain't out here to be writin' our names in the dirt with piss," Winters said. "Now button up your britches and pay attention."

"All right, all right. How much longer before the stagecoach gets here, anyhow? I'm gettin' tired of standin' around."

"Wait a minute, I see it now," Winters said.

"You see the stagecoach?"

"Well, I see a lot of dust flyin' up, and the stage-coach is 'bout the only thing that can do that. Get ready, it'll be here in a few minutes."

The passengers inside the coach heard the sound of gunfire from outside, then they heard the driver calling out to the team. The coach began to slow.

"What was that?" Gladys asked.

"It sounded like a gunshot," Paul replied.

"What are we slowing down for? We ought to speed up," Gladys said.

"I imagine the driver has no choice," Paul said.

The stage came to an abrupt stop, and they heard loud voices. A rider, wearing a handkerchief tied across the bottom half of his face, appeared just outside the stagecoach.

"You folks in the coach," he shouted in a loud, gruff voice. "Come on out of there!"

Cautiously, Paul opened the door and stepped out onto the ground. Then he turned and helped his wife down, then Kenny. Mary exited last.

"What is this? A robbery?" Paul said.

"Well now, ain't you the smart one?" one of the two riders asked. Both men had the bottom half of their faces covered. He held up a canvas bag. "I got the money pouch, and now, I'll be troublin' you folks for whatever money you have."

The outlaw got down from his horse and walked over to them.

"You got the money shipment, isn't that enough for you? Why would you want to take money from the passengers?" the driver asked.

"Let's just say I don't like to leave money on the table."

"I don't have that much money, and I'll need what I have for us to get started in Sorrento. I'm not giving you one red cent," Paul said.

"Paul, give it to him!" Gladys insisted.

"The hell I will," Paul said angrily.

The robber cocked his pistol. "Mister, you'll either hand it to me, or I'll kill you and take it from you."

"All right, all right," Paul said. He took his bill-fold out and handed it over.

"There, now, that's a good boy." The outlaw looked at Mary. "And what about you?"

"I have no money," Mary said.

"How did you buy a ticket with no money?"

"The Indian school where I attended classes provided me with a travel voucher," she said. "That was good for a ticket and meals until I returned home."

"'The Injun school'?" The rider looked at her more closely. "By damn, you *are* a injun, ain't you? Look at you, all dressed up like a white woman. And damn near as pretty, too, I'd say."

"Come on, Coop, we got the pouch and the dude's poke. Let's get out of here."

"Coop?" Mary asked. "You're Coop Winters, aren't you? I've heard of you."

"Injun, you know too damn much." With that, he cocked his pistol and shot her, the bullet striking her in the chest. She fell back against the coach, then slid to the ground as blood gushed from the entry wound, soaking the entire top of her dress.

"No!" Gladys screamed.

Kenny started crying and knelt on the ground beside her. Mary smiled at him and tried to reach for his hand, but couldn't raise her arm. She took a couple of gasping breaths, then died.

"My God, you killed her!" Gladys said.

"Yeah, well, it happens to all of us eventually," the one called Coop said coldly.

"Come on, Coop, we've got the money. Let's get out of here," the other robber said.

When the stagecoach came into town, it arrived at a gallop, with the shotgun guard firing his weapon into the air.

"Holdup!" he shouted. "The coach was held up!"

Those on the street and several who had been inside hurried down to the stage depot, many of them arriving in time to see the dead passenger being removed.

"Who is that?"

"Who was it got shot?"

"Who done it?"

"Mary!" an Indian man shouted. He moved quickly to look down at the young woman.

"I'm sorry, chief," the driver said. The Indian wasn't a chief, and the driver had used the word not as a pejorative but as a term of congeniality.

"Your daughter?" someone asked.

"My daughter," the Indian said. He looked over toward the horse he had brought for his daughter to ride home on. It was decorated with a colorful blanket, feathers, and bits of red and yellow yarn.

"What happened here?" Sheriff Poindexter asked, the last one to arrive on the scene.

"We was held up by Coop Winters and another man," the driver said.

"You sure it was Coop Winters?"

"Yeah, I'm sure."

"How could you be sure, with him wearin' a mask?" Poindexter asked.

"How do you know he was wearing a mask? The driver didn't say anything about the robber wearing a mask," Denham said.

"Well he was wearin' a mask, wasn't he?"

"Yes," the driver said.

"Then how do you know it was Coop Winters?"

"The other fella called him Coop. And the Injun girl had heard of him, so she said his name. And when she did, he shot her."

"How much money did they get?"

"I don't have no idea how much it was. But they got whatever was in the messenger pouch."

"I expect that would be five thousand dollars,"

another man said. This was the banker. "We were getting a money transfer today."

"They also got a hundred and twenty dollars from me," Paul said.

"What was you doin' carryin' so much money?" Poindexter asked.

"We're moving here to Sorrento. That money was to help us get set up."

"Are you Mr. Montgomery?" the banker asked.

"Yes."

"Mr. Montgomery, your bank back in Dallas contacted us about you moving here. We will be happy to loan you the money to get started."

"Thank you," Paul said. "That is very good of you."

"Are you going after the stagecoach robbers, Sheriff?" Denham asked.

"How am I supposed to go after them? I don't know where they are."

"Couldn't you go back out on the road where it happened, then follow the tracks?"

Almost as soon as Denham asked the question, a peal of thunder rumbled through the sky.

"What tracks?" Poindexter asked. "There's a rain comin'. By the time I get out there, the rain will have washed all the tracks away."

"Well, you have to do something," Denham insisted. "After all, you are the sheriff."

"That's right. I am the sheriff, and that means I'll make up my own mind what I have to do, and when I have to do it."

As Denham and Poindexter argued, and the others discussed the robbery at length with the driver and guard, as well as with Paul, Gladys, and Kenny, Mary's father rode out of town with his head bowed. Mary was with him, not riding proudly on the back of her new horse as he had planned, but being pulled behind the horse on a hastily constructed travois.

Not until the first drops of rain started to fall was the crowd broken up.

CHAPTER FOURTEEN

Less than an hour earlier the sky had been clear and blue, but now dark rolling clouds darkened the day and sent jagged bolts of lightning streaking to the ground. Falcon got his slicker out and had just managed to put it on when the rain started. It poured down in torrents, while lightning bolts boomed and snapped, arcing from the sky to the ground.

Falcon could handle the rain, but he didn't like the idea of being in the open while lightning was flashing all around him. Although he could give no scientific explanation as to why, he knew that lightning tended to be drawn toward the highest point. And as a rider on horseback, on a mostly treeless plain, Falcon was the highest point.

Then fortune smiled on him and he saw a cabin ahead. It didn't look occupied; there were no outbuildings around it, and neither barn nor lean-to for stock. There wasn't even an outhouse. Falcon figured that it was probably an abandoned line shack. Whatever it was, it would provide temporary shelter from the rain, and more important, from the lightning.

He saw a flash of light at the window of the cabin and heard the report of a rifle shot. The bullet struck the saddle horn in front of him, which, fortunately, prevented the bullet from hitting him, or his horse. It did, however, startle his horse, who reared up on his back legs, dumping an unsuspecting Falcon to the ground.

"Get out of here!" Falcon shouted to his horse, wanting it to get to safety. He would be in a great difficulty if his horse got killed. With the horse out of harm's way, Falcon pulled his pistol and looked toward the cabin. Realizing that he was exposed, Falcon started running toward a nearby rise, when there was a second shot from the cabin. Falcon spun around, then fell.

"I got 'im! I got the son of a bitch!" someone shouted.

A moment later, two men left the cabin, then came riding up toward him, slowly, confidently.

"You be careful now, Travis."

"Ain't no need to be careful. I hit the son of a bitch dead center. Didn't you see the way he spun around when he went down? Whooee, that was some shootin', I tell you."

* * *

Because Falcon had seen no horses, he thought the cabin was unoccupied. Evidently the horses had been around back.

Falcon was lying on his back with his hand wrapped around his pistol. His hat was over his hand, covering his pistol, and he lay quietly and un-moving as his two assailants approached. They stopped over him, then looked down.

"What do you think, Coop?" Travis asked.

"He ain't dead, Travis."

"He ain't dead, but he looks bad hurt. You bad hurt, mister?" Travis asked. He was narrow faced, hook nosed, and with one eye that didn't quite track with the other one.

"I think I broke my back," Falcon gasped. "I need help."

Coop laughed, a high-pitched cackle of a laugh. Coop was the larger of the two. His most prominent feature was a mouth full of crooked and yellow teeth.

"He needs help. Ha! We shoot 'im, an' he says he needs help, like maybe we come out here to help him, or somethin'."

"Why did you shoot at me?"

"Because you come ridin' up here all fat and sassy," Travis said. "You a bounty hunter, are you? After the reward money?"

"I don't know anything about reward money," Falcon said. "All I was doing was looking for a place to get out of the rain."

"Yeah, well whatever reason it was you had to

come here, you come to the wrong place. You see, here's the thing, mister. We ain't the kind of people who are wantin' to share our house with anyone."

"Really? That doesn't seem all that friendly," Falcon said.

"We ain't exactly what you would call the friendly type," Coop said.

"That's good to know," Falcon replied in a low and strained voice. "I guess maybe I better make sure I don't invite you to my next birthday party."

Coop laughed again. "Did you hear that, Travis? He ain't goin' to invite us to his birthday party," he repeated. "You're a funny man, mister. You know that? I almost hate to have to kill you."

"You know what I think? I think it doesn't bother you at all. I think you're looking forward to it," Falcon said.

"You got that right, mister," Travis said. He aimed his pistol at Falcon and pulled back the hammer, but that was as far as he got before Falcon pulled the trigger on his own pistol. The bullet hit Travis under the chin, then exited through the top of his head. He fell from his horse, dead, before he hit the ground.

"Travis!" Coop shouted. He turned his pistol toward Falcon. "You son of a bitch!" he shouted.

Falcon shot Coop before he could pull the trigger. Standing up then, he looked down at both men. Both were dead, with the rain beating down on them and the water welling up in their open but unseeing eyes.

The rain continued to pour down in large, heavy drops. The lightning increased in frequency until it was almost one sustained lightning flash, a new bolt striking before the previous one left. The thunder boomed in a continuous roar, not unlike the artillery bombardments Falcon could remember.

Taking the reins of the two horses, Falcon hurried toward the cabin, which he was now sure was a line shack. Behind the shack there was a lean-to, and he was happy to see that his horse had found the shelter, coming there of his own accord.

"Good boy, Lightning," Falcon said, rubbing his horse behind its ears. He took Lightning's saddle off but left the bridle so he could secure him to the hitching rail. He unsaddled the other two horses as well.

"No need in you two having to stand here with your saddles," he said to them. "I don't have anything against you just because your riders were a couple of bastards."

There were no other horses in the lean-to, so Falcon was reasonably certain the line shack was empty. Nevertheless, as he thought of the two men who were lying in the mud a hundred yards behind him, he realized there could be another one waiting for him. So, deciding it was better to be safe than sorry, he kicked open the door, then fell to the floor inside, rolling away from the door with his gun at the ready.

His entry wasn't challenged.

Falcon lay on the floor for a moment, making a

slow, thorough perusal of the cabin. Convinced that the cabin was empty, he stood and returned his pistol to the holster. He smelled hot coffee and, looking toward a little pot-bellied stove, saw a pewter coffeepot. It did not take him long to find an empty, clean cup. Pouring himself some of the brew, he took a swallow, then smiled.

"I'll say this," he said aloud. "One of you could make a pretty good pot of coffee."

It was midafternoon before Falcon got started again. He threw the bodies of Travis and Coop over the saddles of their horses so he could take them into town with him. He wasn't sure which body went with which horse, but at this point he didn't think it mattered; they weren't going to challenge him, and the horses accepted their load without complaint.

It was ten miles into town, and the sun had been down over an hour by the time he approached the little municipality. It was dark and everyone was in off the streets. The only indications of life were in the lights that shone from the houses around the edge of town, and from the three saloons that were in town. From the nearest saloon, he could hear a piano playing, the sound of men's voices, and the occasional trills of women's laughter. He saw the *Sorrento Advocate* newspaper office as he passed it by, noticed the window was broken, then rode on until he reached the sheriff's office. Stopping there, he tied the horses off at the hitching rail in front, then went inside.

There was a man, wearing a badge, sitting at the desk. Technically he was sitting, but in reality his chair was leaning back against the wall, his feet were up on the desk, his arms were folded across his chest, and his hat was pulled down over his eyes. He was snoring loudly.

"Sheriff?" Falcon said.

Startled, the chair came forward, and the front two legs hit the floor loudly. His hands slapped the desk in front of him, and he let out a loud hurrumph.

"Sorry about waking you up, Sheriff," Falcon said.

The man swung his legs down from the desk, then pushed his hat back.

"You didn't wake me. I wasn't asleep," he insisted. He rubbed his eyes. "And I ain't the sheriff. The name's Sharp. I'm a deputy. What do you want?"

"I've got two bodies outside."

"Bodies? Who are they?"

"I only heard their first names. One was Travis and the other was Coop."

"Coop? It might be Coop Winters. Where did you find the bodies?"

"It wasn't hard," Falcon said. "They were laying right where they were when I shot them."

"You shot 'em? Both of them?"

"Yes."

"You a bounty hunter?"

"No."

"Then what did you shoot 'em for?"

"Because they were trying to shoot me."

"I'm goin' to have to get the sheriff in on this. He's the only one can authorize the bounty money to be paid. How about you come back tomorrow?"

"All right," Falcon said. "I'll see you in the morning."

The lobby of the town's only hotel was dimly lit by a couple of lanterns, one of which was on a small table next to a settee and the other at the front desk. The desk clerk was reading the newspaper, holding it under the lantern so he could see.

"Would that be the *Sorrento Advocate*?" Falcon asked.

"Yes, sir, you know our paper, do you?"

"Not exactly. But I know Harold Denham."

The clerk chuckled. "He's a Jim Dandy, he is. You got to hand it to Mr. Denham. He sure don't pull no punches when it comes to writin' up stories." The clerk lay the paper down, then stood up. "Are you needin' a room?"

"I am."

"Well, you come to the right place," the clerk said. He chuckled. "Fact is, you come to the only place, seein' as we're the only hotel in town."

"Where can I put my horse?"

"No problem, we got us a livery out back. We

keep fresh water and hay there all the time. No
extry charge."

"Good," Falcon said.

Falcon signed the guest register.

"What brings you to Sorrento?" the clerk asked.

"My horse," Falcon said without looking up.

"Your horse," the clerk said. He laughed. "I
get it, mister, it ain't none of my business. Your
horse," he repeated, and he laughed again. "That's
a good one."

After paying fifty cents, Falcon took care of his
horse, then went upstairs to his room. There was no
lantern, but there was a candle, and Falcon lit it,
then had a look around. The room was very small,
barely large enough to hold the bed, but it was dry
and that suited Falcon's needs for the moment.

He stood at the window for a minute or two and
looked out onto the street, but it was too dark to see
anything other than a few dimly glowing lights.
There was still activity from the saloon, and if
Falcon had not been tired and wet he might have
stopped there for a few minutes. As it was, he went
to bed that night without supper.

When he awoke the next morning, he heard the
ringing sound of a blacksmith's hammer. The store-
keeper next door was sweeping his front porch, and
MacCallister could hear the scrape of the broom.

The blacksmith's hammer and the scratch of
the broom played against each other; the ring and

scratch interspersed with the squeaking sound of the hotel sign, which, suspended from the over-hanging porch roof just below Falcon's window, was answering the morning breeze. From halfway down the street a new edifice was being built, either a house or a business building, and the carpenter's hammer and saw joined the morning symphony of sound.

Falcon lay in bed for a full minute before he got up and walked over to the window to look out over the street of the town he had, thus far, seen only at night.

There were puddles of water in the street, and the mud and horse droppings had mixed together to form pools of ooze. There were planks laid across the street, and he watched as a few people negotiated the planks, which were, themselves, so covered with mud that they were only slightly better than crossing in the street itself.

Down the street a short distance he saw a saloon, advertising itself by a huge, wooden sign that read HOG HEAVEN. Next to the words was painted the car-icature of a pig holding a golden mug of beer, and superimposed over the beer was a large "5¢." Next door to the saloon was a dry goods store. Next to the store was the newspaper, and at the far end of the street was a church.

He also noticed, standing in the middle of the street at the opposite end of town from the church, a gallows, and not just any gallows. This gallows was painted red, and there was a hangman's noose dangling from the gibbet. He didn't think he had ever seen a red-painted gallows before.

He wanted to go see his friend Harold Denham, but decided he would have his breakfast first. Having passed on his supper last night, he was very hungry this morning. Getting dressed, he went downstairs and found the Hungry Biscuit restaurant on the same side of the street, right next door to the hotel.

"Yes, sir, what'll it be for you this morning?" a middle-aged woman asked when Falcon sat at a table. She was wearing a scarf, and when one strand of gray hair slipped out, she pushed it back.

"I'll have about eight slices of bacon, half a dozen eggs, half a dozen biscuits, and maybe some gravy."

The woman smiled. "Whooee, mister, you've got some kind of appetite. Would you be wantin' any grits with that?"

"Grits? Yeah, I'll take some grits." Grits were not something Falcon encountered very often, but he remembered that his mother, who was from Kentucky, would sometimes boil corn in lye until it swelled up and turned white. Then she ground it and made grits.

Half an hour later, Falcon was pleasantly full, and he pushed away from the table with a feeling of contentment. That contentment was interrupted by a loud voice calling to him.

"Mister, are you the one who brought them two dead bodies in last night?"

The voice not only got Falcon's attention, but it got the attention of everyone else in the restaurant as well. All conversation stopped, and everyone stopped eating as they looked on in interest.

The man who had called out to Falcon was wearing a badge. He also had an eye that was so strange looking that it took Falcon a moment to realize that it was missing an eyelid. That fit Jim Courtright's description of Poindexter.

"I am," Falcon answered. "You must be Sheriff Poindexter."

"Yeah, I am. How did you know?"

"I've heard of you."

"Have you now? Well, I want you to come on over to my office. I've got a few questions for you."

"I imagined you would," Falcon replied. "Just let me pay for my breakfast."

CHAPTER FIFTEEN

"Who are you about to hang?" Falcon asked, pointing toward the gallows as he followed the sheriff down to the sheriff's office.

"We don't have anybody waitin' to hang right now," Sheriff Poindexter replied.

"Oh? But you have a gallows there, as well as a hangman's rope."

He chuckled. "Oh, we keep us a permanent gallows in Sorrento 'cause once Judge Dawes sentences a man to hang, why we don't like to mess around. Most of 'em gets hung the same day, and never no later than by the next day. We keep the rope and hangman's noose ready, too."

"Judge Dawes sounds like somebody you wouldn't want to cross."

"You got that right," the sheriff said.

As they approached the sheriff's office, Falcon saw that there were several people hanging around, and when he got closer he saw why they were there. They were all looking at the two bodies that were lying on the porch. The two horses he had brought in were gone.

The sheriff opened the door, then indicated that Falcon should go inside. Falcon did, and the sheriff followed.

"Have a seat there," the sheriff said. It was more of an order than an invitation.

"What's your name?"

"MacCallister. Falcon MacCallister."

"MacCallister? You any kin to the coward that ran from the Alamo?"

Falcon bristled. "Sheriff, that was my father, Jamie. He was with Colonel Bowie's volunteers, and he was ordered to leave the Alamo to take out the last letters and dispatches. And if you knew your history, you would know that he was honored for his service by Sam Houston himself."

"Yeah, I've heard that told, too," Sheriff Poindexter said. "I've also heard of you. You're supposed to be some kind of hero, I'm told."

The sheriff's words were baiting, so Falcon didn't reply.

"Are you a bounty hunter, MacCallister?"

"No."

"Did you know that Cooper Winters and Travis Eberwine were wanted men? That there was a reward of two hundred fifty dollars for each of them?"

"No, I didn't know that. I've never heard of them."

"Then why in Sam Hill did you kill them?"

"Because they were trying to kill me," Falcon replied.

Falcon related the story of how he had been caught in the thunderstorm, had seen a cabin, and was just going to use it to provide shelter.

"They started shooting at me. I shot back."

"And killed both of them," the sheriff said.

"Yes."

"Mister, you must be one hell of a shot."

Again, Falcon didn't reply, though if he had, he could have told the sheriff he didn't have to be that good of a shot since they were right on him when he shot them.

"Now, Mr. MacCallister, here is the big question. Where is the money?"

"What money?"

"The money them two men stole when they held up the stagecoach yesterday. Five thousand dollars. Where is it?"

"I didn't know anything about the stagecoach holdup, and I don't know anything about the money," Falcon said.

"Judge?" Sheriff Poindexter called.

From the back of the office, another man appeared. Wearing all black, the judge was a large man with a porcine face, white hair, blue eyes, and a protruding lower lip.

"This here is Judge Dawes," Sheriff Poindexter said.

Falcon nodded toward the judge, but didn't speak.

"Judge, I'm goin' to ask you to issue me a warrant,

so's I can search this fella. He said he didn't know nothin' about Travis and Coop bein' wanted men. He also says he don't have none of the money them two boys stole. So I aim to search him."

"Consider the warrant issued," the judge said.

"No," Falcon replied. "If you are going to issue a warrant, Judge, I'm going to have to be served. That means you have to write it out."

"The hell you say," Sheriff Poindexter said.

Judge Dawes held up his hand. "The man knows his law. Give me a minute, and I'll write it out."

Judge Dawes sat at the desk, opened the drawer, and pulled out a pre-printed paper. He began filling out the blanks, and a moment later, handed it to the sheriff.

"The warrant has been issued," he said. "Sheriff, do your duty."

Sheriff Poindexter handed the warrant to Falcon, who studied it for a moment, then nodded his head.

"It seems to be in order," he said.

"You're damn right it's in order. I'm the one that issued it," Judge Dawes replied.

"Hold your arms out like this. Straight out by your side, and parallel with the floor," the sheriff ordered.

Falcon complied, and the sheriff began searching him. He stuck his hand down in the shirt pocket, both front pockets and both back pockets of his pants. From Falcon's front pocket, the sheriff took out a pocket knife, two keys, and a few coins. From his left rear pocket he took out a billfold.

Opening the billfold, Sheriff Poindexter whistled.

"Damn, me, look at all this money here?" he said. "Now, this is interestin'. This is awful interestin'."

"How much is there?"

"One thousand and eleven dollars," Falcon said.

"What are you doing with so much money?" Judge Dawes asked.

"I took one thousand dollars from my bank account before I left MacCallister, Colorado," Falcon said. "That would be very easy for you to check. All you need to do is send a telegram to my bank there."

"You've got more than a thousand dollars," Sheriff Poindexter said.

"I got into a game of cards in Glen Rose and won thirty dollars."

"What do you think, Judge?" the sheriff asked.

"Mister MacCallister, what are you doing in Sorrento?" Judge Dawes asked.

"I've come to visit a friend."

"Who is this friend? Will he vouch for you?"

"I expect he will," Falcon said. "It's Harold Denham."

"The newspaper man?" the sheriff asked.

"Yes, I knew him in Colorado."

"Mister, sayin' you are a friend of the newspaper man don't buy you a lot of credit with me. As far as

I'm concerned, he's about the biggest troublemaker there is in this town," Poindexter said.

"I wouldn't know about that. As I said, I knew him in Colorado."

"All right, Mr. MacCallister, you can go," Judge Dawes said.

"Thank you."

"And, don't think I ain't goin' to be a' keepin' my eye on you," Sheriff Poindexter said. "Because I damn sure am."

When Falcon walked back out front, he saw that the number of people gathered around the two bodies had grown considerably. The corpses were still lying on the wooden porch and were now gathering flies.

"That there is Cooper Winters," someone said. "I've seen him before."

"The other'n must be Travis Eberwine," another suggested.

"How come they're still layin' here? I heard that they been here all night long. How come Nunnelee ain't come down to pick 'em up yet?"

"I think the sheriff is wantin' ever'one to see 'em so that he can brag about what a good job he's doin'."

"Say, ain't them the two men that held up the stagecoach and kilt that girl?"

"Yeah, but wasn't no white girl they kilt. Was just a Injun girl is all."

"Plus, they stole more'n five thousand dollars is what I heard."

"They may be layin' here dead on the sheriff's front porch, but I'll bet you anything that the sheriff didn't go out an' hunt 'em down."

"Well, somebody did, 'cause they're both a' layin' here, 'n' they's both of 'em dead."

"I wonder who it was that kilt 'em."

"It was a feller named Falcon MacCallister."

"Never heard of him."

"You ain't? Well I've damn sure heard of him. Never met him, wouldn't know what he looks like, but I've sure heard of him."

Falcon was glad he wasn't recognized by any of the people as he left the sheriff's office, because he didn't want to get into any conversations about the incident. He continued down the boardwalk until he reached the newspaper office. A small bell, attached to the door of the newspaper office, jangled as he pushed it open to walk inside.

"I'm back in the composing room; I'll be with you in a minute!" an unseen voice called.

Falcon glanced around the newspaper office. The first thing he saw was a brick on the floor, surrounded by bits of shattered glass. There was a counter that separated the front of the office from the back, and on the other side of the counter, a steam-powered printing press. There were several signs posted on the wall, advertising the paper and the printing business.

~ QUALITY PRINTING ~

☞ BILLS, POSTERS, CARDS

Inquire for prices.

There was a calendar on the wall with a Currier and Ives print of a train running at night, its headlight stabbing ahead, every window of every car glowing yellow.

There was a distinctive smell to a newspaper office, the smell of processed paper and ink, and this office was no different.

Denham came into the front then. He was wearing an apron that had been white at one time but now was so stained with ink that it looked gray. He was wiping his hands with a cloth on which Falcon could smell kerosene.

"Now, what can I do for . . ." Denham stopped in mid-conversation, then with a broad smile extended his hand. "Well, I'll be damned! Falcon MacCallister. I knew you would come," he said.

"Hello, Harold," Falcon replied, taking Denham's hand. He glanced toward the brick and glass on the floor. "I see you've made friends," he added with a little chuckle.

"If you are talking about the brick, I'm leaving it there because I want everyone in town to know the kind of bastards I have to deal with," Denham said. He pointed to the broken and boarded over window. "Not that they couldn't tell by looking at that."

"Well, if a newspaper doesn't piss somebody off, it simply isn't doing its job," Falcon said.

"I'm glad you see it like that because I've sure as hell pissed off a bunch of folks around here. By the way, I knew you were here. The word has already gotten out that you were the one who brought in the two stagecoach robbers. I wasn't surprised any, because I was damn sure that neither our sheriff nor any of his no account deputies had done it."

"It was me, all right," Falcon said. "But they came after me first, and I had no choice. I didn't know they had robbed a stagecoach, though. I didn't know anything about it."

"They not only robbed the coach, they shot and killed a young Indian girl who was just coming back home from going to school in the East. Beautiful girl, she was, and a fine one, too. Her father is as good a man as you'll meet, Comanche or white."

"Tell me what you've got going on here, Harold," Falcon said.

"We've got a judge and a sheriff who have turned Scott County into their own private fiefdom. They are extorting money from every businessman in town, and from every farmer and rancher in the county. And if it isn't bad enough that they are bleeding us dry, they have let every railroad in the state know that it is going to cost them to come into the county—and that's not only preventing us from growing, it is also killing what little business we have left."

"Has anyone tried to do anything about it?"

Falcon asked. "By that I mean, have you contacted the governor?"

"We've tried, but the governor is not someone who acts with dispatch. While he is examining all the legal ramifications of what is going on here, the noose around our neck just grows tighter. Eb Smalley, who runs the store here, had a friend who was with the Texas Rangers. Eb contacted him, and he came to town. A good man he was too, but . . ."

"'A good man he was'?"

"Sheriff Poindexter killed him."

"Surely, killing a Texas Ranger would get the governor's attention."

Denham shook his head. "I'm afraid not. Judge Small charged Poindexter with murder, tried and acquitted him the same day."

"Double indemnity," Falcon said.

"Exactly."

"What about organizing?"

"We have tried that a few times as well. But that isn't without its problems. For one thing, we aren't always sure of who we can trust, and for another many of those who we could trust are too frightened to do anything about it. One of the reasons I contacted you is I think you might be just the man who can put a little starch in their backbones."

"I'll do what I can," Falcon said. "But courage has to come from within a person."

"I know. And the thing is, most of these people are veterans of the war. They've shown that they have courage when needed. Now it is just a matter of having them reach down inside them so they can find it again. That's why we are planning to have a meeting to discuss this. And we want you to come."

Falcon held up his hand. "I'm not all that good at speaking at meetings," he said.

"You don't have to speak. You won't have to say a word. All I want is for you to be there."

"All right, when is this meeting? And where is it?"

"It's Sunday afternoon. We're doing it on a Sunday because all the businesses are closed anyway, so nobody who comes will be sending a signal by closing up his store."

"Sounds good."

"And we are going to have the meeting out at David Bowman's ranch, the Big Star. The ranchers are being hurt as much as the people in town are, so they are equally anxious to get something done. Also, having it out of town means it is less likely to catch Poindexter's attention."

"I wouldn't count on that," Falcon said. "If Poindexter is the kind of man you say he is, he is going to have his spies out everywhere. I've no doubt but that he already knows about it."

"He probably does know that we are planning a meeting, but he doesn't know when, and he can't know where, because so far, only Bowman and I know that it is going to be at his ranch on Sunday. Neither of us have discussed it with anyone else."

"He may not know yet, but you are going to have to put the word out to the ones you want to attend, and that means he is going to find out."

"Well, let him find out," Harold said defiantly. "It might not hurt for him to know that. Oh, by the way, come back here and I'll give you the first look at the story I wrote about the two you brought in last night. Though why I bothered to write it, I don't know. As fast as news gets around in this town, we don't need a newspaper."

"Sure you do," Falcon said. "Newspapers not only report the news, they also help shape opinion."

"As our Jewish friends say, 'From your lips to God's ear,' " Harold replied. He pointed to the palate. "There it is."

"It's backward; how am I supposed to read that?"

Harold chuckled. "Oh, yeah, I forget sometimes that ordinary people have to have the letters forward. Just a minute, I'll print a page for you."

Harold found a sheet of newsprint, laid it over the palate, and then rolled over it to make a single impression. Pulling the page away, he handed it to Falcon.

Falcon grasped the page at the corners so not to get the still wet ink on him, then moved over to hold it under the light so he could read the story. Harold stood by, smiling and observing Falcon's reaction.

Murderers Caught !

COOPER WINTERS AND TRAVIS EBERWINE
BROUGHT TO JUSTICE

Last week two brigands held up the Fort Worth Stagecoach as it was making its journey to Sorrento. They stole five thousand dollars in money that was being transferred to the local bank, and they killed Mary Little Horse, an innocent young Indian girl who was returning home after two years of attending school in the East.

But the two robbers, Cooper Winters and Travis Eberwine, did not have an opportunity to enjoy their ill-gotten gains, for it was their misfortune to encounter Mr. Falcon MacCallister. Although Mr. MacCallister is a visitor to our area, he is a man well known throughout the West, having won his reputation not only by deeds of derring-do, but because he is a man of unquestioned integrity, honesty, and a willingness to come to the aid of others when they are in distress.

I am happy to say that Mr. MacCallister was invited to visit Sorrento by the publisher of this newspaper, for if ever there was a need for a hero to come to the aid of others, it is here, and now. It is my belief that Mr. MacCallister, working hand in hand with the good, God-fearing and law-abiding citizens of this town and county, will help us to free ourselves from the draconian yoke of oppression which now besets us.

"What do you think?" Denham asked.

"You've sort of thrown down the gauntlet, haven't you?"

Denham chuckled. "You noticed that, did you? I hope Poindexter isn't so damn dumb that he doesn't pick up on it. By the way, where are you going to stay while you're in town?"

"I have a room at the hotel."

"You could stay there, I suppose. But if you want my recommendation, I'd suggest that you check out Mrs. Allen's boardinghouse. Her place is clean and she has a nice stable for your horse. It's just a couple of blocks from here, over on North Ranney Street."

CHAPTER SIXTEEN

The boardinghouse was quite substantial; made of brick, it was two stories high and had a wide, covered veranda out front. Obviously a fine private home at one time, what had been the drawing room was now the lobby and check-in counter. Mrs. Margaret Allen was a small, thin woman, whose gray hair was pulled back and tied in a little bun behind her head. She was wearing wire-rimmed glasses.

"Oh, my, what a handsome man you are," Mrs. Allen said. "You are going to be a hit among all the ladies of the dining table, I can tell you that right now."

Falcon chuckled as he signed in. "Are you this flirtatious with all your guests?"

"Only the handsome ones," Mrs. Allen said. "You wouldn't know to look at me now, but I've turned a few heads in my time."

"What do you mean, in your time? You can still turn a few heads."

Mrs. Allen laughed out loud. "Yes, sir, you are going to be a mighty welcome guest here."

Sheriff Poindexter looked at the map again. It had been drawn by Cooper Winters and Travis Eberwine, and it showed the location of the abandoned line shack where they would meet him and split the money with him.

Poindexter was the one who had informed them of the money shipment. This wasn't the first arrangement Poindexter and Judge Dawes had done. In addition to the taxes they were extracting from the citizens of the town, they were also in partnership with some selected outlaws, though this was just something that Poindexter and the judge knew about. None of the deputies were even aware this was going on.

It wasn't just stagecoach holdups. Over the last two years there had been as many as fifteen hundred cattle rustled from the county ranchers. Poindexter, while seemingly looking for the outlaws, was actually making it possible for them to escape, thus earning a share from each of the jobs pulled.

Originally, Poindexter and Dawes were only going to get twenty-five hundred dollars from the coach holdup. But now, with Winters and Eberwine dead, the entire five thousand would be theirs. Unless MacCallister had found the money and kept it for himself.

Poindexter saw the money bag as soon as he

stepped into the cabin, and he groaned. It was in plain view; there was no way MacCallister could have missed it. It was sure to be empty.

It wasn't empty! Poindexter gasped in surprise, then gave a little shout of excitement when he opened the bag and saw the money inside. Counting it, he found that all five thousand dollars were still there.

For a moment he wondered how MacCallister could have possibly let this get by, then he decided that if MacCallister hadn't known anything about the stagecoach robbery, he wouldn't have known to look for the money. Poindexter stuffed the loot into his saddlebags, then started back to Sorrento.

When Sheriff Poindexter returned to his office, he saw Deputy Sharp reading the newspaper. Sharp looked up when Poindexter came in.

"Have you read the paper today, Sheriff?"

"No. What has Denham said now?"

"This fella MacCallister? The reason he has come to Sorrento is because Denham asked him to come and deal with the"—Sharp struggled over the words as he read them aloud—"draconian yoke of oppression which now besets us." He looked up from the paper. "What does that mean?"

Poindexter chuckled. "That means us. We are the draconian oppressors."

"I'm goin' over to the Hog Heaven," Sharp said, putting the paper aside. Not until he left did the judge come in from his own office, which was behind the sheriff's office.

"Did you get the money?"

Poindexter smiled. "Yeah," he said. "It's out in my saddlebag. We got all of it, Judge. They hadn't spent one cent of it yet. All five thousand dollars."

"Excellent," Dawes said. "By the way, Sheriff, what do you know about this meeting that Denham is having?" Judge Dawes asked.

"What meeting? I don't know anything about it."

"Apparently there is to be a meeting somewhere, soon, and it will involve some of the citizens from town, as well as ranchers and farmers from out in the county."

"What is the meeting about?"

"Well now what do you think it would be about, Poindexter? Why would people from town and the county be meeting? You did read the latest issue of Denham's newspaper, didn't you?"

"Yeah, I read it. Judge, ain't there some way you can close that paper down?"

"It's not that easy. I can play with local and state laws. But freedom of the press is a federal thing, and there's nothing I can do about that."

"What do you think will come out of this meeting?"

"It depends."

"Depends on what?"

"Sheriff, I will leave that up to you."

* * *

Sheriff Poindexter was sitting at a table in the back of the Long Trail saloon. Pogue Allison, who used to be one of his deputies, was at the table with him, along with Ron Mace, Jack Andrews, and Frank Little.

"We didn't get as much money for the cows as we thought we would," Pogue said. "We only got eight dollars a head."

"And if we give you half, that don't leave all that much for us," Mace said.

"That's not my problem," Poindexter said. "You boys are buying protection, and protection ain't cheap."

"Still, it didn't seem hardly worth it," Pogue complained.

"I've got another job for you. A little easier, and I'll give you a hundred dollars apiece when you've done it."

"A hundred dollars?" Pogue asked.

"As soon as the job is done."

"What is the job?"

"There's goin' to be a meetin' of a bunch of so-called *concerned* citizens," Poindexter said, coming down hard on the word "concerned." "Some sort of vigilante committee if you ask me."

"Where is this meetin' goin' to be?" Allison asked.

"It's going to be at the Big Star."

"Same place where we took the cows from," Pogue said.

"Yes."

"And you want us to break it up."

"No, let 'em have their meeting."

"Then I don't understand. If you don't want us to break it up, what is it you want us to do?"

"What do you suppose would happen if while ever'body is meetin' at the Big Star Ranch, that somethin' would happen to one of the other ranches? Don't you think that might cause some folks to think twice before they go to any more meetin's?" Poindexter asked.

"What kind of somethin' happenin'?" Allison asked.

"Oh, I don't know. Maybe something like a fire."

"Ha!" Allison said. "Yeah, now I know what you are talkin' about."

"Here's fifty dollars apiece," Poindexter said. "Take care of that business for me, and there's another fifty dollars."

Allison took the money. "This is goin' to be the easiest and the most fun fifty dollars I ever made."

"I'll not be going to the meeting with you," Falcon said as Denham was getting ready to leave.

"Oh, but I want to introduce you to the others. I want them to know that help is on the way," Denham said.

"Do you think the sheriff knows about the meeting?"

Denham sighed. "I'm sure he does. We have tried to keep it secret, but by now all the ranchers and farmers know about it, which means all the cowboys and farmhands know as well."

"With that many knowing about the meeting, do you really expect the secret to be kept?"

"Probably not," Denham admitted.

"Then that means that there may be someone who will attempt to disrupt the meeting."

"Yes," Denham said. "Which is all the more reason why you should be present."

"Oh, I'll be there," Falcon said.

"Good."

"You just won't know that I'm there."

Now Denham looked confused. "What do you mean?"

"I'm going to be—around—watching."

"Oh," Denham replied. "All right, I guess that will be just as good as you being there."

"It will be better."

As the nearby hills turned from red to purple in the setting sun, Bowman's friends and neighbors began arriving for the meeting. Wagons and buggies brought entire families across the range to gather at the Bowman house. Children, who lived too far apart to play with one another, laughed and squealed and ran from wagon to wagon to greet their friends before dashing off to a twilight game of kick-the-can. The women, who had brought cakes and pies from home, gathered in the kitchen to make coffee, thus turning the business meeting into a great social event. Many of them brought quilts, and they spread them out so that, while the men were meeting, they could work on the elaborate colors and patterns of the quilts they would be displaying at the next fair.

Denham sat in a chair next to an open window. Moths and other bugs beat against the window screen, attracted to the light inside. Outside he heard a mule braying, then as the breeze freshened, the clatter and clank of a responding windmill.

"How old was that young cowboy you buried?" Asa Baker asked. Baker owned one of the neighboring ranches to Big Star. "What was his name?"

"His name was Arnie Jones, and he was only seventeen," Boardman answered.

"Just a boy."

"Yes."

"Did he have any folks?"

"None that we know of. He told us he come from an orphanage in Dallas. Probably some whore's kid who had to give him up. Fact is, he just took the name Jones 'cause he didn't know what it really was. But he was a good kid. It's a shame what happened to him."

There were at least two dozen men present, and after his brief conversation with Baker, David Bowman stepped up to the front of the room and held his hands up to quiet the many conversations.

"Gentlemen, I thank you all for coming. So if you don't mind, we'll get started."

"Get started doing what, David?" Gerald Kelly asked. "I came to this meeting because I agree that something needs to be done, and I sort of hope we can do it. But for the life of me, I don't have an idea in hell what it will be."

"Well now, Gerald, that's why we're holdin' this meeting," Bowman replied. "To see if we can come up with a plan as to what needs to be done."

"David, is this the right time to be doing something like this?" Leon Frakes, a neighboring rancher, asked.

"What do you mean, 'is this the right time'?" Bowman asked.

"I mean, well, yes, we should talk about it, and I reckon that's what we'll be doin' here. But I'm not sure this is the right time, yet."

"Time? Man, we're runnin' out of time! Dawes and Poindexter are bleeding us white with their taxes, and if that isn't enough, the rustlers are having their way with us!" Bowman said. "I'm sure all of you know by now that I just lost two hundred fifty head, plus had one of my cowboys killed."

"David is right," one of the others said. "I've lost fifty head this month myself. The way I see it, either Poindexter is the worst sheriff in all of Texas, or else the son of a bitch is in cahoots with the cattle rustlers."

"That's quite an accusation, Sam," Bowman said. "You got anything to back that up?"

"Nothin' but my gut feelin'," Sam replied.

"Damn me if I don't agree with Sam," one of the others at the meeting said. "I wouldn't be in the least surprised if the sheriff and all his deputies wasn't involved. In all the time the son of a bitch has been the sheriff, has he ever found one stolen cow?"

"Harold, didn't you tell us that you had someone coming, someone who was going to, I believe you said—change the balance for us?" Frakes asked. "Do you really have Falcon MacCallister coming?"

"Yes. Falcon MacCallister. And he isn't just coming, he is already here."

"Well, where is he?"

"He's—around," Denham said without being any more specific.

"How come he didn't come to this meeting?"

"He thought it best not to."

The cowboys and farmhands had also been invited to the meeting because what happened to the ranchers had a direct impact on them. If the ranchers lost their ranches, the cowboys would lose their jobs. However, because the cowboys were working hands and nearly all of them single men, they didn't feel comfortable around the ranchers and their families, so most of them declined, respectfully.

Silver Spur Ranch was one of the smallest spreads in the valley, with only three full-time cowboys. At the moment they were playing cards for grains of corn, and one of them, Shorty Rogers, was winning. Though the corn had no monetary value, and was only a means of keeping a record, that did not lessen the intensity of the game, and Clyde

Barnes and Les Karnes groaned as Shorty won his third successive pot.

"You cheating?" Les asked. "You've got to be cheating."

"I ain't cheatin'," Shorty said. "I'm just better 'n you two, that's all."

"Yeah? Well let's see how you do this time," Clyde said.

The cards were raked in, the deck shuffled, then dealt again.

"You think all them ranchers is goin' to come up with anythin' at this meetin' they got goin' on over to the Bowman place?" Les asked as he dealt the cards.

"I don't know. If they don't, they're all goin' to go out of business and me an' you an' Shorty is all goin' to be lookin' for jobs somewhere else," Clyde said.

"I don't want to go nowhere else. I like it here, just fine."

"Maybe we could wind up workin' for Sheriff Poindexter," Shorty suggested. "I hear tell he's plannin' on buyin' a ranch somewhere."

"Yeah, well, with all the tax money the son of a bitch is collectin', he can probably afford it," Clyde said.

"More 'n likely, though, he would hire his own men. I've got a feelin' we'd all be left out in the cold."

"Yeah, that's probably true," Les agreed. "But the truth is, I wouldn't work for the son of a bitch if he was to pay me double what I'm makin' here at the Silver Spur."

"What about this fella, Falcon MacCallister, that's been brought in?" Shorty asked.

"What about him?" Clyde responded.

"Could be he could take care of the sheriff and the judge," Shorty suggested.

"First of all, how is he goin' to take care of 'em? They're the law. They ain't no count, but they are the law. Besides which, the sheriff has damn near got hisself a regular army of deputies. What could one man do against all them?"

"This ain't just one man. This is Falcon Mac-Callister."

"So it's Falcon MacCallister. What's that supposed to mean? He's still just one man," Clyde said.

"You mean you ain't never heard of Falcon Mac-Callister?" Shorty asked in surprise.

"No, I can't say as I have."

"I ain't never heard of him, neither," Les said.

"Wait a minute," Shorty said. "I want to show you somethin'."

Shorty laid his cards facedown on the table and started toward his bunk. He looked back just as Les was reaching toward his cards.

"Damn it, Les, I seen that!"

"I didn't do nothin'. I was just movin' 'em so they wouldn't fall off the table, is all."

"Uh, huh," Shorty said. He came back, grabbed up his cards, then went over to his bunk. Lifting up his cotton tick mattress, he picked up a paperbound book, then brought it back and dropped it on the table in front of the others. "What do you think of this?" he asked.

The title of the book was: *Falcon MacCallister and the Mountain Shooters*.

"That's just a book. That ain't real," Clyde said.

"Maybe the book ain't real, but the man is. And if he wasn't somethin' kind of special, they wouldn't be writin' no books about him in the first place," Shorty said.

"Yeah, well it don't matter how famous he is, he's still just one man, and I don't see him goin' up against the sheriff and all his deputies all by his ownself," Clyde insisted.

Les started toward the back door.

"Where you goin'?"

"I'm goin' outside to take a piss. That is, unless you want me to piss in here."

"I hope it comes out all right," Shorty said, then he laughed at his own joke. "Do you get it?" he asked Clyde. "I said I hope it comes out all right."

"Yeah, yeah, I get it," Clyde said.

CHAPTER SEVENTEEN

Outside the bunkhouse, four riders stopped on a little hill overlooking the Silver Spur Ranch.

"Do you think there is anyone here?" Frank asked.

"There may be," Pogue replied. "From what I heard, there wasn't many of the cowboys was actually goin' to go to the meetin'. So it's more than likely that someone is here."

Dismounting, the four men moved to the edge of the hill bent over at the waist so they wouldn't show in silhouette, and looked down toward the bunkhouse.

"See anyone?" Pogue asked.

"Yeah, there's someone there," Frank said. "I can see a couple of 'em through the window, sittin' at a table or somethin'."

"Only two? Frakes has three men workin' for him. Wonder where the other one is," Mace said.

"Maybe he went to that ranchers' meeting," Pogue suggested. "No matter. We'll shoot these two. That ought to be enough to scare the rest of 'em off.

Frank, you an' Mace take the one on the left. Me and Jack will take the one on the right. With two of us shootin' at each one of 'em, we're bound to get 'em both."

"I'm ready," Jack replied.

"Me, too," Frank said.

"I'm ready," Mace said.

All four men raised their rifles and took slow, careful aim. Their targets were well illuminated by the lantern that burned brightly inside the bunkhouse.

"On three," Pogue said. "One, two, three." He squeezed the trigger that sent out the first bullet.

Four rifles roared as one.

Shorty died instantly, a bullet coming through the window to crash into the back of his head. Clyde went down with a bullet in his chest. Les, who had just come back into the cabin at that moment, dived quickly to the floor.

"Shorty! Clyde!" he called, but neither man answered.

There was another volley; this time the bullets whistled through the window, slammed into the walls, and careened off the cold stove. Les scooted as far up under his bunk as he could get and lay there with his arms over his head until, finally, the shooting stopped.

"Les!" Clyde called. "Les, I'm real bad shot."

Les crawled across the floor, littered now with

shattered glass from the shot-out window. When he reached Clyde, he saw blood on the injured man's chest. The wound was sucking air, and Les looked away, knowing it would soon be over for his friend.

"What about Shorty?" Clyde asked. "How bad is he hit?"

Les looked over at Shorty and saw him lying very still. His eyes were open, but there was blood and brain matter lying on the floor by the bullet wound in his head.

"He's dead, pardner," Les said.

Les got no reply from Clyde, and when he looked back at him, he saw that Clyde was dead as well.

He heard the sound of galloping horses then, and quickly he darted out the back door and ran through the dark into a small thicket of trees just behind the barn. There were four men, and he watched as, methodically, they began setting fire to the house, barn, cookshack, and smokehouse. They spared the bunkhouse.

Falcon was at least two miles away when he heard the shooting. Because of the echoes, it took him a moment to determine the direction from which the shooting was coming. He rode to the top of a knoll while the firing was still going on to see if he could find out. Then, far to the west, he saw a series of winking lights and knew that they were muzzle flashes.

* * *

Back at the meeting at the Bowman Ranch, the ranchers and farmers, totally unaware of the attack on the Silver Spur, were still discussing the problem and trying to come up with some solution.

"It's time we did something about it," Frakes said.

"We did do something about it. We hired Falcon MacCallister," Bowman said. "Accordin' to Mr. Denham, he is going to be the solution to all our problems. Ain't that right, Harold?"

"That isn't what I said," Denham replied forcefully. "And we didn't exactly hire him."

"What's that?" one of the other ranchers said. "What do you mean you didn't hire him? Ain't he done come here?"

"He came here, yes, but it was of his own accord," Denham said.

"That's not good," Bowman said.

"Why not?"

"It's always better when someone is working for you. That way you have some leverage over them, you can tell them what to do, and they don't have any choice."

Denham chuckled.

"What is it? What did I say funny?"

"When you said 'tell them what to do.' Believe me, nobody ever tells Falcon MacCallister what to do."

"Then what you are saying is we can't count on him to work for us?"

"It is more like he will be working for himself,"

Denham said. "And his goals and ours will be parallel."

"Well, Mr. Denham, you are the one who wanted to get this meeting together. So, what, exactly, do you have in mind?" one of the attendees asked.

"Gentlemen, what we need," Denham began, "is to form some sort of a civic organization that can deal with this."

"You mean like a vigilante committee?" a man named Parker asked.

"No. Well, yes, in essence we will be a vigilante committee, but we cannot and will not refer to ourselves that way."

"What about the Scott County Fusiliers?" someone suggested.

"Fusiliers is too militaristic. We need a more benign-sounding name."

"I've got a suggestion," Bowman said. "Suppose we call ourselves the Scott County Betterment Association."

"Good suggestion," Denham said. "I'll draw us up a charter and do a story about it in the newspaper."

"Excuse me, Mr. Bowman?" someone said, stepping in through the door at that moment. It was one of Bowman's hands.

"Yes, Ben, what is it?" Bowman answered.

"Maybe you folks better come outside here an' look at this," Ben suggested.

The expression in the cowboy's voice caught the attention of the ranchers, and they stopped what they were doing to step out onto Bowman's front porch. Ben pointed toward the distant horizon, but he didn't have to. Everyone's attention had already been arrested by the orange glow of what had to be a large fire.

"That . . . that's your place, ain't it, Al?" someone asked.

"Yes," Al answered in a tight voice.

"Quick!" one of the other ranchers said. "If we get over there in time, we might be able to save some of it!"

"I've got extra buckets in the barn!" Bowman shouted. "Get 'em in the wagons men, an' let's go!"

Falcon stared toward the ranch, now burning, and saw, silhouetted against the flames, four riders. Once he determined which way they were going, he rode quickly to be able to cut them off. Finding a trail through some rocks, he dismounted, ground-tethered Lightning out of sight, then waited for them.

Close in he could hear crickets and frogs. A little farther out an owl hooted, and out on the prairie a coyote howled. But so far he had not heard what he wanted to hear, the drum of horses' hooves, the rattle of the saddle and tack. He was beginning to wonder if he had mistaken their course, when, once more, he got a glimpse them.

He pulled his pistol and checked his load, then waited. When they were close enough, he called out to them.

"That's far enough! You men stop right there!" he called.

"What the hell?" one of the men shouted. "Who is it?"

"What the hell does it matter who it is? Shoot the son of a bitch down!" another called.

The riders pulled their pistols then and opened fire. Falcon returned fire, his first shot knocking one of the men from his saddle onto the rocky ground. All hell broke loose then as the pistols roared and muzzle flashes lit up the night like bolts of lightning.

Even though outnumbered, Falcon had the advantage. He was well positioned on the ground, while the outlaws were astride horses that were rearing and twisting about nervously as flying lead whistled through the air and whined off stone. It was almost impossible for them to get off a shot, even if they had a clear view of their target.

Falcon took down a second rider.

"Where the hell is he?" one of the outlaws shouted in panic.

"Shoot 'im, shoot 'im!" the other yelled.

It only took two more shots, and then it was quiet, with the final round of shooting but faint echoes bounding off distant hills. A little cloud of acrid-bitter gunsmoke drifted up over the deadly battlefield, and Falcon walked out among the fallen outlaws, moving cautiously, his pistol at the ready.

It wasn't necessary. All four men were dead, and the entire battle had taken less than a minute.

* * *

In the east the sun had risen full disc. A dozen wagons were parked in the soft morning light, and in the wagons, nestled among quilts and blankets, slept the children of the families who had come to help fight the fire. The light of day now disclosed the damage the fire had done. The house had been completely destroyed, but it could have been worse. The smokehouse, cookshack, bunkhouse, and barn had not been as thoroughly involved in flames, and they were saved, first by Les's efforts and then by the united effort of all who had come to help.

Martha Frakes stood in her husband's arms, weeping softly. Harold Denham stood nearby, looking at the destruction with eyes that were wide and sad. The Frakes, like everyone else out here, were covered with soot and ash from the blackened ruins of their home. On the ground under a tree sat a pitiful pile of what few belongings they had managed to pull from the ashes. Most of their belongings were burned and twisted beyond recognition, but here and there a few things had survived the flames, and their bright, undamaged colors shined incongruously from the pile of smoking, blackened rubble. The cast-iron cook stove stood undamaged, almost defiantly, in the midst of what had been the kitchen.

Everyone was tired and covered with a great sadness for the two young cowboys who had been killed. In addition to their deaths, the death of a home was also particularly hard, because this was an area where homes and people were few and far between.

"How many were there?" one of the ranchers asked Les. It was the first chance there was for interrogation because the entire night had been passed in the unsuccessful attempt to fight the fire.

"There was four of 'em," Les answered.

"Did you recognize any of them?"

Les, who had helped fight the fire, was, like the others, covered in soot and ash. He walked over to the well and brought up a bucket of water, then took a long drink from the dipper, not yet having answered the rancher's question. He wiped the back of his hand across his mouth, leaving a clean swipe through the soot.

"I'm not real sure," Les finally said. "I was hiding under my bed in the bunkhouse, remember? And besides that, it was dark. But, when they set fire to the main house, it lit up the yard some, and that's when I got a pretty good look at one of them. I wouldn't swear to it, you understand, but I'm pretty sure I saw who it was."

"Who was it?" Denham asked.

"I believe it was Pogue Allison."

"Pogue Allison? Are you sure?" Denham asked, his face plainly showing his intense interest.

"Well, like I said, I don't know if I could swear to it," Denham hedged. "But it sure looked like him."

"Who is Pogue Allison?" one of the other ranchers asked.

"Pogue Allison is one of Poindexter's deputies," Denham said.

"He was a deputy," Bowman said. "But seems to me like he got fired last month. It had somethin' to do with the whores, I believe."

"Yes, in addition to the scam the sheriff and the judge are running on the whores, Pogue Allison had his own game going," Denham said. "But he was a deputy."

"That doesn't mean the sheriff was behind this," another rancher pointed out.

"Maybe not. But it sure doesn't mean he is innocent of this, either," Bowman insisted.

"There's someone comin' in!" someone called, and the men who had fought the fire all night long now stirred themselves to meet the rider.

"Maybe it's the arsonists come back!" another shouted.

"No, wait, he's leadin' a string of horses. Ain't no arsonist goin' to come back to where he started a fire leadin' horses. What is it, a pack train?"

"It's Falcon MacCallister," Denham called. "Don't anyone get excited."

"Look what's on the horses. It's bodies."

CHAPTER EIGHTEEN

As Falcon rode into the front yard of the burned-out house, he saw the men gathering together to meet him. He stopped near one of the wagons, then climbed down from his horse and, taking his canteen from the pommel, walked over to the well to fill it. All eyes were on him, not only the men, but the women and children as well. The men crowded down close, the women hung back, and the children were back farther, in some cases hiding behind their mothers' skirts, peering out around them with wide, curious, and in some cases, frightened, eyes.

"Mr. MacCallister, you want to tell us what all this is about?" Bowman asked.

Falcon filled his canteen, then took a long Adam's apple–bobbing drink. He lowered the canteen and looked toward the burned-out house, then nodded back toward the four horses.

"They are the ones who did this," he said.

"How do you know they did it?" Bowman asked.

Falcon put the top on his canteen and hooked it over the pommel.

"I saw them coming away from the fire."

"If you saw them, why didn't you stop them?" another asked.

"By the time I saw them, it was too late. They had already set the fire. Whose house is this?"

"It was my house," Leon Frakes said.

"I'm sorry about your house. Sorry I didn't see them in time to stop them."

Bowman walked over to the four horses and was checking each of the men by grabbing a handful of hair and lifting the head.

"This one is Pogue Allison," he said. "You were right, Les."

"I thought it was him I seen," Les said. He looked over at Falcon. "I'm glad these sons of bitches are dead. I just wish it had been me instead of you that shot him. They killed Clyde and Shorty."

"What are we going to do with the bodies?" Bowman asked.

"We'll take them into town," Denham suggested.

"If we do that, the sheriff might try and charge Mr. MacCallister with murder," Bowman said.

"No, he won't," Frakes said. "Not if he thinks Les and I killed them while they were attacking us, killing Clyde and Shorty, and burning down my house."

When Falcon and the others returned to town, they brought the bodies of the four arsonists and the two cowboys who were killed with them. The two cowboys were brought in in the back of a wagon. The wagon stopped at Nunnelee's Funeral parlor. The bodies of the four arsonists, which were thrown over the backs of their horses, continued on. This macabre procession got everyone's attention, so that by the time they reached the sheriff's office, there were at least one hundred people gathered around to see what this was all about.

"Look there. That's Ron Mace."

"And that's Jack Andrews."

Sheriff Poindexter and Deputy Sharp came out of the office then, and they stepped down off the boardwalk to examine the bodies.

"Pogue Wilson, Ron Mace, Jack Andrews, and Frank Little," Poindexter said as he examined each one of them. He looked up at Falcon.

"You know all these men, do you, Sheriff?" Falcon asked.

"Indeed I do. People seem to have a habit of dying around you, don't they, MacCallister?"

"He didn't have nothin' to do with this, Sheriff," Les said. "These sons of bitches kilt Clyde and Shorty."

"And then they set fire to my house and barn," Leon Frakes added.

"So we kilt 'em," Les said.

"Who killed them?"

"We all did," Bowman said.

"All of you?"

"Yes, all of us. We were having a meeting at Leon Frakes's house when they attacked. They were killed, fair and square."

Poindexter's one-lidded eye squinted. "What do you mean you were having a meeting at Frakes's house? I thought the meeting was at your house."

"What give you that idea?"

"I don't know. I guess I just heard it somewhere."

"I guess you did."

"All right, I've seen 'em. Take 'em down to Nunnelee's place."

Frakes nodded, and the four riders who were leading the horses over which a body was draped started back down the street toward the funeral home.

"MacCallister," Poindexter said.

Falcon looked at him, but said nothing.

"How much longer arc you going to stay around town?"

"As long as it takes," Falcon answered.

"As long as what takes?"

"As long as it takes to finish my business."

"Yeah, well, don't make that be too long. I'm beginning to find you"—he paused for a moment as he looked for the word—"tiresome."

"I'm sorry you don't seem to be enjoying my company that much."

As the crowd around the sheriff's office began to break up, Falcon and Denham rode back down to the newspaper office, dismounted, and went inside.

"Sheriff Poindexter was behind that fire, just as sure as a gun is iron," Denham said. "I'd like to take a club and just bash that son of a bitch right in the head."

Falcon chuckled. "And here I thought you were a peaceful newspaperman."

"I'm peaceful until I get riled. Then I'm not all that peaceful anymore."

"So I see."

"Well, I'd better get to work," Denham said. "I've got a newspaper to get out."

"And I think I'll get on back to the boarding-house. Mrs. Allen told me we're having chicken and dumplings for supper, and I don't want to miss that."

Denham laughed. "You better watch that old lady, Falcon. Chicken and dumplings? She's setting her cap for you."

There were four other guests staying with Mrs. Allen. Three women and one man. Two of the women, Mrs. Ring and Mrs. Sherman, were, like Mrs. Allen, widows. And like Mrs. Allen, they were in their mid-sixties. The youngest of the three was unmarried and had never been married. This was Barbara Clinton, and she was an attractive woman in her mid-forties.

The man's name was Captain Jerry Aufdenberg. Aufdenberg had commanded a Confederate Raider during the war, sometimes sailing with Admiral

Rafael Semmes. Aufdenberg was in his early sixties, and it was obvious that there was some sort of relationship going on between Captain Aufdenberg and Barbara Clinton.

"Miss Clinton was in the theater in New York for a while," Mrs. Allen said after she had introduced all of them.

"Interesting," Falcon said. "You may know my brother and sister . . . ,"

"Andrew and Roseanne MacCallister!" Barbara said, interrupting Falcon in mid-sentence. "Yes, indeed, I do know them! I have appeared on stage with them. Oh, what wonderful performers they are! And, what wonderful people! In fact, I do believe I have heard them speak of you."

"I hope you didn't believe anything they said. I'm not nearly as bad as all that."

"Ha! You should hear them speak of you. According to both of them, you hung the moon."

"Well now, aren't we fortunate to have him among us," Captain Aufdenberg said.

"Don't be jealous, now, Captain," Mrs. Ring said. "I'm sure that Mr. MacCallister will be here but a short time only. And when he leaves, you will still be here, and still be the lord of this castle."

The others, including Captain Aufdenberg and Falcon, laughed.

"Have any of you read today's paper?" Mrs. Allen asked.

"I haven't read it yet," Captain Aufdenberg said.

"Mr. Denham is at it again. Tweaking the sheriff. I think he should be more careful. I am frightened for him."

Vandals Kill Two, Burn House and Barn

FOUR NIGHT RIDERS ARE THEMSELVES KILLED

They rode out of the night, four despicable brigands, announcing their arrival with a volley of gunfire that struck down Shorty Rogers and Clyde Barnes, two fine young men who were in the prime of their lives. Then, not content with murder, the hooligans continued their perfidious activity by setting fire to the home, barn, and bunkhouse at the ranch of Leon Frakes.

This newspaper is happy to report, however, that the four arsonists, Pogue Wilson, Ron Mace, Jack Andrews, and Frank Little, were themselves killed before the horrific activity of the night ceased. The readers may well recognize the names of these four men, for all of them have, at times, been deputies to Sheriff Poindexter. Though Sheriff Poindexter will claim that the men were not working for him at the time, and to be sure none of the four were found with a badge. However, the mere fact that he has employed such men as these underscores the complaint the citizens of Sorrento have with Sheriff Poindexter's heavy-handed policies.

Sorrento and Scott County

BETTERMENT ASSOCIATION FORMED

In a recent meeting held in the home of Rancher Leon Frakes, a proposal was advanced, and passed, that a Betterment Association for both Sorrento and Scott County be formed. Eb Smalley was elected as president of the association, and David Bowman vice president. Doc Gunter is the treasurer and this editor, Harold Denham, is the secretary. The purpose of the Betterment Association will be to improve the lives of our citizens by bringing about the best business and political environment possible.

To achieve that purpose, we intend to dedicate ourselves to the task of ending the reigns of Sheriff Poindexter and Judge Dawes, to replace them with upright citizens who will serve us ably.

After supper, Falcon excused himself and walked down to the Hog Heaven, which Denham told him was "a gathering place for convivial people, or, put another way, the best and the brightest of Sorrento."

Falcon was sitting at a table with Denham and Doc Gunter when Poindexter came in. Falcon watched him come in, noticing that the sheriff entered a saloon the same way he did, backing up against the wall and pausing for a moment as he perused the place.

"What does that son of a bitch want now?" Denham asked.

Doc Gunter chuckled. "I'd say he's read your paper today and isn't pleased by it."

Poindexter came straight toward the table where the men were sitting. "Denham, what do you mean by printing the kind of stories you printed today?"

"What are you doing here, Sheriff? I thought the Long Trail was your hangout. And if you read the stories, the answer to your question is evident. I mean to get you and Judge Dawes out of office, as quickly as I can."

"You're treading on dangerous ground here."

"No, Sheriff, I'm treading on hallowed ground, the hallowed ground of freedom of the press, freedom of speech, and freedom of the ballot."

Poindexter paused for a moment, wheezed a couple of times, then continued. "Well, all I got to say is, you had better watch your step. I've got my eye on you."

"Hell, Poindexter, that bug-eyed piece of glob you call an eye is always on everybody. You can't help it, 'cause you can't close it," Denham said.

The others in the saloon heard that, and they all laughed. Then, plunging on because he didn't like being the butt of anyone's jokes, he turned to Falcon.

"MacCallister, you got a telegram. It says that the horse you want to buy is for sale."

"Tell me, Sheriff. If that telegram was for me, how is it that you know what it says?"

"There ain't no secrets from me in this town, MacCallister."

"Apparently not."

"So I reckon you'll be wantin' to get back to it, before someone else buys that horse you're wantin'."

"No, I don't think so. I've changed my mind. I don't want it anymore."

"Then why did they send you the telegram?"

"I thought I wanted the horse, but now I don't."

Poindexter stared at Falcon for a long moment, as if trying to decide if there was more to this telegram than met the surface. But, not able to get to the bottom of it, he turned his attention back to Denham.

"You just watch what you print in that paper. You hear me? You just watch."

CHAPTER NINETEEN

"I've got a feeling, Falcon, that that telegram you got yesterday didn't have a damn thing to do with you buying a horse."

The two men were in the newspaper office, Denham having slept there all night to protect his paper.

"What makes you think that?"

"I don't know. As I said, it's just a feeling that I have. And I'm pretty sure that Poindexter has that same feeling."

"You may be right."

"So, what is it? What did the telegram mean?"

"It means I've been appointed a Deputy United States Marshal."

"Hot damn!" Denham said, smiling broadly and hitting his fist into his hand enthusiastically. "Now you've got 'em. That gives you all the authority you need."

"Yes, but I don't want anyone else to know, yet."

"I don't know why you should feel that way."

"I think that if I keep it quiet, at least until I need the authority, I can get more accomplished."

"All right, if that's what you want, I won't say a word." Suddenly a big smile spread across Denham's face. "Hey, I've got an idea. What if you were appointed city marshal for Sorrento? That would give you some authority to sort of move around and look at things. And Poindexter wouldn't be worried because he would realize that as sheriff, his position would be superior to yours. But what he wouldn't know, is that in addition to being a city marshal, you would also be a U.S. Marshal, over him?"

Falcon laughed. "Sounds a little convoluted, doesn't it?"

"Yeah, that's what makes it so great."

"How do I become city marshal? Isn't that an elective position?"

"Ordinarily, it is. We had an elected city marshal, but he was so intimidated by Poindexter that he resigned. The city charter says that the mayor has the authority to appoint a new city marshal until the next election. He hasn't appointed anyone yet, because there's nobody in town who will take the job."

"All right," Falcon said. "Suppose we go meet the mayor."

"You mean you'll do it? You think it's a good idea?"

"Yeah, I think it is a fine idea."

In addition to being mayor of Sorrento, Joe Cravens was also a pharmacist and owner of the Sorrento Apothecary. Before Denham took Falcon down to see him, he stopped by to pick up Smalley and Doc Gunter.

There was a very pretty young girl in the store, sweeping the floor. She smiled when Falcon, Denham, Smalley, and Doc Gunter went in.

"Hello, Mr. Denham, Mr. Smalley, Dr. Gunter," she said. She looked at Falcon but didn't call him by name.

"This is Falcon MacCallister," Denham said.

"I thought you might be," Julie replied with a dimple-producing smile. "I read about you in the paper."

"Julie, what are you doing here, anyway? Shouldn't you be in school?" Denham asked.

Julie laughed. "I graduated from school last year. I'm working for Daddy now."

"You can't meet any young men working here," Smalley said. "You should come down to my store and work for me."

"Oh, I don't think Daddy would like that."

"Is your daddy in?" Denham asked.

"He'll be right back. He walked down to the post office to—oh, there he is now."

When Cravens came in, he looked nervously at the men who were gathered.

"Julie, you can go on home now," he said.

"I haven't finished sweeping the floor."

"I'll take care of it."

"All right." Julie threw another smile toward Falcon as she started out. "It was nice meeting you, Mr. MacCallister."

"The pleasure was all mine," Falcon replied.

Cravens waited until his daughter was gone before he spoke to the group. "What is it? What do you men want?"

"Joe, why is it that we do not have a city marshal?" Denham asked. "The way it is now, without a city marshal, Poindexter has too much authority over us."

"You know why we don't have a city marshal. Larry Wallace resigned, and nobody else has agreed to serve in the position. Why, I doubt if we can even get someone to run for the job in the next election."

"If someone agreed to take the position, would you appoint them?"

"I—I'm not sure I have that authority."

It wasn't until then that Denham showed him the bound sheaf of papers he was carrying. He raised it up and showed the cover to Mayor Cravens.

CITY CHARTER
Sorrento, Texas
Adopted Sep. 18, 1873

"Do you recognize this?"

"It's the city charter."

Denham began to read. "Paragraph two, City officers. Slash b, City Marshal. The city marshal shall be an elective position. If for some reason the city marshal is unable to complete the term, the mayor shall have sole authority to appoint an interim marshal who will serve with full authority until the next regularly scheduled election. At that time the appointed marshal must run for reelection."

"All right," Mayor Cravens said. "But it's like I told you, nobody has agreed to take the position."

"I'll take the job," Falcon said.

"You . . . you are the one who brought in the two stagecoach robbers, aren't you?"

"Yes. And the four arsonists."

"I thought there were several of you who brought them in."

"There were several of us. But we didn't bring them in until after Mr. MacCallister had already— subdued them."

"Subdued them?"

"Killed them," Falcon said.

Cravens pulled a handkerchief from his pocket and wiped the sweat from his brow. "Oh, my," he said.

"Swear him in, Mayor," Doc Gunter said. "Or so help me, I'll tell everyone of my patients that all your potions are poison."

"No, no, I—uh—will swear him in. Hold up your right hand."

Falcon held up his hand.

"Do you swear you'll perform the duties as city marshal to the best of your ability?"

"I do."

"You are now the city marshal of Sorrento. Just a minute, I have a badge over here."

Mayor Cravens walked over to a bench and began moving beakers, mortars, pestles, and test tubes around until he found what he was looking for. He came back with a large star, upon which were imprinted the words CITY MARSHAL.

Falcon put the badge on, and the others shook his hand in congratulations.

It was early the next morning, and though most self-respecting roosters had announced the fact long ago, half a dozen cocks were still trying to stake a claim on the day. The sun had been up long enough for the morning light to change from gold to white, and here and there were signs of Sorrento rising.

Falcon could eat at the boardinghouse, and occasionally he did, but more often he preferred to eat downtown because it kept him more in touch with everyone. When he stepped into the Lonely Biscuit Café this morning, there were several people who noticed the marshal's star on his chest and, though Falcon could see the reaction in their faces, nobody said anything to him. He took a table, and the owner of the café, who was also the waiter, came over to him.

"Yes, sir, Mister—or is that Marshal—Mac-Callister?"

"It is Marshal. City Marshal."

"Well, congratulations, Marshal. What can I get for you?"

"I'll just have a cup of coffee now," Falcon said.

"Mr. Denham, Mr. Smalley, and Doc Gunter will be joining me shortly, and we'll order breakfast then."

"Very good, sir," the owner said.

Falcon was halfway through his coffee when Denham and the others came into the café. Denham was carrying a newspaper.

"I thought you might like to see this article," Denham said, showing him the paper.

"It's only a little after seven," Falcon said. "You must have gotten a very early start this morning."

"I did. I want the whole town to know that we have a new marshal."

The waiter returned, and the men ordered, eggs, bacon, and biscuits. Then, as they waited for their meal, Falcon read the article.

New City Marshal Appointed

Yesterday, Falcon MacCallister raised his hand and took the oath of office for the position of city marshal for the city of Sorrento, Texas. Marshal MacCallister is a man of immense capability and, even before assuming the position of city marshal, brought to justice Cooper Winters and Travis Eberwine, the stagecoach robbers and murders.

Because we now have a marshal, the authority Sheriff Poindexter currently exerts within the city limits will be much reduced. Our citizens can breathe easily now, without fear of the harsh

and capricious enforcement we have
heretofore been subjected to. It can only
be hoped that Sheriff Poindexter will
realize that his authority over the citizens
of Sorrento has been greatly diminished,
thus making our lives easier.

CHAPTER TWENTY

The previous town marshal had shared the sheriff's office and the county jail, but Denham, Smalley, and Doc Gunter, as well as a few other leading businessmen of the town, didn't think that was a good idea. They bought a small building that was next to the apothecary and within a few days were able to convert it into a marshal's office and jail.

Denham insisted that the mayor have a grand opening of the new office and jail, and he printed an article in his paper inviting the whole town to turn out to see the mayor hand the key to Falcon. More than one hundred of the town's citizens showed up. Sheriff Poindexter and his deputies were there as well, though they stayed well back from the crowd, holding themselves detached from the event.

"Ladies and gentlemen," Denham said, addressing the crowd. "I want to thank all of you for coming today to celebrate the grand opening of our new City Marshal Office and City Jail. Before the mayor hands the key over to Marshal Mac-Callister, I would like to invite him to say a few words. Marshal?"

Falcon nodded at Denham, then he stepped out onto the porch of the office and jail. His marshal's star, which was larger than that worn by Poindexter or any of his deputies, shone brightly in the morning sun.

"I want to thank the mayor for appointing me to this position," Falcon said. "And it is my intention to serve the town of Sorrento to the best of my ability. Thank you."

Mayor Cravens handed Falcon the key, Falcon used it to open the door, everyone applauded, then the crowd broke up. Denham hurried back to write the story, Smalley returned to his store, and Doc Gunter to his office.

When everyone else left, one person remained behind. It was Sheriff Poindexter.

"Something I can do for you, Sheriff?" Falcon asked.

"MacCallister, I don't know what this was all about," Poindexter said with a little wave of his hand. "But don't be getting any ideas about your authority. As the county sheriff, you have to answer to me."

"And I will, for anything outside the town limits," Falcon said. "Inside the town limits, I am the primary law enforcement officer."

Poindexter raised his hand and pointed his

finger at Falcon. "Just don't get in my way," he warned.

Even as Poindexter was leaving, Denham returned. The two men didn't speak as they passed each other.

"Let me guess," Denham said after Poindexter was gone. "He's letting you know that he is the sheriff, and you are just a city marshal."

"Something like that," Falcon said. "I pointed out that, inside the town limits, I am the primary law enforcement officer."

Denham laughed. "Good for you. I knew this was a good idea."

As the two men were talking, Les Karnes came in.

"Hello, Les," Denham said.

"Mr. Denham," Les replied. "Marshal, I wonder if you would like to hire a deputy."

"Why? Would you be interested?"

"Yes, sir, I would," Les said. "Until Mr. Frakes gets back on his feet, he don't have no work for me to do. I've got to get on somewhere. And I figured, well, maybe you could use a deputy."

"What about it, Harold?" Falcon asked. "Am I authorized to have a deputy?"

"Yes, indeed, you are."

"All right, hold up your right hand, Les, and say I do."

Les held up his hand and smiled. "There ain't no ladies around here that I'm a' marryin' by sayin' 'I do,' is there?" he asked.

"None that I can see," Falcon replied with a chuckle.

"All right. I do."

"The mayor didn't give me any deputies' badges, but I'm sure he has one, so we'll walk over and get it."

"Oh, say," Denham said. "I was about to ask you if you might like to go to the theater with me tonight? As a matter of fact, both of you should go."

"The theater? Yes, I enjoy going to the theater," Falcon replied. The theater was in Falcon's family, and though he had never done anything on stage, his brother and sister, Andrew and Roseanne, were internationally known stars of the stage. They appeared regularly in New York, London, and Paris, and had made frequent tours throughout the United States.

"Yes, well, it isn't entirely just for enjoyment," Denham said. "One of the reasons I want you to come tonight is so you can see what we have been putting up with under Poindexter. There is gunplay in the theater nearly every night. I have personally counted over one hundred bullet holes in the curtains and screens around the theater, as well as on the advertising posters."

"Gunfights?" Falcon asked.

"No. So far it has been just drunken cowboys letting off steam, and nobody has been hurt, but if we don't put a stop to it, someone is sure to get killed."

"Why hasn't Poindexter done anything about it?"

"There's no money in it for him," Denham said. "Poindexter's enforcement of the law goes only as far as he can see a way to make money."

"All right, I'll go. Les and I will both go. But let's do this, shall we? Before the show tonight, we'll post signs ordering everyone to surrender their guns upon coming into the theater," Falcon said.

"Good idea. I'll print them up in my shop and help you post them."

"Come on, Les, we'll walk down to see the mayor and get you a deputy's badge," Falcon said.

"Wow," Les said. "I never thought I would be wearing a lawman's badge."

"A deputy's badge?" Cravens said. "Yes, I know I have one, I saw it when I found your badge."

"Good. As of now, Deputy Karnes is on the city payroll."

"Oh," Cravens said. "Uh, that's going to be a problem."

"Why should it be a problem?"

"The deputy is a volunteer position. There's no money allocated to pay a deputy."

The smile left Les's face. "You mean I ain't goin' to get paid? I got to have me a job that pays money. How else am I goin' to live?"

"I take it there is pay for the marshal's position?" Falcon asked.

"Oh, indeed there is. Forty dollars a month."

"I will forgo my salary. I want you to see to it that the forty dollars a month goes to Deputy Karnes."

"Forty dollars a month?" Les gasped. "That's a fortune!"

"Well, I don't know if I can do that," Mayor Cravens said.

"You can do it," Falcon insisted.

From the mayor's office, Falcon and Les walked down to the newspaper office. Several of the townspeople greeted them along the way.

As they passed a grocery store, they saw Julie Cravens carrying a bag of groceries toward a buckboard that was drawn up out front.

"Excuse me, Marshal," Les said as he hurried toward the pretty young woman.

"Miss Julie, may I help you with that?" Les took the bag from her and put it in the buckboard.

"Why, Mr. Karnes," Julie said. "You are a law officer now?"

"Yes, ma'am, your pa just give me the badge. I'm the deputy city marshal. So if you have any problems with anything, why, you just come to me and I'll take care of it."

"Well I will, Mr. Karnes, thank you."

Les helped her into the buckboard.

"Uh, Miss Julie, there's goin' to be a dance Saturday night at the Cattlemen's Association Hall. Will you be going?"

"That is my intention, Mr. Karnes."

Les smiled broadly. "Good. Then I'll see you there. I hope you save a dance for me."

"I would be delighted to," Julie said as she snapped the reins to move the team forward.

Les tipped his hat to her as she drove off. When he turned, he saw Falcon standing nearby, watching with bemused enjoyment. Falcon was smiling at him.

"That's Julie Cravens," Les said. "She's the mayor's daughter. I just thought I would help her get the groceries in the wagon is all."

"Oh, I don't blame you, Les," Falcon said. "A pretty girl like that shouldn't have to load her own groceries now, should she?"

Denham was already printing the signs when Falcon and Les stepped into the newspaper office, and he held one up for Falcon's approval.

By Order of the City Marshal:
NO FIREARMS ALLOWED
Inside Theater.

"What do you think?" Denham asked.

"It looks good," Falcon said. "I don't think there's much chance of anyone not understanding it."

That night Falcon stood leaning against a post at the rear of the Malone Theater. Les had taken a walk around the inside of the theater and returned to stand next to Falcon.

"How are things looking?"

"There are four men down front, passing a bottle back and forth around and talking a little loud."

"Are they armed?" Falcon asked.

"Yes, they are. But they are sheriff's deputies."

"My sign didn't say everyone check their guns but sheriff's deputies. It said everyone. I think I'll just mosey on down there by them."

Suddenly, the band played a fanfare and, amidst shouts, hoots, and whistles, the theater owner walked out onto the stage. He stood in front of the closed curtains and held his hands up, asking for quiet.

"Ladies and gents," he called.

"There ain't no ladies present!" someone from the audience yelled, and his shout was greeted with guffaws of laughter.

"Oh, yeah? Well, what do you call me, you low-assed, pig-faced son of a bitch?" a painted woman replied.

There was more laughter, but the theater owner finally managed to get them quiet again. "Lovers of the theater," he said. "Tonight we have an especially thrilling show for you."

The audience applauded and whistled.

"We begin our show with the loveliest dancing girls to be found in all of Texas. Here they are, the *Dames de charme!*"

Amidst a great deal of whistling and stamping of

feet, six beautiful and scantily clad young women began the show. After the girls performed, there was a comedy act between a mustachioed man and a beautiful, innocent young girl. It was set up as a drama director, describing to his ingénue, the particulars of her role.

DIRECTOR: In the first scene, my dear, the young man grabs you, binds you with rope from head to foot, then smothers you with hugs and kisses.

YOUNG WOMAN: Is the young man tall, dark, and handsome?

DIRECTOR: Yes, he is. Why do you ask?

YOUNG WOMAN: Because if he is tall, dark, and handsome, he won't need the rope.

The joke was concluded with a drum-roll, then loud laughter from the audience. There were a few other jokes of that ilk, then a man billed as the "World's Greatest Magician" made his appearance. He introduced his assistant, a lovely young woman who looked suspiciously like one of the *dames de charme.*

"And now, friends, I shall perform a feat the likes of which you have never seen before. My lovely assistant will fire this pistol at me, and I will catch the bullet with my teeth!"

Falcon had seen the trick before, and he knew how it worked. The magician's assistant would fire blanks while the magician would jerk his head back in a bit of ham acting, then spit out the bullet he held concealed in his mouth.

Suddenly, one of the "deputies" stood up and pointed a revolver toward the stage.

"Catch this one, professor!" he shouted.

Quickly, Falcon managed to reach him just in time to deflect his shot, while the terrified magician and his assistant hurried from the stage to the guffaws of the audience. One blow from Falcon's big fist knocked the deputy out, and Falcon turned to the others.

"I believe I had a sign posted out front telling everyone to check their guns. Now I'll be taking yours."

"Mister, who are you to tell us to give up our guns? We're sheriff's deputies."

"I'm the city marshal."

"I told you, we're sheriff's deputies. We don't have to listen to no city marshal."

"Yeah, you do. Now take off those gun belts."

"You want my gun belt, you're goin' to have to take it. Because I ain't . . ."

The deputy didn't get to finish saying whatever it was that he wasn't going to do, because without another word Falcon drew his pistol and brought it down on the deputy's head. Now, with his pistol in hand, he pointed to the remaining two.

"Drop your gun belts," he said.

They complied, meekly, and even relieved the two unconscious deputies of their gun belts.

"Would you get their gun belts please, Deputy?"

"Yes, sir, Marshal, I'd be real pleased to take 'em."

"Get those two on their feet," Falcon said, pointing to the two who were coming to, but still on the floor.

"What are you going to do with us?" one of the men asked.

"You four are going to have the honor of being the very first occupants of our new city jail," Falcon said.

"The hell you say! You ain't puttin' us in no city jail. I told you, we are sheriff's deputies!"

"Let's go, sheriff's deputies," Les said, giving one of them a slight shove.

"Folks, I'm sorry for the disturbance," Falcon said loudly. "We'll get these men out of here now and let you enjoy the rest of the show."

The audience applauded and even as Falcon and Les led the four sullen men through the lobby, the orchestra began playing music again as the show resumed.

City Jail Put to Use for First Time

Four Men Use the Accommodations

For too long now, ruffians have made it difficult for the citizens of our fair city to enjoy the theatricals, which from time to time visit Sorrento. Indeed, some traveling troupes have made it known that they would not return out of fear of injury from these ruffians. Boorish behavior, obscene shouts, unwanted physical contact with the actors and actresses, and indiscriminate gunfire have become the norm at the Malone Theater.

But now, thanks to Falcon MacCallister, our new city marshal, order has returned. Last night's Programme of the Grand Combination of the Celebrated Artists, Heckemeyer and Vaughan, Robert Wilkerson the elocutionist, with comedy, dancers, vocalists, and pianist, was interrupted when Albert Russell attempted to employ his pistol in the direction of Professor Heckemeyer during one of the acts. He was interrupted by the timely intervention of Marshal MacCallister and Deputy Karnes.

The marshal and his deputy took Russell and his three companions, Josh Peters, Harry Toombs, and Lou Hamilton, in custody, depositing them in the city jail. Our readers will recognize that Russell, Peters, Toombs, and Hamilton are deputies for Sheriff Poindexter, and many is the businessman who has come under their rough treatment when they have been dispatched to collect taxes.

CHAPTER TWENTY-ONE

The next morning, Falcon was sitting at the desk in the marshal's office writing something on a sheet of paper when Deputy Sheriff Sharp came into the city marshal's office. As soon as he came in, the four deputies who were back in the cell yelled at him.

"Sharp! Get us out of here! He ain't got no right to arrest us!" Toombs called.

"What do you think you are doin', MacCallister?" Sharp asked. "Why are these men in jail?"

"Last night I posted signs saying that no guns would be allowed in the theater," Falcon said.

"So?"

"So they came into the theater with guns."

"Yeah, they are sheriff's deputies. They can wear a gun anywhere they want to."

"No. In my town, they can wear guns only where I say they can. They violated the law, and I put them under arrest."

"The sheriff ain't goin' to like this, MacCallister.

He ain't goin' to like it one bit. If I was you, I'd turn those men a' loose, right now."

"Would you now?" Falcon asked.

Sharp stared angrily at Falcon as Falcon returned to his task at hand. After a moment, Falcon looked up.

"You're still here, Sharp?"

Sharp raised his hand and pointed a finger at Falcon. "You ain't heard the last of this," he said.

"I don't reckon I have."

Sharp glared at him for just a moment longer, then he turned, angrily, and started toward the door.

"Hold on there, Sharp!" Toombs called from the cell. "You ain't goin' to just leave us in here, are you?"

Sharp didn't answer.

"MacCallister, you'd better let us out of here, if you know what is good for you," Toombs said.

"You boys just relax for a while," Falcon said. "You aren't going anywhere."

Standing, Falcon folded the paper he had been writing on and stuck it in his shirt pocket.

"Hey, what about supper? Are you goin' to feed us any supper?"

"You had breakfast and dinner, didn't you? Don't worry, you aren't going to starve."

Falcon left the office and walked down to the newspaper, where he found Denham laughing and talking with two other men.

"Ahh, here he is now. Gentlemen, may I present

Marshal MacCallister. Falcon, this is Ken Cole and Jim Myles. They are members of our city council."

"City council, are you? Good, good, you are just who I want to see. How many are on the city council?"

"There are five of us," Denham replied.

"Us? You are on the city council?"

"Yes. So are Eb Smalley and Doc Gunter."

"Good, good. Now, let me ask you this. Do we have a city attorney?"

"I guess that would be Burt Gillespie, wouldn't it?" Cole asked.

"No," Denham said. "Gillespie is the prosecuting attorney for the county. As far as I know, we don't have a city attorney."

"Is there another lawyer in town? One we could appoint as the city attorney?"

"James Earl Van Arsdale," Myles said.

"Who is nothing but a damn drunk," Cole added.

"No, now, that's not necessarily the case anymore," Denham said. "Since he got drawn into acting as prosecutor in that sham murder trial for Poindexter, he has quit drinking. And if truth be known, he is one of the smartest men I know."

"We're going to need a city attorney for what I have in mind," Falcon said.

"What do you have in mind?"

"I've written out a list of city ordinances I would like to propose," Falcon said, taking from his pocket the sheet of paper he had been working on.

"I tell you what." Denham looked up at the clock

on his wall. "About this time of day, I generally meet Eb and Doc over at the Hog Heaven for a beer. Ken, why don't you go to Eb's store and ask him to come down here? I'll get Doc and James Earl Van Arsdale. We'll just have us a council meeting."

"What about Mayor Cravens?" Myles asked. "Shouldn't he be there if we're goin' to have a council meeting?"

"Good idea, Jim. How about you stop by for him, tell him what this is about. I'll get us a table set up in the back."

"The only thing, isn't the mayor the one who calls a city council meeting?" Myles asked.

"Ordinarily, that would be so. But if the mayor gives you any trouble, you tell him we are going to have a city council meeting with or without him. And we will be able to pass whatever ordinance we want."

Myles laughed. "Yeah, that'll get his attention, all right."

Half an hour later, Falcon, Mayor Cravens, Harold Denham, James Earl Van Arsdale, and the entire city council were gathered around a table in the back of the composing room of the office of the *Sorrento Advocate*.

"All right, gentlemen, you called this meeting," Mayor Cravens said. "Now, suppose you tell me what this is all about."

"The first thing we want is for Mr. Van Arsdale to be appointed city attorney," Denham said.

"James Earl Van Arsdale? Are you serious? You know how he is. We all know how he is."

"I wish you wouldn't speak of me as if I weren't here," Van Arsdale said. "And, strictly speaking, Mr. Mayor—you would have to say that is how I was. I have been sober for two weeks. I intend to remain sober."

"Intention and doing it are two different things," Mayor Cravens said.

"You aren't being fair, Joe. I've known many people who have beaten the devil."

Cravens ran his hand through his thinning hair and looked at Van Arsdale. "Do you think you are up to the job?"

"I would like to be given the chance," Van Arsdale said.

"We can't pay you anything."

"Yet," Denham said.

"What do you mean, 'yet'?"

"The marshal has some ideas he wants to put before us," Denham said.

"What kind of ideas? Nothing that is going to cost the city any money, I hope. I warn you, we have very little money in the treasury."

"On the contrary, Mayor. The plan I have will make the city some money."

Mayor Cravens smiled. "Well now, I'm all for that," he said. "Let's hear what you have."

"My first proposal is to make prostitution legal within the town limits."

"I don't know," Mayor Cravens said. "I'm not sure the church people would take to that. Why would you want to do a thing like that, anyway?"

"I have two reasons," Falcon said. "The first reason is, if we make prostitution legal, we can charge a license fee for anyone who is in the business."

"Oh, I don't know. With these monthly fines they are all paying now, like as not adding an additional fee would just . . ."

Falcon interrupted the mayor in midsentence.

"That brings up my second reason. If we make it legal, then Poindexter and the judge will no longer be able to fine them."

"Ha!" Smalley said, slapping his hand on the table. "I like that. I like that a lot! I . . ." Smalley looked over at Van Arsdale. "Is that right? If we make it legal for the whores to do business, that Poindexter can't fine them anymore?"

"If it is legal, he will have no authority to levy a fine against them, that is true," Van Arsdale said.

"How much will we charge for the license?" Mayor Cravens asked.

"How much is the fine?"

"From what I hear, it is ten dollars," Cole said. "Every month."

"Sometimes more than once a month," Myles said.

"That would be one hundred twenty dollars a

year each. I suggest we charge them a one-time-only fee of thirty dollars for a year's license," Falcon said.

"Yeah," Denham said. "Yeah, the whores are going to like that. They are going to like that a whole lot."

"The next thing we need to change is the taxes," Falcon said.

"Look here, with all the taxes our people are paying to the sheriff, we can't possibly add any more," Mayor Cravens said.

"What if we take away all of the taxes being imposed now and replace that with a five percent tax on all the businesses?"

"How are we going to do that?" Smalley asked.

"We are going to pass another city ordinance that prohibits the county from collecting any tax other than a one percent sales tax."

"Is that legal?" Myles asked.

"It will be legal as soon as the city council passes the ordinance," Van Arsdale said. "Of course, they can always challenge it."

"Challenge it? Challenge it how?"

Van Arsdale smiled. "They would have to challenge it in the Texas State Supreme Court. So far, the only precedent of counties to collect taxes is a modest property tax . . . which is assessed at a fixed, yearly rate. What they have been doing will never stand the test in the Supreme Court. Which means, they won't challenge it."

"They may not challenge it in the Supreme Court," Myles said. "But don't forget, Poindexter has been using his deputies to collect taxes. And they have been doing it by direct threat."

"You let me handle that," Falcon said.

"What do you mean?" Myles asked.

"If any deputy attempts to collect taxes, other than a property tax, which by the way, we will assume has already been paid for this year, I will put him under arrest."

"Ha!" Smalley said. "Now that I want to see!"

"You will see it," Falcon promised. "The very first time an attempt is made, after the ordinances are enacted, and after those ordinances are published in the paper."

"And," Van Arsdale added quickly, "filed with the state government."

"Why do we have to do that?" Mayor Cravens asked.

"Once they are filed with the state government, they then have the authority of the state, which supersedes the authority of the county. That way, the county can't claim a superior position over us, and can only overturn the statutes by appealing to the state."

"What if the taxes they have been charging are filed with the state government?" Doc Gunter asked.

Van Arsdale smiled. "Do you think the state government would validate laws that allow a county to collect taxes as capriciously as Judge Dawes and Sheriff Poindexter do?"

"No," Doc said. "No, by damn, I don't think they would."

"So, what you are saying is, we can pass any ordinance we want, and as long as we file it with the state government, it will take precedence over county laws?" Mayor Cravens asked.

"Yes, as long as those laws pertain only to a jurisdiction within the city limits of Sorrento, and, unless, and until, those laws are challenged in court."

"Oh, that's not good. If it goes to court, Judge Dawes can just throw them out," Myles suggested.

"No. Since he is a county judge, and would be a party to the lawsuit, it cannot be settled in his court."

Mayor Cravens smiled broadly. "You know what? Hiring you as city attorney may just be the smartest thing I've done as mayor."

"What do you say, Mayor, that we get these ordinances passed?" Denham suggested.

It was no surprise to Falcon when he returned to the city jail to find Sheriff Poindexter waiting there for him.

"Look here!" Poindexter said angrily. "What are my deputies doing in jail?"

"They brought guns into the Malone Theater last night," Falcon said.

"That was in direct violation of my orders."

"Your orders? Who the hell are you to give orders?"

"I'm the city marshal, or haven't you heard?" Falcon said. "And I posted a notice in the front of the theater last night that all guns had to be checked before anyone could enter. They violated that notice."

"Let them out."

"I will, as soon as they pay their fines."

"Fines? Judge Dawes hasn't imposed any fines on these men."

"Judge Dawes has no authority to impose fines within the city limits. Only I have that authority."

"What? Where the hell do you get that idea?"

"They are being fined one hundred dollars each. They can either pay the fines or spend the next thirty days in jail."

"Sheriff!" Toombs called. "Pay our fines! Don't leave us in here!"

"One hundred dollars each," Falcon said. "That's a total of four hundred dollars. If, as you say, they are your deputies, then I'm sure you won't mind paying it."

"The hell I will!" Poindexter said. He pointed at Falcon. "You are going to let these men out, and you are going to let them out now, or else you will settle with me."

Falcon turned to face Poindexter, letting his hand hang loosely near his pistol. "Now just when would be a convenient time for us to settle this little dispute? Is now all right with you? Because right now would be just fine with me."

Poindexter glared at him, and for a moment Falcon was sure the sheriff had a notion to draw against him. But something held him back and the notion passed. Falcon, who was very adept at reading facial and body language, knew exactly when Poindexter made the decision not to challenge him.

"Now is not the time. But the time will come," he said, starting toward the door.

"Sheriff, no!" Toombs and the other three prisoners called out to him. "No, don't leave us here!"

"You boys just hang tight," Poindexter said. "I'll be back."

CHAPTER TWENTY-TWO

City Council in Special Meeting

NEW ORDINANCES PASSED

In a special meeting conducted by Mayor Joe Cravens, much business was conducted. The appointment of Falcon MacCallister as City Marshal was confirmed by unanimous consent of the council. Marshal MacCallister's appointment of Les Karnes as Deputy Marshal was also confirmed. In addition, James Earl Van Arsdale was hired as City Attorney for the town of Sorrento.

Following these important appointments, the city council passed the following ordinances, which will take effect immediately.

(A) ORDINANCE PERTAINING TO
    PROSTITUTION:

1. Prostitution will be legal within the
   city limits of Sorrento, providing that
   those engaged in the profession
   adhere to the regulations herein
   listed.
   a. Each person engaged in the
      profession will obtain from the city
      a license for operation.
   b. Each person engaged in the
      profession will be examined by a
      doctor once per month.
2. The licensing fee will be thirty dollars
   per annum without regard to the
   venue in which the profession is
   being practiced. It shall be illegal for
   any fines to be assessed provided the
   above requirements are met.

(B) ORDINANCE PERTAINING TO
    TAXATION:

1. Effective immediately, all residents
   and businesses are exempt from any
   county taxation, with the exception of
   1% property tax to be paid once per
   year. All taxes paid in the year instant,
   shall be deemed as payment in full
   said property taxes.
2. To the city shall be due a 5% tax
   applied to all businesses, said tax to
   be assessed one time per year.

(C) ORDINANCE PERTAINING TO LAW
       ENFORCEMENT:

1. Effective immediately, all local
     law enforcement will be handled
     by Marshal MacCallister or Deputy
     Karnes. The county sheriff or
     any sheriff's deputy will, when
     investigating a crime that
     occurred outside the city limits,
     go through the marshal or the
     deputy marshal before making
     any arrests within the city limits.

The town's reaction to the new ordinances was immediate and enthusiastic. On the very first day, within an hour after the paper was printed, Falcon went in to the Hog Heaven and ordered a beer. He put a nickel on the bar, and Beeson shoved it back.

"Uh, uh. You drink free, here," Beeson said.

"No, I appreciate the offer, but I'll pay for my own drinks," Falcon replied. "If I don't, how would I be any different from Sheriff Poindexter?" Falcon shoved the nickel back toward Beeson.

"Yes, sir, I reckon you do have a point there," Beeson said, taking the nickel, then drawing a beer from the keg behind the bar.

Just then Les Karnes came into the saloon. "Marshal, Deputy Sharp come down to the jail. He's paid the fine for all four of them, so I let 'em out. I hope that's all right."

"As long as their fine was paid, you did the right thing," Falcon said.

The new ordinance against the collection of taxes was tested that very day. Falcon had just started to drink his beer when a man came into the saloon looking for him. He was in his mid-forties, with thinning hair and thick glasses. There was a pencil stuck behind his ear.

"Marshal MacCallister?"

"Yes? What can I do for you?"

"My name is Deckert, Marshal. Hodge Deckert. I'm a clerk in Mr. Smalley's store. There's a couple of the sheriff's deputies over there now, and they are demanding that he pay four hundred dollars in taxes. Marshal, that's more tax than he's been payin' for a whole year, and they're sayin' he has to pay it now."

"Thanks, Mr. Deckert, I'll look into it."

Leaving his unfinished beer on the bar, Falcon left the saloon and walked quickly down to Eb Smalley's store, walking so fast that Deckert had to break into a trot to keep up with him. When he pushed through the door of the store, he saw Sharp and Toombs in the back, glaring at Smalley.

"Smalley, you are either goin' to come up with four hunnert dollars in taxes, or I'm goin' to pistol-whip you and take the money from you. That way you'll wind up without the money, and with a headache."

"Good afternoon, Mr. Smalley," Falcon said. "I

am in the market for a new shirt, and I wonder if you might show me a few."

"Not now, MacCallister," Sharp said with a growl. "I've got business with Smalley at the moment."

"Oh? Well, if you are buying something, I'll be happy to wait. I don't want to get in the way of Mr. Smalley making a sale. What are you buying?"

Sharp laughed, a low, mocking, guttural laugh.

"I ain't buyin' nothin'. I'm collectin' some tax Mr. Smalley owes. It's exactly four hunnert dollars." Sharp looked over at Falcon and smiled. "Four hunnert dollars. I reckon that amount should be a little familiar to you, shouldn't it?"

"Oh, I see. Now, let me get this straight. You figured that you would pay the fine for Toombs and the other three men, then make it up by trying to collect it in tax money. Is that right?"

"Well now, you ain't quite as dumb as I thought you was," Sharp said. "Here you got it all figured out, ain't you? Sheriff Poindexter was some upset about havin' to come up with the four hunnert dollars, and he told me to collect it in taxes. Onliest thing is, he didn't say I was to get it all in one place. That was my idea. So I come here for it."

"Mr. Smalley, you are a good businessman," Falcon said. "How much money would you say you have paid Sheriff Poindexter since January of this year?"

Smalley opened a ledger book and ran his fingers down the columns. "I have paid them two hundred and seventy-five dollars."

"And what is the latest appraised value of your land and store?"

"I have twelve hundred dollars in it, not counting my inventory."

"All right, that means your property tax assessment at one percent comes to—twelve dollars. You have paid two hundred seventy-five dollars, that means you have overpaid by two hundred sixty-three dollars. Sharp, do you have two hundred sixty-three dollars on you?"

"What?" Sharp asked with a surprised expression on his face. "What the hell are you talking about?"

"I'm talking about the money Sheriff Poindexter has extorted from Mr. Smalley this year. You have collected two hundred sixty-three dollars more than you are authorized. Now, if Mr. Smalley wants to, he can forgive that debt. But he has every right to demand that the money be returned. Mr. Smalley, would you like to have that money back?"

"Yes, sir, I would."

"All right, Sharp, Mr. Smalley has asked that his money be returned." Falcon held out his hand, palm up. "Give it back."

"Are you crazy? I don't have that kind of money on me."

"That's all right. Technically, you don't owe it, anyway. Sheriff Poindexter does. You might tell him that there is going to be an accounting."

"Oh, yeah, there's going to be an accounting all right. I think you can depend on that."

Suddenly, and unexpectedly, Sharp went for his

pistol. But he didn't even clear the holster when he saw the gun in Falcon's hand, the draw so fast that Sharp wasn't sure Falcon hadn't been holding the pistol all along.

"Do you really want to go through with this?" Falcon asked.

Sharp pulled his hand away from the gun, then held both hands out, as if pushing Falcon away.

"No!" he said. "No, I ain't drawin' on you."

"Good idea." Falcon holstered his gun. "I suggest you go tell the sheriff that he owes Mr. Smalley two hundred sixty-three dollars."

"I can't tell him that. He's goin' to ask me why, and I don't know what to tell him."

Falcon saw, on the counter, a small stack of newspapers for sale. He put a nickel in the bowl beside the papers, picked one of them up, and handed it to Sharp. "Show him this article."

Sullenly, Sharp and Toombs left the store. Falcon watched them leave, then looked back toward Smalley, who had a broad smile on his face.

"Oh, that was good to see," he said. "Didn't you think so, Hodge?"

Hodge Deckert, the man who had summoned Falcon, was standing back in the corner, behind a counter.

"Hodge? Hodge, where are you?"

"I'm here, Mr. Smalley," Hodge said. "I, uh, didn't know if there would be shooting or not."

"Well, I think you can come out now. It would appear to me that the excitement is over."

* * *

There were three saloons in Sorrento: the Hog Heaven, the Long Trail, and the Brown Dirt Cowboy. Sheriff Poindexter spent so much time in the Long Trail that there were some who, jokingly, made the remark that he had moved his office there.

Like the other two saloons, the Long Trail paid taxes, and the bar girls who worked there paid their fines each month. But when the Long Trail paid its taxes, it was merely transferring money from one pocket to another. That was because, though very few people knew it, Sheriff Poindexter was the owner of the Long Trail saloon.

Poindexter was sitting at "his" table in the back corner of the saloon playing solitaire when Sharp and Toombs came in.

"Have you collected all the taxes already?" he asked as he put a red jack on a black queen.

"We ain't collected no taxes at all," Sharp said.

"What do you mean, you ain't collected no taxes?"

"Ever'one says they don't owe no taxes. And Smalley, he says we owe him—how much was it did he say, Toombs?"

"He says we owe him two hundred sixty-three dollars back from what he has overpaid in taxes."

"What? All right, I'll handle him. What about the others?"

"They didn't nobody pay any taxes. They say that there's been a new law passed that says they don't have to pay us no taxes at all, except a one percent property tax, once a year."

"What law are they talking about? I never heard of no law like that."

"I reckon it's this law," Sharp said, showing Poindexter the newspaper article.

Poindexter read the article, and the more he read, the angrier he got. "We'll see about this," he said.

"Legally, there is nothing we can do about it right now," Judge Dawes said after reading the article.

"What do you mean, legally we can't do anything about it? You are the judge."

"I am a county judge, and I can try felony cases. But I have no jurisdiction as to the legality or illegality of city ordinances. In order to overturn these ordinances, we would have to take the case to the Texas Supreme Court."

"Well, why don't we do that?" Poindexter asked.

"Dewey, if we took this case to the Supreme Court, and some of our own activity came under scrutiny, we would both be out of office and in jail. Now, do you want that?"

"No. But, what are we going to do about this? We can't let them get away with this?"

"You might find some way to persuade the mayor to issue an executive order overturning this new ordinance," Judge Dawes suggested.

"Can the mayor do that?"

"Oh, I'm sure the city council would challenge it in court. My court," he added with a smile.

"But how are we going to get the mayor to do that?"

"The mayor has a daughter, doesn't he? A lovely young girl of about sixteen or seventeen, I believe?"

"Yeah, what about it?" Poindexter asked.

"Nothing. I was just making an observation, is all," Judge Dawes said.

CHAPTER TWENTY-THREE

Although the dance was sponsored by the Cattlemen's Association, it was an event that involved the entire town. The band that would provide the music arrived by stagecoach from Fort Worth in midafternoon, their arrival greeted by all the young people of the town.

Then, that evening, as the band tuned their instruments, the high skirling of the fiddle and the thump of the bass fiddle could be heard, even before the first person arrived at the dance.

"Marshal, I know that we have to be there to sort of keep an eye on things, and to keep order," Les said. "But will it be all right if I have a few dances with Miss Julie?"

Falcon chuckled. "Les, I think if I said no, you'd probably turn in your deputy star."

"Well, no, sir, I wouldn't do that," Les said. "But I would be some disappointed, that's for sure."

"Well, you can keep your star, and you can dance. It will be perfectly all right."

"Thanks!"

That night the Cattlemen's Association Hall was brightly lit with hanging chandeliers and wall sconce lanterns, while inside the young men and women of the town and county were gathered in several groups, waiting for the music to begin.

"Ladies and gents, choose your partners and form up your squares!" the dance caller shouted.

Les found Julie, and they joined the first square to be formed.

Once all the squares were formed, the music began, while the caller began to shout, dancing around on the platform in compliance with his own calls, bowing and whirling about as if he had a girl and was in one of the squares himself. The dancers moved and swirled to the caller's commands.

Les danced two more sets with Julie, but because she was a pretty, and popular, girl, others came around afterward so that, for the next several dances, Les stood on the side and watched the activity.

As there were no dance cards being used, Les managed to dance with Julie about every third dance, and it became such a routine that Julie started waiting for him, turning down invitations until he arrived. Then, just as he was approaching, he heard Julie turn down Deputy Toombs.

"What do you mean you won't dance with me? I

been watchin' you all night; you've danced with just about ever' cowboy in the county and that worthless buzzard Karnes. You may be the mayor's daughter, but that don't mean you're too good for me."

"It's not because I'm the mayor's daughter that I'm too good for you, Deputy Toombs. Any woman in the county is too good for you," Julie said.

"Yeah? Well, you're goin' to dance with me whether you want to or not. Otherwise, you ain't goin' to like what happens next."

"Julie, I believe this is our dance," Les said, coming up to her.

"I do believe it is," Julie said with a relieved smile.

"I told you, you was goin' to dance with me!" Toombs said angrily, and he grabbed her by the shoulder. That was as far as he got, because Les laid him out with a powerful right cross to Toombs's jaw.

Toombs's loud voice had already drawn the attention of the other dancers, and when they saw Les knock him down, they applauded.

Les offered Julie his arm, and they started to walk away thinking, as did the others, that it was over.

"Karnes!" Toombs shouted, having gotten to his feet. "I'm going to settle this, here and now." Toombs had a pistol in his hand, and he was pointing it at Les.

"I don't have a gun, Toombs," Les answered easily. "I don't wear a gun when I'm on the dance floor."

Toombs smiled, though it wasn't a smile of mirth. "Well now, ain't that just too bad. Because I do have a gun."

"What a coincidence," Falcon said, "so do I."

"This ain't your fight," Toombs said.

"Yeah, it is," Falcon said. "I just made it my fight."

Toombs lowered his pistol. "I—I don't want no trouble," he said.

"Then I suggest you leave."

"You got no right to throw me out of this dance," Toombs said angrily.

"Yeah, I do. You'll either walk out, or I'll kill you and have you carried out. Either way, you are leaving."

Toombs glared at Falcon, but he didn't challenge him. Instead, he holstered his pistol, and to the derisive laughter and a few catcalls from the others at the dance, he left.

The night creatures called to each other as Deputies Sharp and Toombs sat astride their horses just on the edge of town. A cloud passed over the moon, then moved away, bathing in silver the little town that rose up like a ghost before them. As they came into town, they rode toward a big white house that stood at the end of the street. With its cupolas, dormers, balconies, porches, and gingerbread trim, the house was shining brightly in the moonlight. The property was surrounded by a white picket fence, which enclosed not only the house, but a carriage house and stable as well. A neatly lettered sign in front of the house read JOE CRAVENS.

"Let's go," Sharp said. "We'll tie the horses off in

the stable at the back of the property. That way no one will notice a couple of strange horses hangin' around the house."

The two men continued on, avoiding the main street so that they approached the house from a direction that provided them with the least chance of being seen. When they reached the stable behind the big white house, they dismounted, then tied their horses off just inside the carriage house. One of the stabled horses snorted.

"What was that?" Toombs asked.

"You ain't never heard a horse snort before?"

"Yeah, it just startled me, is all."

The two men left the stable, then moved across the backyard, picking their way through the shadow of the trees in order to avoid the bright moonlight. The back door to the house was locked, but Sharp stuck his knife in between the door edge and the lock plate and had it open in a couple of seconds.

Quietly, and quickly, they stepped inside. The curtains were open and the shades were up, so a bright moonlight spilled into the room, casting a silver glow on the big cook stove that occupied one side of the room, giving back a faint aroma of the pork it had cooked for supper. There was a white cloth at one end, and as they walked by Toombs lifted the cloth. Under the cloth was half a cherry pie.

"Hey, Sharp, look," Toombs whispered. He broke off a piece of the pie.

"Leave it, we don't have time for that."

"I ain't goin' to leave it. It's cherry pie. That's my favorite."

Toombs raised the pie to his mouth and took a big bite. Some of the pie broke away and fell to the floor, but he stuck the rest of it in his mouth, then, chewing it, followed Sharp through the rest of the house.

The moonlight that allowed them to navigate through the kitchen illuminated the parlor and showed, clearly, the bottom of the stairs. They started up the stairs and were on the third step when there was a sudden whirring sound, followed by four "bongs." It was the clock, striking four a.m.

"Son of a bitch," Toombs whispered. "That scared the bejesus out of me."

"Keep quiet," Sharp warned.

They continued to the top of the stairs. Slowly, quietly, they moved to the nearest bedroom, then opened the door. The same splash of moonlight that had illuminated the parlor also illuminated this room, and they could see a woman, sleeping alone.

"That's her," Toombs said.

Quietly, Sharp and Toombs moved on into the room, then stood over Julie's bed, looking down at her. She was wearing a silk sleeping gown and, because it was very warm, she was sleeping on top of the covers. Even in the moonlight, Toombs could see her nipples pushing against the silk, and he felt a sudden, powerful erection. For a moment he was ready to forget what he was here for, but he managed to put the urge down. He pulled his pistol from his holster, then he bent down and clamped his hand over her mouth.

Julie awoke with a start and, looking up, saw Toombs staring down at her. She tried to scream only to have it cut off by increased pressure from Toombs's hand.

"Don't you be doin' no screamin' now," Sharp hissed. "You just lie there real quietlike, and you won't get hurt."

Julie's eyes were opened wide in terror.

"I'll bet you're wishin' you had danced with me now, ain't you?" Toombs asked.

"Where at's the mayor?" Sharp asked.

Julie continued to stare at the two of them with fear-crazed eyes.

"Is your pa in the house?"

Julie made no attempt to answer, and Sharp cocked his pistol.

"Shake your head yes or no, girl," Sharp said gruffly. "Is your pa in the house, or ain't he?"

Julie shook her head yes.

"I'm goin' to have Toombs take his hand away now," Sharp said. "You make a sound, I'm goin' to blow your brains out. Then I'm goin' to kill your pa and your ma. Do you understand that?"

Julie nodded.

"All right, Toombs, take your hand away."

Slowly, he pulled his hand away.

"What . . . what do you want?" Julie asked in a small, frightened voice.

"We want you to come with us."

"Is this because I didn't dance with you?"

"Nah. We was goin' to come get you tonight whether you danced with me or not," Toombs said.

"What—what do you want with me?"

"I want you to do what I say without askin' so damn many questions," Sharp said. "Now, get out of bed and get dressed."

Julie nodded, then got out of bed. Seeing the clinging silk gown made Toombs's erection grow stronger, and he was having a difficult time concentrating on what he was doing.

"I can't get dressed with you in here."

"Oh, yes, you can."

"Turn your backs."

"Not on your life. Get dressed, and be quick about it."

"Julie?" a woman's voice called.

"Who is that?" Sharp hissed.

"That's my mama."

"Julie, are you all right?"

"If you want her to live, she better not come in here."

"I'm fine, Mama," Julie answered. "I must have just called out in my sleep."

"All right, honey, if you say so," Julie's mother called back.

Julie turned her back to the intruders and took off her nightgown. Sharp and Toombs saw only her backside, but that was almost more than they could take. They watched, entranced, as she got dressed. Then she turned toward them.

"I'm dressed," she said.

"Let's go."

"Look what you have done!" Mayor Cravens said the next day when he came into the marshal's office. "They took her, and it's all your fault!"

"Easy, Mayor, what are you talking about?" Falcon asked.

"Julie is gone! We woke up this morning and she didn't come down to breakfast; her mother went up to get her. Julie was gone, but Emma found this."

"Julie is gone?" Les asked anxiously. "What do you mean 'gone'?"

"I mean somebody took her during the night," Mayor Cravens said. He showed a note to Falcon. "This was lying on her pillow," he added.

Mayor, if you want to see your daughter alive again, you will issue an executive order overturning the ordinances recently passed by the city council. We will not stand by and see such evils as prostitution legalized in our town.

Citizens for a Moral Town

"Marshal, we have to get her back!" Les said anxiously.

"We will," Falcon said. "Tell me, Mayor, have

you ever heard of this group, Citizens for a Moral Town?" Falcon asked.

"No. I'm sure it was just formed."

"When is the last time you saw your daughter?"

"Last night, after we got back from the dance, and just before she went to bed. But she was still home at four o'clock this morning, because Emma heard her cry out, and that was just after I heard the clock strike."

"Your daughter cried out?"

"Yes, but when Emma called to her, she said it was just a dream."

"It was no dream. That was when whoever took her, took her."

"Why didn't she say anything?"

"Because they probably told her that they would kill you and her mother if she said anything."

"Yes. Julie would do that to protect us. And now I'm going to do everything I can to protect her. I'm calling a special meeting of the council, and I'm going to issue an executive order revoking every ordinance that was passed."

"I'll come to the council meeting with you," Falcon said.

"Me, too," Les said.

"Citizens for a Moral Town my ass," Smalley said with a snort after he read the note. "I don't believe there is such a group."

"Of course there is no such group. Poindexter

is behind this, I would bet my last dollar," Denham said.

"I don't care who is behind it. Whoever is behind it has my daughter, and I'm not going to stand by and do nothing. I hereby issue an executive order negating everything passed by the council in our last meeting."

"You can't do that, Mayor," Van Arsdale said. "You don't have the authority."

"But I have to, James Earl," Cravens said. "Don't you see that? I have to! My little girl's life is at stake."

"What about this?" Denham suggested. "Suppose the mayor issues the executive order and you, James Earl, acting at the behest of the city council, immediately challenge it. We'll have to take it to court."

"Judge Dawes's court? Are you serious? We've all agreed, haven't we, that he is the one behind this? Either he or Sheriff Poindexter, which, for all intents and purposes is the same thing," Van Arsdale said.

"Oh, I'm sure he is. But this could buy the mayor a little time. And if it comes to Julie's safety, then I say we should do it," Denham said.

"You know Judge Dawes will uphold the executive order, don't you?" Smalley asked.

"Yes, but for now, I see no other recourse. Issue the order, Mayor. I'll print it in the paper."

"Will you also print that the order is being challenged?" Van Arsdale asked.

"Yes."

"Good. And, for as long as the challenge is in effect, the ordinances will also remain in effect."

"What does that mean?" Mayor Cravens asked.

"That means that you have issued the order, but nothing will change until the final court decision," Van Arsdale explained.

"You know that Judge Dawes will make an immediate ruling, so that will accomplish nothing," Doc Gunter said.

"He can't make a ruling on it until it is brought before his bench," Van Arsdale said. "And it is going to take me a few days to prepare the case."

"What about Julie?"

"She will be safe as long as they think they can use her," Falcon said.

"Yes, but how long will that be?"

"Long enough for me to find her," Falcon said.

"You mean long enough for us to find her," Les said.

"Les, I know you want to go, but believe me, I can do better on my own."

"But I've got to do something," Les said.

"You can keep order in town while I'm gone."

"Are you sure you can find her? You've got to promise me you will find her."

"I'll find her," Falcon said. "I have done things like this before."

"When are you going to start?" Mayor Cravens asked.

"Right now."

"If it will help you, her horse is also missing. I'm sure they took it when they took her. It's a sorrel."

"Yes, thanks, that will help."

Falcon accompanied the mayor back to his house. There, they found a shaken Emma Cravens being comforted by several of the neighbor ladies.

"Marshal MacCallister is going to find Julie for us," Mayor Cravens said to his wife.

"Oh, please find her, and bring her back safely," Emma said.

"I will get her back for you," Falcon promised.

CHAPTER TWENTY-FOUR

About five miles north of town, Sharp, Toombs, and Julie arrived at an arroyo. They stopped, and Sharp whistled, mimicking the call of a quail.

The call was returned, and Peters and Hamilton rode out of some brush to meet them.

"Well, I see you got her," Peters said. "Did you have any trouble?"

"No trouble at all," Sharp said. "Is everything all set up?"

"Yeah, there's food and coffee at the shack," Hamilton said.

"Good, because you are trading places with me," Sharp said.

"What do you mean I'm trading places with you?" Hamilton asked. "Nobody has told me that."

"Well, I'm the senior deputy, and I'm telling you. Me 'n' you are trading places. I'm goin' back into town with Peters, you are goin' to go on with Toombs and the girl."

"Why?"

"Why? Because I said so, that's why. Unless you know something I don't know," Sharp added.

"Like what?"

"Like maybe there's someone tryin' to set up an ambush for us or somethin' and you know about it," Sharp said.

"No, why would you say that?"

"Good. Then you won't have no problem goin' on with Toombs and the girl, will you?"

"No. I won't have no problem."

"Besides, I'm ridin' a horse with a tie-bar shoe. There's no doubt in my mind that MacCallister will be following us, and if he is, he'll hook on to that tie-bar shoe. And when I start back to town, like as not, MacCallister will follow me. That will give you three a chance to get away."

"Yeah," Hamilton answered. He smiled as he realized the cleverness of that. "Yeah, that will be a great idea."

"Yeah, and I've got an even better idea," Sharp said.

"What's that?" Toombs asked.

"Me 'n' Peters are goin' to wait right here for MacCallister."

"Wait for him? What do you mean, wait for him? What are you going to say to him when he shows up?" Toombs asked.

"Oh, we won't be sayin' nothin' to him," Sharp answered. "What I aim to do is, I am goin' to shoot the son of a bitch soon as he gets in range."

* * *

Hamilton and Toombs went on with the girl, while Sharp and Peters stayed back to see if they were being followed. They waited for more than an hour, and nobody showed up.

"Maybe we were wrong. Maybe MacCallister ain't comin' for the girl," Peters said.

"He'll be here," Sharp said.

"How do you know? He's just another city marshal, and I ain't never knowed no city marshal to take one step out of town."

"Yeah, but MacCallister ain't like no other city marshal we've ever seen."

"I don't know he . . . ," Peters started to say, then he stopped. "Wait a minute. I see the son of a bitch now."

As Peters had said, MacCallister was coming toward them, unerringly following the tracks.

"I tell you what, that bastard is one good tracker," Sharp said. "Look at him come."

"He won't be doin' no more trackin' after I get through with him," Peters said. Peters snaked his rifle out of the saddle sheath, then rested it across the top of a rock and took aim.

"Don't shoot yet," Sharp warned him. "Let him get closer."

"What do you mean 'let him get closer'? Mac-Callister ain't the kind of man I want too close to me," Peters said. He pulled the trigger, the rifle barked, and the kick rocked his shoulder back.

* * *

Falcon had followed the tracks to an arroyo about seven miles north of town. He found evidence that the three riders had waited there until they were joined by two more riders. It also appeared that the horses separated at this spot. Three went north and two, it appeared, were still here. One of the tracks that had not gone with the other three was the same tie-bar he had been following. What was going on here? He dismounted to examine the droppings of one of the horses that had continued north.

That horse had been eating oats.

He smiled. Julie's horse had been eating oats. The other horses had been eating hay. Whoever was riding the tie-bar horse was one of those who had taken Julie from the house, and Falcon definitely wanted him. But Julie's horse went north, and his first priority was to find her.

But two sets of tracks had not gone on and that meant they were still here. Falcon turned in his saddle to have a look around when a rifle cracked and he heard the deadly whine of a bullet frying the air right by his head. Luckily he had just changed positions in his saddle at almost exactly the same moment the rifle was fired. Had he not done this, he would be dead.

"Damn it! I told you to wait! You missed!"

Peters saw MacCallister dismount and run in a zigzag toward a small rise. He shot again, just before MacCallister got there, but missed this time as well.

"He got his rifle out of the saddle holster before he sent his horse to runnin' off, didn't he?" Sharp asked.

"Yes."

"Uh, huh. I told you to wait. Now he's got a rifle, and position, and I ain't plannin' on stayin' around."

"Me, neither," Peters said, following Sharp back to where their two horses were ground tethered.

After Falcon dived over the top of the knoll, he rolled over to the other side, then he came back up to peer over the top of the little hill to try to see where the shooter was.

He saw no one.

Falcon slipped back down, then he put his hat on the end of his rifle and poked it up over the top of the knoll. He held it there for a long moment, hoping to draw fire, but nothing happened. Then, when he was absolutely certain there was no one there, he moved cautiously to where the ambusher had been.

Whoever had been there was gone, but Falcon found the spent brass casings of a couple of .44-40 shells jacked out of the rifle by the assailant after firing.

It took Falcon a couple of minutes to find his horse. Lightning was standing quietly down in a ravine. Falcon remounted, then started after the tracks heading north.

Toombs and Hamilton had brought Julie to a little cabin, about ten miles out of town.

"You sure this is the place?" Toombs asked.

"This is the place. Me and Peters come out here earlier and got it all set with food and coffee inside."

"How did you know about this place?"

"Poindexter told us about it."

"I wonder how the sheriff knew about it?"

"I guess he just stumbled onto it. I think it was a linc shack at one time," Hamilton said. "Damn, I gotta piss like a Russian racehorse. Ooops, sorry, little lady," he added.

Toombs laughed.

"What you laughin' at?"

"I'm laughin' at you for apologizin' for sayin' you have to take a piss."

"A man should always be polite in front of a woman, don't you know that?"

"What do I need to know that for? Onliest time I'm ever with a woman is when I am payin' for her, and if I'm payin' for her, then there ain't no need to be polite," Toombs said.

"That's 'cause them's whores. This here girl ain't no whore. You do appreciate it, don't you girl, my bein' polite and all?"

"Please," Julie said quietly. "Please, just untie me and let me get down."

"Sure thing, Little Lady. We don't mean to discomfort you none more'n we have to," Hamilton said easily.

Hamilton reached up and cut the rope, then Julie got down. She had no idea how far they had come, but this was the longest she had even been on a horse in her entire life. Even when they had stopped for a few minutes and Hamilton took Sharp's place, she had been forced to stay on the horse. She was sore all over, and her back was hurting.

With Hamilton holding on to her arm, she went into the little cabin. Once inside, Toombs lit a lantern.

"You think that's smart? Lighting a lantern like that?" Hamilton asked.

"What's wrong with it? You want to sit here in the dark?"

"What if someone comes lookin' for us? They'll see the light."

"Who is going to come looking for us? Mac-Callister? He is a city marshal; he has no jurisdiction out here. You know who has jurisdiction out here? We do." Toombs pointed to himself with his thumb. "And if anyone would happen by, we'll just tell them that we have taken the girl into protective custody."

"That won't work. She'll tell them otherwise."

"No, she won't," Toombs insisted. "Because she

knows that if she does say anything, we'll kill whoever it was that asked the question. You won't say anything, will you, girl?"

"No," Julie answered, her voice weak with fear and exhaustion.

"I'm goin' to go outside and take me that—uh—take a look around," Hamilton said. "I'll be right back in."

"You want something to eat?" Toombs asked Julie after Hamilton stepped outside.

"No, thank you," she replied.

"Have it your own way," Toombs said. He tore off a piece of bread that was on the table, then cut some dried meat and began eating.

When Hamilton came back inside, he saw that Toombs was eating and the girl wasn't.

"You offer her any food?"

"Yeah, I did," Toombs replied, the words muffled by the fact that his mouth was full. "She said she didn't want none."

"You got to eat somethin'," Hamilton said, offering Julie a piece of dried meat.

"That looks awful," Julie said. "Why did you take me away from my parents? You are lawmen. You are supposed to protect people."

"We are protectin' you," Hamilton said. "That's why we're tryin' to get you to eat."

"Protecting me from what? Anyway, I'm not hungry."

"How come you ain't hungry? I know you didn't have no breakfast. And we ain't et nothin' all day."

"Hell, if she don't want to eat, so be it," Toombs said. "It ain't no skin off my ass, that's for sure."

"She's got to eat sometime," Hamilton said. "She ain't goin' to be worth nothin' to us if she starves herself to death."

"What do you want with me, anyway?" Julie said. "If you're wantin' Papa to pay money to get me back, I have to tell you, he doesn't have much money. I heard him and Mama talking the other night. The store is going through some hard times right now."

"It don't have nothin' to do with money, girlie. This has all done been thunk out for us," Toombs said.

Despite her condition and situation, Julie chuckled. "That figures."

"What figures?" Toombs asked.

"It figures that this would have to have been thought out for you by someone else. It is quite apparent that neither of you have enough intelligence to do it."

"What does that mean?" Toombs asked. "What is she saying, Lou?"

"She is saying that we are dumb."

"She is, is she?"

Suddenly, and totally unexpectedly, Toombs brought the back of his hand sharply across Julie's face. Instantly, her nose began to bleed.

"I'll not have any more of your smart-mouth talk, girl," Toombs said angrily. "This ain't like last night, where that fool city marshal snuck up on me and put a gun in my back. Now it's just you and me, and before I'm finished with you, you'll wish dancin' is all we were doin'." He rubbed his crotch. "Yes, sir, when the time comes, me 'n' you is goin' to have us some fun. Do you hear me?"

Julie put the back of her hand to her nose in an attempt to stop the bleeding.

"I said, do you hear me?!" Toombs shouted, and he raised his hand to hit her again.

"No, please, I hear you."

"No more smart talk?"

"No more," Julie said.

Toombs stared at her for a moment, then once more he grabbed his crotch. "You should 'a been with us this mornin', Lou," he said. "Would you believe I seen this girl butt naked?"

"Did you?" Hamilton asked.

"Oh, yeah. And I tell you what. She's tittied up 'bout as good as any whore I've ever seen, exceptin' maybe for Big Tit Hannah."

Hamilton laughed. "You ain't never goin' to see no one with titties like Big Tit Hannah."

Hamilton took out a handkerchief and handed it to Julie.

"Thanks," Julie said as she held the handkerchief to her nose. "How long?"

"How long what?"

"How long are you going to keep me here?"

"For as long as it takes," Toombs answered.

* * *

Shortly after he left the arroyo where he had been fired upon, Falcon quit following the trail. He quit following the trail because he knew where it was leading. He would be willing to bet anything that they were going to the same cabin where he had encountered the stagecoach robbers. In fact, he was betting the young girl's life, because he quit following the trail and swung wide of it so he could approach the line shack unobserved.

An hour later, just as darkness was falling, he saw the line shack. This time, he was approaching from the back. There were no windows in the back of the shack, so he was almost positive that he had not been seen. He knew they were here, because there were three horses tied up in the lean-to behind the shack.

Falcon tied Lightning off to a low growing mesquite tree, then moved on down to the line shack. He climbed up onto the roof, then walked over to the smoke stack and put his ear to the opening. He could hear the conversation from inside the cabin.

"As long as we've got to be out here watchin' over this girl, seems to me like we ought to have us a little fun," one of the two men said.

"What do you mean?"

"You know what I mean. Ever since I seen her naked this mornin', I been wantin' to try me some of that."

"Yeah, well, you got an advantage over me. You done seen her naked. I ain't."

"Well, hell, that ain't no problem, we can take care of that right now. Hey, you, girl. Take your clothes off."

"No, please, no," the girl's pleading voice replied.

"Take 'em off now, or I'll shoot you in the leg and take 'em off you myself. You goin' to get naked, girl, one way or the other. Either with a shot leg, or without one. Now which is it to be?"

Falcon cupped his hands around the top of the smokestack, then spoke into it in a stentorian voice.

"Leave the girl alone!"

"What the hell? Who said that?" Falcon heard one of the voices ask.

"I don't know," the other answered.

"Leave the girl alone!"

"Who the hell is that?"

"I'm gettin' out of here."

"What about the girl?"

"To hell with her. I ain't stayin' around here any longer."

Falcon stood up then and walked across the roof to the front of the cabin. He watched as Hamilton and Toombs came running out of the cabin with pistols in hand.

"Hello, boys," Falcon said easily.

"You! It was you, wasn't it? You son of a bitch!" Toombs shouted. Both he and Hamilton raised their pistols and fired. Falcon felt the shock wave of the two bullets passing by him, then he shot back, getting two shots off so fast that they sounded like one.

Both Toombs and Hamilton went down.

Falcon stood on the edge of the roof for a moment, looking down at them to make certain neither of them represented any danger to him. Then he jumped down from the roof and pushed open the door to go inside.

He saw the mayor's daughter sitting on the edge of the bed. Her eyes were wide with fright. When she saw Falcon, though, the fright turned to an expression of relief, and she smiled broadly.

"Marshal MacCallister."

"Hello, Julie. I've come to take you back to your mama and papa. That is, if you are ready to go," Falcon said.

"I've never been more ready to go in my life," Julie said.

Falcon nodded toward the open door. "Were those men the only two here?"

"Yes, sir. There were two more, but they left before we got here. The two men that were with me. Where are they, now?"

"Don't worry about them coming back. They are dead."

"You killed them?"

"Yes."

"I never thought I would be glad someone is dead, but I'm glad," Julie said.

"Are you all right?"

"Yes, I am now. But if you hadn't come when you did, they were going to, I mean . . ."

"I know what you mean, sweetheart," Falcon said.

"But that's not anything you have to worry about now. Do you think you are up to riding?"

"I . . . I'm pretty sore," Julie said. "But I don't care. If that's what it takes to get out of here, yes, I'm ready to ride."

"It's too late to go all the way back now. We're going to have to get some rest tonight and start back tomorrow morning."

"Marshal MacCallister, can we go somewhere else to rest?" Julie asked. She hugged herself and shivered. "I don't think I could stand to spend the night here."

"All right. We'll find a nice place to camp out on the way back."

When they went outside, Julie gasped as she saw the two bodies. "What—what are you going to do with them?"

"I'm going to throw them on their horses and take them back with us."

"No, please don't."

"They can't hurt you now."

"I—I just don't want them to go with us. Please?"

Julie was so insistent with her entreaty that Falcon acquiesced. "All right," he said. "I'll pull them inside the cabin so the critters can't get after them, and I'll tell Poindexter where they are. He can come get them."

CHAPTER TWENTY-FIVE

Everyone in town had heard about the kidnapping of the mayor's daughter, and when they saw her riding into town alongside the new town marshal, word spread quickly. So, by the time they reached her house, more than half the town had turned out to greet her, including Les who came up to ride alongside her.

"Thank God, child, you are safe!" someone shouted.

"Are you all right, Julie?"

"We've been praying for you."

Word had reached Emma Cravens even before they got to the house, and she came running down the street to meet them, her arms spread wide.

"Julie! Julie! Oh, thank God you are home!"

Julie dismounted and hugged her mother.

"Let me through! Let me through!" Mayor Cravens called as he came running up the street from his drugstore. He joined Emma and Julie, putting his arms around both of them. After a moment, he looked up at Falcon, who was still in the saddle.

"Marshal MacCallister, I can't thank you enough," he said. "You brought my daughter back. There is no way to thank you for that."

"I'm glad it turned out all right," Falcon said. Then, with a nod, he rode back to Mrs. Allen's boardinghouse, where he put Lightning into the stable, removed his saddle, rubbed him down, and gave him a good supply of oats before he went inside to take a bath.

When he came down to the parlor of the boardinghouse half an hour later, freshly bathed and wearing clean clothes, Sheriff Poindexter was waiting for him.

"I am told that you brought the mayor's daughter back, safe and sound," Poindexter said.

"Yes."

"That's good. Where did you find her?"

"I found her in the same shack that Coop Winters and Travis Eberwine were using."

"You don't say."

"Interesting, don't you think, that she was taken there?"

"Yes, I suppose you could call it interesting. You could also say that you were out of your jurisdiction. I could arrest you, you know, for exceeding your authority."

"Oh, I didn't go there as a city marshal," Falcon said easily.

"You didn't?"

"No, it's like you said, a city marshal has no authority outside of the city limits. No, sir, I had just told the mayor that I thought I might take a ride around the area, just to have a look around, and what do you know, I found her."

"You should have come to me then and let me make the arrest."

"Oh, that wasn't necessary; I had the authority to deal with it."

"What do you mean? You just admitted that as city marshal you have no authority outside the city limits."

"Ah, yes, that's as the city marshal. But you see, I am also a Deputy United States Marshal. And it was as a Deputy U.S. Marshal that I handled the case."

"U.S. Marshal? You are a Deputy U.S. Marshal?" Poindexter asked in a tight, choked voice.

"Yes. Oh, didn't I tell you, when I arrived?"

"No."

"It must have just slipped my mind."

"Well, at any rate, I'm glad the young Cravens girl is back home. The poor girl must have gone through quite an ordeal. Do you have any idea who kidnapped her?"

Falcon leaned back against the doorjamb that led into the dining room, and he crossed his arms across his chest.

"Funny you would ask me that," he said.

"Why would you say it is funny?"

"Because I figured you already knew."

"What kind of damn fool response is that? How is it that I'm supposed to already know?"

"Because it was two of your deputies who did it."

"Are you telling me that two of my deputies kidnapped Julie Cravens? Who? Who did it? I want to know, because the first thing I plan to do is put them under arrest."

"No need for that, Sheriff."

"What do you mean, no need for it? If they kidnapped the girl, of course they will be put under arrest. And they will be tried."

"I said there is no need for it, because I've already tried both of them. I found them guilty, and I executed them."

"You—you executed them?" Sheriff Poindexter replied, emphasizing the word "executed."

"In a manner of speaking, I did. They both fired at me, and I returned fire. They missed, but I didn't."

"Who were they?"

"Hamilton and Toombs."

Poindexter shook his head. "I could have guessed," he said. "Nothing but troublemakers, those two were. Where are they now?"

"I moved their bodies into the shack to keep them away from the critters."

"You just wasted your time," Poindexter said. "They'll be food for the worms pretty soon now anyway, so you may as well have let the coyotes and buzzards get a head start on them. I'll get Sharp and Peters out there to bring them back."

"That's interesting."

"What's interesting?"

"That you didn't ask me where the shack was."

It took Poindexter a moment to realize the significance of what Falcon had just said, and he frowned and pointed a finger at Falcon. "Mac-Callister, I don't like you. You got off on the wrong foot with me, and, U.S. Deputy Marshal or not, me 'n' you are going to have an accounting someday. And that day may come sooner than you think."

"I sincerely hope so," Falcon replied calmly.

Julie Cravens Safely Returned

GIRL HAS HARROWING TALE TO TELL

Deputy United States Marshal Falcon MacCallister, who is also the Sorrento City Marshal, brought back to the arms of her loving parents, the young daughter of our esteemed mayor.

Young Miss Cravens states that she was awakened at shortly after four o'clock of the morning on two days previous. After being forced to be quiet on pain of seeing her parents murdered before her very eyes, the brigands who came in the middle of the night took her prisoner.

The most shocking thing of this story, dear readers, is the identity of the two kidnappers. They were Harry Toombs and Lou Hamilton. Yes, the same two who swore an oath to protect the people they serve, when they pinned on the badges of deputy sheriff.

Sheriff Poindexter has disavowed any association with the two brigands herein mentioned. There is no need for Judge Dawes to issue warrants pursuant to the arrest of Toombs and Hamilton, their final accounting now being given before He who will one day judge us all. Both Toombs and Hamilton fell victim to the accurate shooting of Marshal MacCallister. When he effected the rescue, a short but deadly gun battle took place, during which balls, energized by Marshal MacCallister, snuffed out the lives of Toombs and Hamilton. This newspaper applauds the action of Marshal MacCallister, and condemns Sheriff Poindexter for not more properly vetting those whom he has deputized.

"Did you order that done?" Judge Dawes asked Sheriff Poindexter.

"I didn't order it. It was an idea that the deputies came up with on their own."

"But you made no effort to stop them."

"No. It seemed like a good idea to me. And it worked; Mayor Cravens issued an executive order repealing the ordinances."

"And he has since rescinded that order. The ordinances are once more in force."

"I also didn't expect MacCallister to get involved.

I thought he was just a city marshal. I had no idea that he was also a Deputy U.S. Marshal."

"We need to get rid of MacCallister," Judge Dawes said.

"How are we going to do that?"

"We need to get rid of MacCallister," Judge Dawes repeated, this time slowly and distinctly.

"Have you got any ideas in mind?"

"What do you know about a man named Loomis Drago?" Judge Dawes asked.

"Drago? You mean the bounty hunter?"

"That's who I mean."

"I've heard of him, of course. I expect nearly everyone has heard of him."

"If he knew there was a high enough reward on MacCallister's head, he might be persuaded to try and collect."

"Reward? What reward?"

"The five-thousand-dollar reward I'm putting on him for killing two sheriff's deputies."

"Judge, where are we going to get five thousand dollars?"

"You know where we will get it."

"Judge, that's all we can afford. You plan to spend it all to get rid of MacCallister?"

"Which is worth more to you? The money we got from the stage holdup, or your life?"

"Well, I guess if you put it that way."

"We can always get more money, Sheriff. We can't get another life."

"All right, I see your point. And you think Drago can do the job for us?"

"I do. Mail this letter," Dawes said, handing Poindexter an envelope, already addressed and sealed. "This will inform Drago that the reward has not yet been made public. That will give him exclusive access."

Poindexter looked at the addressee. "This ain't to Drago. This is to some judge down in Laredo."

"He is a retired judge, actually," Dawes said. "He will get the message to Drago."

Hank Owens rode into the sleepy little border town of El Indio, slowly, sizing it up as he did so. The north side of the town was the American side. It was made up of whipsawed lumber shacks with unpainted, splitting wood turning gray. The south side of town was the Mexican end of town, and it was dominated by sand-colored adobe buildings. There was one, rather substantial-looking, brick building with a sign over the door that identified it as the COMMERCE BANK. Owens figured the bank might offer some promise. He would spend a couple of days in town, checking it out.

Owens rode up to the hitching rail in front of the Border saloon. Dismounting, he patted his tan duster a few times, sending up puffs of gray-white dust, then he walked inside. He found a quiet place at the end of the bar, ordered a beer, and then began formulating a plan for robbing the bank.

At the other end of the bar a dark-haired, dark-eyed man tossed his whiskey down, then ran his finger over the scar that stretched from his right eye down to his chin. This was Loomis Drago, and he had recognized Owens from the moment Owens walked in. The last paper he had seen on Owens said he was worth five hundred dollars. Drago was low on cash right now, and five hundred dollars sounded pretty good.

"Would your name be Hank Owens?" Drago called.

Owens didn't look up from his beer.

"I asked you a question, mister. Would your name be Hank Owens? I'm askin' you real nice, and I expect an answer."

Drago's voice was loud and authoritative, and everyone in the saloon recognized the challenge implied in its timbre. All other conversations ceased, and the drinkers at the bar backed away so that there was nothing but clear space between Drago and Owens. Even the bartender left his position behind the bar.

Owens looked up from his beer. "You expect an answer, do you?"

"I do."

"Here's your answer. I'm not who you think I am. You've got me mixed up with somebody else."

"I don't think so. I know who you are. I've seen paper on you. You're a bank robber and a murderer."

"If you think you know who I am, why did you bother to ask?"

"Because I wanted to be sure."

"Well, you can't be sure, can you? 'Cause I'm tellin' you, I'm not who you think I am."

"I'm sure enough that I'll be takin' you to the local sheriff for the reward."

Owens wiped the beer foam from his lips with the back of his hand. "Mister, that's big talk, unless you think you can back it up."

"I reckon I can back it up," Drago said.

"How do you propose to do that?"

"I propose to kill you, then collect the five hundred dollars that's offered for your carcass," Drago said. The words came easily, as if spoken by a man of supreme confidence.

Owens set his beer mug down, then stepped away from the bar. He flipped his duster back so that his gun was exposed. He was wearing it low and kicked out, the way a man wears a gun when he knows how to use it.

"You've got a big mouth, mister," Owens said. "I reckon it's about time you and me got this thing settled."

Drago stepped away from the bar as well. Like Owens, Drago wore his gun low and kicked out.

"What might your name be, mister?" Owens asked.

Drago smiled at him. "The name is Drago," he said. "Loomis Drago."

Up until now, Owens had been cool and confident in dealing with this barfly. But when he heard the name "Drago," his manner changed sharply. He had heard of Loomis Drago, who some called the devil's acolyte because of his tendency to send outlaws to hell.

Drago noticed the sudden change in Owen's demeanor, and he smiled, a cold, evil smile. That fear had just given him the edge he counted on. "Well, now, unless I miss my guess, I'd say you've heard of me."

Owens no longer had a stomach for conversation. He was fast and had won many previous shoot-outs, but he had never come up against anyone like Drago before. He knew his only chance was to make a sudden and unexpected draw, and that is exactly what he did, pulling his pistol in the blink of an eye.

For just the blink of an eye he thought it might have worked, but Drago had his own pistol out a split-second faster, pulling the hammer back and firing in one fluid motion. In the close confines of the barroom, the gunshot sounded like a clap of thunder.

Owens's eyes grew wide with surprise at how fast Drago had his gun up and firing. Drago's shot caught Owens in the chest, and he fell. The still unfired pistol clattered to the floor and slid away from him. He stretched his arm out toward the gun, but Drago stepped on his hand, then smiled down at him as the life faded from Owens's eyes. Drago reholstered his pistol and turned back to the bartender.

"I just earned myself five hunnert dollars," he said. "I reckon I'll spend some of it, setting up drinks for ever'one in the bar."

"Yes, sir, Mr. Drago," the bartender replied, and, with a happy shout, everyone in the saloon rushed to the bar to give their order.

CHAPTER TWENTY-SIX

Having responded to the letter, Loomis Drago came to Sorrento and was now sitting in Sheriff Poindexter's office.

"With a reward this high, how come there is no paper out on this man?" Drago was rolling a quirley.

Judge Dawes was also in the office, and he answered Drago's question.

"It's a rather tricky situation. He is the town marshal."

"The town marshal, and he is a wanted man?"

"Not in the traditional sense. Let's say that his status is more narrowly constructed than that of the normal fugitive," Judge Dawes said.

"Judge, I don't know what the hell you are talking about," Drago said. "Is there a five-thousand-dollar reward out for him or not?"

"In a manner of speaking there is. But the reward has not been made public. Only you are aware of it."

"How come you ain't makin' it public?"

"Because I thought you might be able to handle it better if nobody else got in your way. You have a, let us say, unique method of bringing in the men you go after."

Drago lit the cigarette he had just rolled, then spoke around the puff of smoke. "It ain't all that unique. If a feller is wanted dead or alive, then it's easier to bring 'em in dead."

"Yes," Sheriff Poindexter said. "You might say that's why we think you would be very good for this job."

Drago smiled. "I'll be damn. You want the son of a bitch dead, don't you?"

"To put it bluntly, yes. But it is worth five thousand dollars, and as a sitting judge, I can guarantee you will not be prosecuted for killing him."

"Who is this Falcon MacCallister? I've never heard of him."

"It's not likely that you would have heard of him," Poindexter said. "He's pretty much of a nobody."

"If he's a nobody, why are you willing to pay me five thousand dollars to kill him?"

"He has become an impediment to good order in Scott County."

"All right, you can quit frettin' about it. I'll take care of him. Where will I find him?"

"He is the town marshal," Judge Dawes said. "How hard can it be to find a man who is walking around town with a star on his chest?"

Drago nodded. "All right, I'll find 'im, and I'll kill 'im for you."

Poindexter waited until Drago left, then he turned to Deputy Russell. "Al?"

"Yeah?"

"You go back him up."

Russell went over to the rifle rack and took out a Winchester. "If I'm going to back him up, I ain't goin' to be real close while I'm doin' it."

Drago's opportunity came that same afternoon. He was in the Brown Dirt Cowboy, playing cards with three others, when Falcon MacCallister came into the saloon. Drago knew who MacCallister was because he was greeted by several of the saloon patrons. But just to make certain, he asked the others who were at his table.

"Is that MacCallister?"

"Yes, he's our new city marshal," one of the men said. "And he is a real Jim Dandy, too."

The owner of the saloon was a woman named Big Tit Hannah. In her youth, she had been a very successful whore, aided in her avocation by that part of her anatomy that had earned her the sobriquet. She moved over to the bar to stand beside Falcon.

"Jimmy, the first drink for the marshal is on me," she said. Then she turned to Falcon. "And before you refuse, this doesn't have anything to do with giving you free drinks because you're a lawman.

This has to do with what you did for the mayor's daughter."

"All right," Falcon replied with a smile. "In that case I'll accept. I'll have a beer, Jimmy."

"Yes, sir, one beer coming up."

"Why are they taking on over him like that? What makes him so special?" Drago asked the others he was playing cards with.

"Well, to start with, the judge and the sheriff was bleeding us all dry from taxes, and MacCallister stopped it," one of the players said.

"And then, two of the sheriff's deputies kidnapped the mayor's daughter, and MacCallister not only found her, he killed the two deputies, then brought her back."

"Wait a minute. Are you saying he killed two sheriff's deputies? How come he isn't in jail?"

"Because them was two of the most no-account bastards you ever seen. Remember, they had just kidnapped a girl."

"I'll tell you how no acount they were," one of the other players said. "When they brung 'em back into town and buried 'em out at the cemetery, there wasn't a soul who showed up for the buryin' except for the grave digger that works for Nunnelee."

"Yeah, not even the sheriff showed up."

"You folks talk about him like he's some big hero or something," Drago said.

"In my book, he is."

Drago stood up, then walked over to stand at

the opposite end of the bar from Falcon. "Whiskey," he said.

The bartender poured a glass, and Drago tossed it down in one quick swallow. Then he turned toward Falcon.

"MacCallister?" he called.

His voice was loud and challenging, so much so that it got the attention of everyone else in the saloon. All conversation stopped as everyone looked toward the man who had just called out.

"Miss Hannah, I've got a feeling you should step away," Falcon said.

Hannah moved quickly to get out of the way, as did all the others who had been standing at the bar. Jimmy, the bartender, moved out from behind the bar.

"Do you have something on your mind, mister?" Falcon asked.

"Folks around here are tellin' me that you are a hero. You are a hero because you killed a couple of men. Are you a hero, Mr. MacCallister?"

Falcon didn't respond.

"Well, I've killed a few myself," Drago continued. "So I guess that makes me a hero, too."

Falcon remained silent.

"Let me introduce myself to you, Mister Mac-Callister. My name is Loomis Drago."

Drago had not introduced himself at the table where he had been playing cards, and this was the first time anyone in the saloon had heard his name. There was an immediate reaction to it.

"Drago? You mean we was playin' cards with Loomis Drago?" one of the cardplayers asked, his voice reflecting his awe.

"They say he has killed nineteen men," another said.

"What's he doin' here?" a third asked.

"What do you want, Drago?" Falcon asked.

"I want you to die, MacCallister."

"You've just made a mistake, Drago. You have threatened an officer of the law. So now I'm going to ask you to unbuckle your gun belt and come with me."

"Suppose I don't unbuckle my gun belt. Suppose I draw on you. What will you do, Mr. MacCallister?"

"I will kill you," Falcon said easily.

MacCallister's calm, almost expressionless reply surprised Drago, and the smile left his face. This wasn't the way he was supposed to react. His adversaries always showed fear of him, and he used that as his edge.

"Mr. City Marshal, do you have any idea who I am?"

"I believe you just said your name is Drago."

"That's right. Loomis Drago."

The expression on Falcon's face remained fixed and unmoving. Now it was Drago who was getting a little uneasy.

"Are you tellin' me the name Loomis Drago don't mean nothin' to you?"

"I've never heard of you," Falcon said.

"Bartender, do you know who I am?"

"Yes, sir, I know who you are," Jimmy answered from near the piano, where he had moved when the confrontation began.

"You had better tell this—this city marshal about me before he bites off a hell of a lot more 'n' he can chew."

"Loomis Drago is a gunfighter, Marshal. He's killed more men than you can count in gunfights. Including Bing Short, who ever'one thought was the fastest gun there was."

"You are partly right," Drago said. His smile could only be described as an evil sneer. "The only difference is, I know exactly how many I've killed. And it looks to me like I'm about to kill me another one."

"I told you to unbuckle your gun belt," Falcon said. He had given no reaction of any kind to the information that he was confronting a deadly and skilled gunman.

Drago raised his arm and pointed his finger at Falcon. "Marshal, I'm about to teach you a lesson. It's too bad you aren't going to live long enough to appreciate it."

A cold, humorless smile spread across Mac-Callister's face. "Drago, you have just made a big mistake," Falcon said.

"Have I? And what mistake would that be?"

"You've pointed at me without a gun in your hand."

"Don't you worry about my gun, Marshal," Drago said confidently. "I can get to it fast enough if I need to."

"It's like I said. You don't have a gun in your hand, and I do."

"What?"

Falcon drew then, his draw so fast that it was a blur. One moment Drago was taunting, challenging Falcon, and a split second later the black hole at the business end of the barrel loomed large in Drago's face.

"No! Wait!" Drago shouted. He put both arms up. "I ain't goin' to draw! I ain't goin' to draw!"

Falcon put his gun back in his holster.

"Mr. Drago, I want you to leave now. You are no longer welcome in my saloon," Hannah said.

"You ain't heard the last of me," Drago said.

"Marshal, look out!" one of the bar girls shouted.

Looking up toward the second-floor landing, Falcon saw Deputy Russell aiming a rifle at him. Drawing and turning toward him, Falcon fired at the same time Russell fired, the bullet crashing into the bar behind Falcon. Falcon fired back, and Russell tumbled over the banister, then fell fifteen feet to the floor below.

Falcon couldn't say whether he heard Drago drawing his pistol, saw him out of the corner of his eye, or just felt it with that almost extrasensory intuition developed over a lifetime of exposure to danger, but somehow he knew. He turned toward Drago, who had planned to take advantage of the fact that Falcon was distracted.

Again two guns roared, and again, Falcon's shot found its mark. Drago fell to the floor with a bullet hole in the middle of his forehead. Falcon stood there holding the still smoking gun, while smoke from the four discharges gathered in an acrid cloud just under the ceiling of the saloon. He held the pistol for a moment longer, looking around the saloon to see if there was any further challenge.

There was not.

"He's dead," Sharp told Poindexter a moment later.

Poindexter smiled. "Drago killed him, huh?"

"No. MacCallister killed Drago."

"How the hell did that happen? I thought Drago was supposed to be fast with a gun. And where was Russell? Didn't he back Drago up?"

"Yeah, well, here's the thing, Sheriff. Russell is dead, too. Falcon kilt both of them."

Judge Dawes smiled broadly. "Now we've got him just where we want him," he said.

"What do you mean? I sent two people after him, and he killed them both," Poindexter said.

"'Killed.' That is the operative word," Dawes said. "He killed them both. I want you to arrest him. I will try him for murder."

"The whole saloon seen it, Judge," Poindexter said. "They are going to testify that it was in self-defense."

"You just arrest him, and bring him to my court. I'll take care of finding him guilty."

"That new ordinance they passed says I can't arrest nobody in town anymore."

"Except for felonies," Dawes said. "I will write a warrant charging MacCallister with first-degree murder. That is a felony. You have every authority to arrest him."

Poindexter, Sharp, and Peters, armed with shotguns, waited until Falcon went into the Hungry Biscuit for his evening meal. Then, all three rushed into the restaurant with their shotguns leveled toward Falcon.

"No need to be bringin' his order to him, Ellie Mae," Poindexter said. "He'll be takin' his supper in the county jail. You are under arrest, MacCallister."

"May I inquire as to the charge?"

"Yeah, you can inquire. You are being charged with double homicide. You murdered Loomis Drago and Albert Russell. Now, take that gun belt off, real slow, put it on the table, stand up, and put your hands behind your back."

Harold Denham was just closing up his office when, through the recently replaced front window, he saw Poindexter and two of his deputies, all carrying shotguns, walking Falcon MacCallister down the street. Falcon's hands were handcuffed behind his back.

"Damn!" he said aloud. "This doesn't look good."

CHAPTER TWENTY-SEVEN

Word that Falcon had been arrested spread quickly throughout the town, and when the citizens learned that he was about to be tried for murder, the courtroom was filled to capacity. Those who couldn't find seats in the courtroom stood along the walls and at the back of the room. There were at least another one hundred people gathered outside the courtroom, unable to get inside and unwilling to leave.

It was a hot day, and the windows were open to allow some air to circulate, though the room was so crowded that the open windows did little to alleviate the heat. Most of those present were holding fans, and there was a steady wave of fans throughout the gallery.

Falcon was brought into the court through the side door. His hands were chained in front of him, and he was wearing leg irons.

"Oh!" Lucy Smith said. "Oh, look at the way they are treating him."

"That ain't fair, Sheriff!" someone shouted. "There ain't none of the other defendants been chained up like that."

"Quiet!" Poindexter yelled. "The next person who says anything is goin' to be kicked out."

There were no more shouts, but an angry buzz continued as the men and women in the gallery talked among themselves.

James Earl Van Arsdale was standing at the defendant's table waiting for Falcon, and he pulled the chair out to help Falcon be seated.

"How are you doing?" Van Arsdale asked. "Are you all right?"

"I'm fine, thanks," Falcon said.

"Hear ye, hear ye, hear ye! This here trial is about to commence, the honorable Theodore Dawes presidin'," Sheriff Poindexter, who was also acting as the bailiff, shouted. "Everybody stand respectful."

There was a rustle of clothes and a scrape of chairs as everyone in the courtroom stood. Judge Dawes came out of a back room. After taking his seat at the bench, he adjusted the glasses on the end of his nose, then cleared his throat.

"Is the accused represented by counsel?"

"He is, Your Honor," James Earl Van Arsdale said. "I am representing him."

"Objection, Your Honor," Gillespie said.

"Objection? What are you objecting?"

"James Earl Van Arsdale is the city attorney. Since he represents the city, I think it improper that he represent MacCallister."

"Your Honor, Falcon MacCallister is the city marshal, and the shooting which has precipitated this case was done in the performance of his duty. Therefore, as he is a city official, I not only have the right to represent him, I have the obligation to do so."

"Are you drunk, Mr. Van Arsdale?" Judge Dawes asked.

"I beg your pardon?"

"It's not a hard question, Counselor. I asked if you are drunk."

"I am not drunk, Your Honor."

"Approach the bench and let me smell your breath."

"Your Honor, I protest to the effrontery of that request."

"That isn't a request, Counselor, that is an order. Now you will either come up here on your own, or I will have the sheriff and a deputy bring you here."

"Your Honor, request permission to approach the bench, as well," Gillespie said.

"For what reason?"

"I am prosecuting this case. I believe that I should know, firsthand, whether or not my adversary is intoxicated."

"That won't be necessary, Mr. Gillespie. I will make the determination."

"Very good, Your Honor."

"Mr. Van Arsdale, if you will?"

Van Arsdale got up from behind the defendant's table and walked up to the bench. Stepping up onto the little platform, he walked around behind the bench, then blew his breath in Judge Dawes's face.

"I don't smell any liquor. You may be seated."

"Your Honor, you have not ruled on my objection as to having a city attorney represent the defendant," Gillespie petitioned.

"Your objection is overruled. Mr. Van Arsdale may act as counsel for the defendant. Bailiff, would you publish the charges please?"

"Your Honor, comes now before this court, Falcon MacCallister, who is charged with murder in the first degree of Loomis Drago, and murder in the first degree of Albert Russell."

"Would the bailiff please bring the accused before the bench?"

The sheriff walked over to the table where Falcon was sitting with Van Arsdale.

"Get up, MacCallister," he growled. "Present yourself before the judge."

Falcon shuffled up to stand in front of the judge. Van Arsdale went with him.

"Mr. MacCallister . . . ," Judge Dawes started, but Van Arsdale interrupted him.

"It is Marshal MacCallister, Your Honor. And it is necessary to our defense that he be addressed as such."

"Very well. Marshal MacCallister, you have been charged with murder. How do you plead?"

"Not guilty, Your Honor."

"Your plea is heard. Be seated."

Falcon shuffled back to the table, then looked over toward the jury. *Voir dire* had been a joke. The jury pool was handpicked by the judge and prosecuting attorney, and it didn't matter who was challenged or preempted, the result was the same: a jury that was stacked in favor of the prosecution.

Gillespie rose from his chair behind the prosecutor's table and, hooking his thumbs into his suspenders, approached the jury.

"Gentlemen of the jury, the case before you today is particularly heinous, because it pertains to an officer of the law, a man who has sworn to uphold the law, to protect and defend the citizens who are subject to that law.

"Marshal Falcon MacCallister violated that oath of office when he, with malice and aforethought, gunned down two men. He was wearing the badge of his office even as he was committing the crime of murder, killing in cold blood, Loomis Drago and Albert Russell.

"This wasn't a random killing. Prosecution will prove that he had motive for killing both men. He had his first encounter with one of the deceased when he brutally pistol-whipped Deputy Russell while Russell and his friends were trying to enjoy a theatrical at the Malone Theater.

"And what, you may ask, was the reason for the pistol whipping?

"It was as simple as an exercise in power. Mac-Callister had just been appointed to the position of City Marshal, and as a way to project his newfound authority, he decreed that there be no guns in the theater except his own. This was despite the fact that Albert Russell was himself a deputy sheriff, an officer of the law, duly authorized to be armed at all times. He didn't just arrest Deputy Russell, he pistol-whipped him.

"I believe that it was a residual of this bad feeling between them that motivated his recent killing of Albert Russell.

"The killing of Loomis Drago is easier to understand. Loomis Drago was a man with a reputation for being skilled in the use of firearms, a man who had, many times, faced armed and desperate men in deadly confrontations. Always, I may add, in the performance of a legal duty, because Loomis Drago was what is known as a regulator, a concerned citizen who, on his own, helped rid the State of Texas of wanted criminals. Yes, he received a bounty for the men he captured or killed, but no less a personage than Governor Roberts himself has stated that, 'without the bravery and patriotism of the individual bounty hunters, our law officers would be overwhelmed.'

"Loomis Drago was one of those valiant few, the civilian who puts his life on the line to bring to justice the most dangerous and hardened criminals in our state.

"Judge Dawes had issued a warrant against Falcon MacCallister dealing with the deaths of Deputies Harry Toombs and Lou Hamilton.

Drago was attempting to serve that warrant when the altercation took place.

"MacCallister had a double motive for murdering Drago. He killed him to prevent the warrant from being served, and he killed him for another, more sinister reason. You see, gentlemen of the jury, Falcon MacCallister enjoys a reputation similar to Drago, in that he has killed many men in deadly disputes. Indeed, he is the hero of many a popular dime novel."

Gillespie pointed dramatically toward Falcon. "But how can he stay a hero if there is another man who can draw his pistol faster, and shoot more accurately—a man who has been tested and emerged victorious in many gun battles? There is only one way, and that is to eliminate he who is your rival.

"And that, gentlemen of the jury, is exactly what Falcon MacCallister did. He assured his position in the folklore of gun fighting by murdering the very man who was the biggest threat to his position. I will prove all these contentions during the course of this trial, and you will have no recourse but to find the defendant guilty as charged."

With a smug look of satisfaction, Gillespie returned to take his seat behind the prosecutor's table.

"Damn good job, Gillespie, good job," one of the jurors called.

"Your Honor, I object!" Van Arsdale shouted. "And I ask that this juror be replaced."

"*Voir dire* has been completed," Judge Dawes

said. "However"—he turned in his seat to face the jury—"I will have no more outbreaks from any juror. The next juror who speaks without permission will be removed and held for contempt."

"Sorry, Judge," the guilty juror said.

"Mr. Van Arsdale, your opening remarks?" Dawes said, turning his attention back to the defense table.

Van Arsdale walked toward the jury and measured the hostility in the eyes of the twelve men sitting there. He knew all twelve of them, knew that all were considered to be in the sheriff's camp. Instead of addressing them, he aimed his remarks at the gallery, where he knew he would get a much more favorable reaction.

"Not too long ago, I stood right here in this same position, not as defense counsel, but as prosecutor in a case involving Sheriff Poindexter. Sheriff Poindexter had just shot and killed a Texas Ranger . . ."

"Objection!"

"Sustained. Limit your opening remarks to your case, Counselor. The case you cited is not relevant."

"Yes, Your Honor." Van Arsdale suppressed a smile. The judge had sustained the objection, but he had already put the thought in the minds of the people in the courtroom. And he was playing to them, more than to the jury, since he knew the jury was stacked.

"It is interesting to note, is it not, in the prosecutor's opening remarks, we learn that this case doesn't deal just with the noted killer Loomis

Drago? There was another who was killed in the same incident. Al Russell.

"You see, it was not just Loomis Drago who attempted to kill Marshal MacCallister, but Deputy Al Russell as well. But Russell wasn't facing Marshal MacCallister. Russell was standing on the second-floor overlook, armed with a rifle."

Van Arsdale took a bullet from his pocket and held it out, first briefly, for the jury, then more leisurely so that the gallery could examine it.

"This bullet was taken from the bar, not two inches from where Marshal MacCallister had been standing. It is a forty-four, forty-caliber bullet, the same caliber bullet as fired by the Winchester Deputy Russell was using when he attempted to kill Marshal MacCallister.

"We will prove that Marshal MacCallister was not only acting in his official capacity as an officer of the law, but that the shooting was justified because it was in self-defense."

After Van Arsdale sat down, prosecution called Deputy Sharp as its first witness.

"Did you see the shooting?" Gillespie asked.

"Yeah, I seen it. I seen it all."

"Please tell the court what you saw."

"MacCallister was standin' there at the bar, drinkin' a whiskey, when he looked up and seen my friend Al Russell standin' up on the upstairs landin'. Al was just standin' there lookin' down on the rest of the folks that was in the saloon. He liked to do that, you know, just look at people. Al was a good sort who liked people. Well, the next thing you know,

MacCallister seen him. And I don't know, maybe he was still mad about the little fracas they had at the theater that time whenever MacCallister pistol-whipped Russell for no reason at all. Anyhow, without so much as a fare-thee-well, MacCallister pulled out his pistol and shot poor ol' Al. Then he turned his gun on Loomis Drago and shot him, too."

"Did either of those men draw on him?" Gillespie asked.

"Not that I seen."

"Thank you. No further questions."

Van Arsdale didn't rise from his chair as he asked the question. "Mr. Sharp, I have a list of everyone who was in the saloon at the time of the shooting. Why is it that I don't find your name?"

"I was standin' just outside, lookin' in through the door."

"No further questions."

"Redirect?" Judge Dawes asked.

"Deputy, why were you there?" Gillespie asked.

"I knew that Drago was going to try and bring MacCallister in for questioning about the killing of two of the sheriff's deputies, so I was there just to make sure ever'thing went all right."

"But it didn't go all right, did it?"

"No, sir, it sure as hell didn't."

"Call your next witness, Mr. Prosecutor," Dawes said.

"Your Honor, I don't feel that any further witnesses are necessary. Prosecution rests."

"Defense, your first witness."

"Defense calls Miss Hannah Butrum."

"Hannah Butrum? Who is that?" someone asked.

The woman who walked up to the witness stand to be sworn in was very modestly dressed, but even the most modest dress could not conceal her ample bosom.

"I'll be damn! It's Big Tit Hannah!" one of the men in the jury said, and the courtroom erupted in laughter.

Judge Dawes used his gavel. "I will have order in my court!" he demanded.

Hannah was sworn in, then she took her seat in the witness chair.

"Miss Butrum, you heard the testimony of Deputy Sharp. Does his testimony give an accurate portrayal of the events as you witnessed them?"

"No, it does not," Hannah said. "Mr. Drago confronted Marshal MacCallister, and while they were talking, Deputy Russell took a shot at Marshal MacCallister."

"And where was Deputy Russell?"

"He was up on the second-floor overlook."

"What happened after he took his shot?"

"Marshal MacCallister shot back. And while he was doing that, Drago was drawing his own gun, so Marshal MacCallister turned and shot him, too. It was all in self-defense."

"Thank you, Miss Butrum."

Van Arsdale called half a dozen witnesses, all of whom described the events leading up to the shooting. To a witness, they testified that Russell had fired first and that Drago drew his gun on Falcon as he was responding to the challenge from Russell.

In his closing argument, as he had in his opening statement, Van Arsdale addressed, not the jury, but the gallery. It was his hope that, in so doing, he might bring enough pressure on the jury to make the right decision.

"You heard the account of every witness, men and women that you all know, men and women who have absolutely no reason to lie. And these testimonies, even though they came from different people, and from different positions within the saloon, indeed, from different stations in life, have given us testimony that has layered truth upon truth, until you are forced to come to the only conclusion possible.

"The unfortunate incident that took place in the Brown Dirt Cowboy was clearly justifiable homicide. And here is the bottom line, gentlemen of the jury. Had Mr. MacCallister not been an officer of the law, but merely an ordinary citizen who dropped in for a beer . . . the shooting would still have been justifiable by reason of self-defense.

"If you return any verdict other than not guilty, you will be acting contrary to the facts of this case, abundantly established. Your duty is clear. You must find Marshal MacCallister not guilty, by reason of justifiable homicide."

The gallery applauded and cheered, and an angry Judge Dawes pounded his gavel so hard that it broke and the head of it flew into the jury box, hitting one of the jurors in the nose.

"I will fine the next person who makes so much as one sound!" Dawes said angrily.

The gallery grew quiet.

"Mr. Prosecutor, your closing statement, please."

"Your Honor, gentlemen of the jury, there is no need for me to grandstand and play to the crowd as did Mr. Van Arsdale. These people aren't going to decide this case, you are. And I ask that you not let them decide this case for you. Pay no attention whatever to their outlandish response to Mr. Van Arsdale's pitiful attempt to take from you your rights as a juror.

"Though I called only one witness, defense called several witnesses. But let us examine the quality of these witnesses, shall we? His lead-off witness, the one on which he bases most of his case, was Miss Hannah Butrum. I daresay most of us didn't even know Miss Butrum's real name. We know her only as Big Tit Hannah.

"Consider the veracity of the witnesses, a deputy sheriff, duly sworn by oath to uphold the law and tell the truth, and Big Tit Hannah, who is nothing more than a whore.

"I called only one witness, because there is only one truth. And that truth, as Deputy Sheriff Sharp pointed out, is that MacCallister, known to have been holding a grudge against Al Russell, killed him with malice and aforethought. MacCallister is also known to be a prideful man. It is easy to understand how such a man might be jealous of Loomis Drago. It is not difficult then to imagine that Mac-Callister killed Drago in order to enhance his own résumé.

"There is but one verdict you can find in this

case, and that is the verdict of guilty. And for the crime of murder, there is but one sentence, and that is that MacCallister be hanged by the neck until he is dead."

"Gentlemen of the jury," Judge Dawes said, "you may be excused to consider the verdict."

Half an hour later, the jury returned and took their seats in the jury box.

"Have you reached a verdict?"

"Yeah, Your Honor, we have. We find the son of a bitch guilty."

"Bring the defendant before the bench."

Sheriff Poindexter walked over to the defendant's table.

"Get up," he said gruffly.

Falcon stood and, with his chains rattling, walked over to stand before the judge.

"You have been tried and found guilty by your peers. I sentence you to death by hanging, the execution to be carried out two o'clock tomorrow afternoon."

"No!" someone shouted from the gallery.

"Your Honor, request an extension so that I may file an appeal."

"File your appeal, Counselor, but there will be no extension. The prisoner will be hanged at two o'clock tomorrow afternoon. Court is adjourned."

"That ain't right!" someone shouted. "That ain't in no way right!"

CHAPTER TWENTY-EIGHT

Miscarriage of Justice

Yesterday, Theodore Dawes directed a packed jury to return a decision in a case that, by comparison, would make the Spanish Inquisition appear to be a paragon of jurisprudence. The jury, and the judge, discarding the testimony given by honest men and women, relied instead on the perjury of Deputy Sharp to find Marshal Falcon MacCallister guilty.

And what was Marshal MacCallister guilty of? He was guilty of defending himself when attacked both by Deputy Russell and the infamous murderer, Loomis Drago.

The counsel for defense, James Earl Van Arsdale, presented his case brilliantly, sufficient to convince everyone present of the justness of his cause. Everyone but the jury, who, if the judge had told them that the sun rose in the West, would have returned a verdict of same.

Mr. Van Arsdale entered a plea for a sentencing delay of sufficient time to allow him to file an appeal. The appeal was filed, even though the delay was denied. All we can hope for from the appeal now is the validation of our belief that Marshal MacCallister is innocent of all charges, and that the trial was a mockery of justice.

But that validation, when it comes, will be too late for Marshal MacCallister, who is scheduled to be hanged today, at two o'clock.

HANGING TODAY
2 o'clock
Public Invited.

Word that Falcon MacCallister was to be hanged reached into every corner of the county, and ranchers and farmers began streaming in to voice their protests. They stood in a crowd around the gallows, some of them holding up signs to display their belief that this was wrong.

"This isn't a hanging, this is a murder!" Leon Frakes shouted.

"I've written the governor about this!" David Bowman added.

Two blocks from the gallows, Deputy Sharp

walked back to the cell where Falcon MacCallister
lay waiting to be conducted out to the gallows.

"Here's your last meal," Sharp said. "Steak, fried
taters, a mess of greens, and biscuits. If it was up to
me, I wouldn't feed you nothing but bread and
water, but the sheriff wanted to be nice to you."

"That's very good of the sheriff. Did you bring
catsup?" Falcon asked.

"Of course I brung catsup. You can't very well have
fried taters without catsup." Sharp laughed. "And
I've noticed that the prisoners that's about to get
hung purt' nigh always don't eat their meal, so I
wind up eatin' it for 'em. And I like catsup with taters."

Falcon took the food, then returned to his bunk
and sat down.

"I tell you the truth," Sharp said, turning his back
to the cell and walking to the front window to look
out onto the street. "I do believe they's more folks
that has come into town to watch your hangin' than
any hangin' we've ever had before. Yes, sir, this is
goin' to be quite a show."

Sharp heard a gagging sound from behind him.

"What's the matter, you chokin' on somethin'?"
Sharp asked, heading back toward the cell.

He saw Falcon lying back on his bunk. His
throat was covered with blood, and his arm was
draped down off the bunk onto the floor. The knife,
its blade smeared with blood, had fallen from his
open hand.

"Sumbitch!" Sharp shouted. Unlocking the door,
he ran into the cell. "What the hell did you do that
for? You done spoiled ever'one's fun!"

Sharp leaned down to get a closer look at the blood-smeared throat, when all of a sudden Falcon's hand came up from the floor grabbed him by the collar and jerked his head down so that it slammed hard against the table where the food tray was setting.

Deputy Sharp fell to the floor, knocked out, and Falcon, after wiping the catsup from his neck, stepped outside the cell and locked the door. Then, rifling through the sheriff's desk, he found his pistol and holster belt. Putting it on, he stepped out through the back door of the jail and walked back to the jail livery, where he found his horse and saddle.

This Horse and Saddle to Be Sold
after the Hanging

"Hello, Lightning," Falcon said quietly. "Happy to see me?"

Saddling his horse, Falcon MacCallister rode slowly and quietly down the alley toward the end of the block. He could hear Sheriff Dewey Poindexter talking from the platform of the gallows to the gathered crowd.

"Yes, sir, folks, as long as I am your sheriff, there ain't no outlaw in the country goin' to be safe in this here county, no matter how bad they might be. And this here feller we are hangin' today, Falcon MacCallister, has prob'ly kilt more men that John Wesley Hardin."

"But I ain't never before heard nothin' bad

about Falcon MacCallister," someone said. "I've read about him in books. He's a folk hero!"

"They've made a hero out a' Jesse James, too, 'n' he ain' nothin' but a thievin' murderin' outlaw. Don't believe ever'thing you read in books."

When Falcon was clear of town, he urged his horse into a rapid, ground-eating lope.

The crowd gathered around the gallows and heard someone yelling, but he was too far away and his words too indistinct for them to hear clearly. Then they saw that it was Deputy Sharp, and as he got closer they could understand him quite easily.

"He's escaped! MacCallister is gone! He broke out of jail!"

The crowd broke into immediate cheers.

"I knew it!"

"Ha!" Les Karnes said, hitting his fist into his hand. "I knew damn well you couldn't hold him!"

"Sheriff, I wouldn't much want to be in your shoes now," Eb Smalley said.

"What do you mean? What are you talking about?"

"You've made an enemy of Falcon MacCallister. I can't think of any man in America who I would least want as an enemy than Falcon MacCallister."

"You think MacCallister is going to stay around here? I'd be willin' to bet you five to one that he's headin' out to California or some such place."

"Maybe he is. Or, maybe he's going to come back into town to settle up, once and for all."

* * *

"What are we going to do?" Poindexter asked Judge Dawes.

"We don't have a problem," Judge Dawes said.

"The hell we don't! This son of a bitch has more lives than a damn cat."

"Ahh, but now he is an escaped, convicted murderer. I can put out a reward on him that will be valid all over the state. He'll have bounty hunters buzzing around him like flies on a cow pile."

"But what if he comes back here?"

"Do you suppose you could round up ten more deputies if we offered to pay them two hundred and fifty dollars apiece?"

"For two hundred and fifty dollars apiece, I could get forty men," Poindexter said.

"I think ten men will be enough. It's going to cost you twelve hundred and fifty dollars."

"Wait a minute! What do you mean it's going to cost me twelve hundred and fifty dollars?"

"That is your share," Judge Dawes said. "I shall be putting the same amount. Surely that is not too much to pay for your own life. For if he does come back to town, and I think that he will, who do you think he will be coming after?"

"He'll be coming after you," Poindexter insisted, then, hesitating for a moment, he added, "and me. All right, I'll come up with my share."

* * *

"Now we are right back where we started," Smalley said. "Only maybe it's worse. All Mac-Callister did was stir up the pot."

"I wouldn't give up on him yet," Denham said.

"You don't think he's going to come back here, do you? Don't get me wrong, I don't blame him. I mean now he is a convicted murderer."

"You know damn well that trial was a farce," Denham said. "He's no more a convicted murderer than I am."

"Still, if he comes back here, it will be his death warrant. Have you seen all the deputies Poindexter has now? They are all over the place," Travers said.

"I've not only seen the deputies, I also see that every deputy he hired came from Judge Dawes's jury pool."

"Yes, and they've started collecting taxes again. Not only that, they've raised the taxes so that they are higher than they ever were," Smalley said. "I don't know how much longer I can hold on here. I would leave today, if I could sell my store."

"I may leave whether I can sell my place or not," Travers said.

"Well, if the town dries up, there sure won't be a need for a newspaper," Denham said.

"There's always a need for a good newspaper," Falcon said, and at the unexpected sound of his voice, everyone looked toward the back of the saloon. They saw Falcon standing just by the back door.

"Falcon!" Denham said. "If you aren't a sight for sore eyes!" Then the smile faded. "Wait a minute! What are you doing here? Poindexter has hired ten new deputies, and I hear he will be paying a bonus to whichever one of them gets you. That's ten, no, with Poindexter, Sharp, and Peters, that's thirteen. Thirteen to one."

"Thirteen to two," Les said, stepping in through the back door then. Les was carrying a shotgun.

"Even so, thirteen to two, that's not very good odds," Doc Gunter said.

"Maybe not, but it's the only odds we have," Falcon said.

"Where do we start?" Les asked.

"Suppose we surround them?" Falcon proposed.

"Surround them? With two people?"

"In a manner of speaking. I will come into town from the east of Front Street, you come in from the west. That way we'll have them from both sides."

"Surround them," Les said. He laughed, broke down the shotgun to check the loads, then snapped it closed again. "All right, Marshal, let's surround them."

"I'm not the marshal anymore, Marshal Karnes, you are. I'm just a deputy."

Les nodded, then the two men went out the back door.

"What do you think they are going to do?" Travers asked.

"I'm not sure. But I wouldn't want to be wearing a deputy sheriff's badge right now," Denham said.

Scarns and Evans were two of Sheriff Poindexter's new deputies. Both men had served as jurors many times, but before becoming deputy sheriffs their work ethic had been spotty at best. Scarns had tended bar for a while in the Long Trail; Evans had worked as a hostler from the freight company. Now they were enjoying their new position.

"What I like is, we can have us any whore we want, any time we want," Scarns was saying.

The two men were walking down the board sidewalk and had just walked by the bank, when, about sixty feet in front of them, Falcon MacCallister stepped out from behind a building to confront them.

"It's MacCallister!" Scarns shouted as his hand dipped toward his gun. Evans drew as well, but Falcon's draw was faster. Only two shots were fired. Only two shots were needed.

Leaving the two bodies where they fell, Falcon stepped back off the street, into the space between the land office and the shoe store. A ladder was leaning up against the shoe store, and Falcon made use of it, climbing up onto the roof of the store. He walked up to the false front and watched as two more deputies came running down the street with guns drawn. Falcon didn't know either of them by name, but he remembered them from having served on the jury that convicted him.

"Son of a bitch!" one of the two men said. "That's Scarns and Evans!"

"What happened here?" the other asked.

"I killed them," Falcon said from the top of the shoe store.

"It's MacCallister!"

Again, Falcon faced two men. Unlike Scarns and Evans, though, these two already had guns in their hands. They began shooting, and one of the bullets clipped the edge of the false front, sending a splinter into Falcon's face.

Falcon shot back and both men fell.

Another deputy, drawn by the shooting, saw Falcon on top of the shoe store. He had a rifle and drew a careful bead on Falcon. Before he could pull the trigger, though, there was the loud bang of a shotgun blast. Les had come up alongside him and was no more than ten feet away when he pulled the trigger. The sheriff's deputy fell with half his head blown away.

Falcon looked down toward Les, and with smiles, the two men exchanged waves. Falcon held up one hand with five spread fingers, indicating that they had accounted for five of Poindexter's men.

Falcon climbed back down the ladder.

"I've got you now, you son of a bitch!" Peters shouted. Peters was standing back in the alley, and like Les, he was carrying a shotgun. He let loose a blast just as Falcon dropped to the ground and rolled away. The shotgun blast cut one leg of the ladder in two, and it fell. Falcon rolled once, getting out of the way just as Peters threw away the now empty shotgun and fired at Falcon with his pistol. The bullet hit so close that it kicked dirt into Falcon's face. Falcon returned fire and, as in his previous encounters, his bullet found its mark.

Falcon hopped back up and was on his feet, even as Peters was collapsing with a bullet in his heart.

CHAPTER TWENTY-NINE

By now word had reached Poindexter and Judge Dawes that MacCallister was back in town, and making quick order of his deputies.

"Countin' Peters, he's done kilt six of 'em," Sharp said. "Well, he's only kilt five; Karnes has kilt one."

"You had better do something, Poindexter," Judge Dawes said. "He's coming for you."

"It ain't just me he's comin' for, Judge," Poindexter said. Poindexter was standing at the window of his office, looking out into the street.

"You've got to stop him."

"Sharp, get a rifle and climb up on top of the Brown Dirt. When he comes up the street this way, you'll have a clear shot at him."

"Yeah," Sharp said. "I'd like nothing better than to be the one who kills this son of a bitch."

"Wait until you have a good clear shot, and don't miss," Poindexter said.

"I ain't goin' to miss," Sharp said.

* * *

There were five of the new deputies remaining now, and they had learned better than to be walking down the middle of the street. Three of them were now walking on the north side of the street.

Falcon appeared in front of the three, then, seeing them, he ran into the tinsmith's shop. The three deputies ran down to the tinsmith's shop and began firing through the windows into the shop, shooting repeatedly until the window came crashing down.

"Hold it! Hold it! Quit firing!" one of the three shouted.

The shooting stopped, and the three men stood there holding smoking pistols.

"I'm goin' inside. Bill, you go around the left side of the building. Lee, you go around the right side."

The three men reloaded and started their probes.

After Falcon ran into the tinsmith's shop, he ran out the back door, even as the deputies began blasting away out front. Running down the alley for a few buildings, he came back toward the street, getting there just as the three men started in and around the building.

Falcon returned to the tinsmith shop, then stepped out into the middle of the street, facing the shop.

"He ain't here!" one of the men called.

"He ain't here, either!" another answered.

The three men came back to the front of the shop, one coming up each side and one coming out the door. That gave them a spread that made them difficult targets for one man, but Falcon didn't care.

"I'm here," he said.

"Son of a bitch! Shoot him! Shoot him!"

The guns roared, as they all started shooting. The three men were not nearly as proficient as Falcon, and they were also on the verge of panic. All three went down.

Falcon heard the roar of a shotgun and, turning quickly to his left, saw Les take down one of two more deputies who had been advancing on him. Falcon got the second one.

Les smiled and stuck out his hand toward Falcon. Falcon took his hand, then he heard yet another shot, this time the crack of a rifle. Looking up, he saw Mayor Joe Cravens standing in front of his drugstore, holding a smoking rifle. Looking across the street, and up on the top of the Brown Dirt Cowboy, he saw Deputy Sharp drop his rifle, then stagger toward the edge before falling off the roof and crashing through the overhang below.

"He's one of the sons of bitches who grabbed my daughter out of her own bed," Cravens said.

"They're dead!" Judge Dawes said. "They're all dead! What are we going to do now?"

"There's only one thing left to do," Poindexter said. He took his pistol out and checked the loads, then he put it back in his holster. "I should have done this the first day he came into town."

Poindexter walked out into the street, then stood in the middle, his arms hanging by his side.

"MacCallister!" he shouted.

Falcon looked toward him.

"You got enough guts to face me man to man?"

Les and Mayor Cravens got out of the way, and several of the other town citizens who, by the gunfire, had been drawn out into the street to see what was going on, now scrambled to get out of the way as well. They got out of the way, but they didn't leave. They knew this was going to be a gun battle people would be talking about long from now.

"Hello, Sheriff," Falcon said. "I was wondering if we would meet up again."

"You know, Falcon, you were a foolish man to come here and get involved in this. This isn't your town; you have no stake here. Why the hell did you come here and make a mess of everything?"

"I didn't have anything better to do," Falcon answered easily.

"Nothing better to do than get yourself killed?"

"You've got nothing left, Poindexter. Why don't you drop the gun belt and give yourself up. Unlike the trial you and the judge gave me, I expect you would get a fair trial."

"Do you now?" Poindexter said. "The only trial I want now is by the gun. Because after I kill you, the deputy marshal . . ."

"He's the marshal now."

"All right, the marshal. After I kill you, the marshal, the mayor, and that interfering newspaperman, things will get back to the way they was around here."

"I don't think so."

"You don't think things can get back to the way they was?"

"I don't think you can kill me."

Suddenly, and with no warning, Poindexter drew his pistol. He was fast, as fast as anyone Falcon had ever faced. He beat Falcon to the draw and got his shot off. Falcon felt a blow to his left arm, then he fired back. He saw a spray of blood as his bullet hit Poindexter in the middle of his chest. Poindexter fell back, a little cloud of dust billowing up around his body.

Everyone in town cheered, and they came running out into the street, many of them going toward Poindexter to make certain he was dead, and the others coming toward Falcon.

"The judge!" somebody yelled. "Get the judge!"

Judge Dawes had watched the gun fight through the window of the sheriff's office. Panic stricken at the way the fight turned out, he grabbed a double-barrel shotgun and a satchel, then ran out the back door. He planned to go to the livery stable to get a horse, but there were too many people between him and the livery. When he turned back, he saw others coming toward him, so he turned away from them.

Dawes ran out into the street, still holding the shotgun in one hand and the satchel in the other. He was chased and taunted by the crowd.

"Give it up, Dawes!" someone yelled. "Your day is over! We're goin' to get a real judge in here."

With every escape route denied him, Dawes ran out into the street, brandishing the shotgun.

"Stay away!" he yelled. "I'm ordering you to stay away!"

"You aren't giving orders anymore, Dawes," Denham said. "We've held a special election, and you are no longer the judge."

"Stay away!" Dawes shouted again. "I'll shoot anyone who comes near me!"

Dawes kept backing away from the slowly advancing crowd, until he backed into the steps leading up to the gallows. Still brandishing the shotgun, he climbed the steps, keeping a wary eye on the crowd.

"Put down that shotgun, Dawes!" someone yelled.

"Someone bring me a horse!" Dawes shouted. "A horse! Someone bring me a horse!"

"Why? You aren't going anywhere."

Les started up the steps after him, holding out his hand.

"Give me the shotgun, Judge."

"No! Get back! Get back!"

Les reached the top step and started toward Dawes.

"I'm warning you!" Dawes said. He took several steps back, then, backing into the hangman's noose that was dangling from the gibbet.

"Ahh!" he shouted. Judge Dawes twisted around, and as he did so, two things happened. The noose dropped around his neck and, reflexively, he pulled the triggers on the shotgun. The shotgun blast hit the lever that operated the drop. The lever moved, and the floor opened under the judge. He fell through. The judge's scream was cut off, and the crowd gasped in surprise as they saw what happened. Then it was deathly quiet, save for a creaking sound as the judge turned slowly at the end of the rope.

Les stepped over for a closer look.

"Is the son of a bitch dead?" someone asked.

"Yeah," Les said.

There was a loud cheer from the crowd.

Les reached down to pick up the satchel the judge was carrying. Opening it, he pulled out a canvas bag. The bag was marked BANK OF SORRENTO, and it was filled with money.

"I'll be damned," someone said. "I believe that's the money from the stage holdup."

Falcon was sitting on a chair in the drugstore. His shirt was off and there was a bandage around his left arm.

"You were lucky," Doc Gunter said. "The bullet went all the way through. I've got you sewed up, and the mayor had plenty of iodine."

"You enjoyed using it, too, didn't you? It burned like the blazes."

"Better a little burning than for the wound to start festering," Gunter said. "Make sure you keep it clean, and when you get back home, have your doctor take the stitches out and dose it up again with iodine or carbolic acid. Either one will do. And keep doing that until it is healed."

"Whatever you say, Doc."

Denham, Smalley, and Travers were in the drugstore as well. So was Les Karnes.

"Mr. Mayor," Falcon said.

"Yes?"

"Don't you think Marshal Karnes has earned a pay raise? If for no other reason, then for getting back the money shipment that the bank lost."

"A pay raise? Well, I must say, he did acquit himself well. But a pay raise?"

"Look at it this way, Mayor. You do want him to make enough money to take care of your daughter, don't you?"

"My daughter?"

Julie and her mother were also in the drugstore, and Julie walked over to stand close to Les, who put his arm around her.

"For heaven's sake, Joe, are you the only one in town who didn't know about this?" Emma asked.

The others chuckled.

"A pay raise." Cravens smiled. "Well, under the circumstances, I suppose a pay raise is in order."

As Falcon rode out of town the next morning, heading for Fort Worth where he would take a train back to MacCallister, he passed by Nunnelee Funeral Home.

"Marshal! I wish you would stay around a while longer," Nunnelee shouted. "You've been just real good for business."

There were fourteen wooden coffins lined up in front of the funeral home, and those who had gathered out of morbid curiosity laughed as Falcon threw them a wave and rode on.

Turn the page for an exciting preview!

*The novels of William W. Johnstone and
J. A. Johnstone have set the standard for
hard-hitting Western fiction. In his new series,
this master storyteller trains his sights on Texas—
and the men and women who sowed their
sweat and blood into the land.*

In Hangtree, Texas, any day could be your last.
For on the heels of the Civil War, Hangtree is
drawing gamblers, fast women, and faster
gunmen. Amidst the brawls and shooting, the
land-grabbing and card-sharking, two men barely
hold the boomtown together: Yankee Sam Heller
and Texan Johnny Cross. Heller and Cross can't
stand the sight of each other. And Hangtree
needs them more than ever.

Comanche war chief Red Hand leads a horde of
warriors on a horrific path of bloodshed and
destruction, with Hangtree sitting right in
Red Hand's path. For a town bitterly divided,
for Heller and Cross, the time has come to unite
and stand shoulder to shoulder—and fight, live,
or die for their little slice of hell called Hangtree.

SAVAGE TEXAS: A GOOD DAY TO DIE

by William W. Johnstone
with J. A. Johnstone

Coming in September 2012
Wherever Pinnacle Books are sold.

CHAPTER ONE

On a night in late May 1866, Comanche Chief Red Hand took up the Fire Lance to proclaim the opening of the warm weather raiding season—a time of torture, plunder, and murder. For warlike Comanche braves, the best time of the year.

Six hundred and more Comanche men, women, and children were camped near a stream in a valley north of the Texas panhandle, on land between the Canadian and Arkansas rivers. The site, Arrowhead Rock, lay deep in the heart of the vast, untamed territory of Comancheria, home grounds of the tribal nation.

The gathering was made up mostly of two main subgroups, the Bison Eyes and the Dawn Hawks, along with a number of lesser clans, relations, and allies.

Red Hand, a Bison Eye, was a rising star who had led a number of successful raids in recent seasons past. Many braves, especially those of the younger generation, were eager to attach themselves to him.

Others had come to hear him out and make up their own minds about whether or not to follow his lead. Not a few had come to keep a wary eye on him and see what he was up to.

All brought their families with them, from the oldest squaws to the youngest babes in arms. They brought their tipis and personal belongings, horse herds, and even dogs.

The Comanche were a mobile folk, nomads who followed the buffalo herds across the Great Plains. They spent much of their lives on horseback and were superb riders. They were fierce fighters, arguably the most dangerous Indian tribe in the West. They gloried in the title of Lords of the Southern Plains.

Farther southwest—much farther—lay the lands of the Apache, relentless desert warriors of fearsome repute. During their seasonal wanderings Comanches raided Apaches as the opportunity presented itself, but the Apache did not strike north to raid Comancheria. This stark fact spoke volumes about the relative deadliness of the two.

The camp on the valley stream was unusual in its size, the tribesmen generally preferring to travel in much smaller groups. The temporary settlement had come into being in response to Red Hand's invitation, taken by his emissaries to the various interested parties. Invitation, not summons.

A high-spirited individual, the Comanche brave was jealous of his freedom and rights. His allegiance was freely given and just as freely withdrawn.

Warriors of great deeds were respected, but not slavishly submitted to. A leader gained followers by ability and success; incompetence and failure inevitably incited mass desertions.

It was a mark of Red Hand's prowess that so many had come to hear his words.

The campsite at Arrowhead Rock lay on a well-watered patch of grassy ground. Cone-shaped tipis massed along the stream banks. Smoke from many cooking fires hazed the area. The tipis had been given over to women and children; the men were elsewhere. Packs of half-wild, half-starved dogs chased each other around the campgrounds, snarling and yapping.

The horse herds were picketed nearby. Comanches reckoned their wealth in horses, as white men did in gold. The greater the thief, the more he was respected and envied by his fellows.

For such a conclave, an informal truce reigned, whereby the braves of various clans held in check their craving to steal each other's horses . . . mostly.

North of the camp, a long bowshot away, the land dipped into a shallow basin, a hollow serving as a kind of natural amphitheater. It was spacious enough to comfortably hold the two hundred and more warriors assembled there under a horned moon. No females were present at the basin.

To a man, they were in prime physical condition. There was no place in the Comanche nation for weaklings. Men were warriors, doing the hunting, raiding, fighting, and killing—sometimes dying.

Women did all the other work, the drudgery of the tribe.

The braves were high-spirited, raucous. Much horseplay and boasting of big brags occurred. It had been a long winter; they looked forward to the wild free life of raiding south with eager anticipation. An air of keen interest hung over them as they waited impatiently for Red Hand to take the fore.

At the northern center rim of the basin stood a triangular-shaped rock about twenty feet high. Shaped like an arrowhead planted point-up in the ground, it gave the site its name. Among Comanche warrior society, the arrowhead was an emblem of power and danger, giving the stone an aura of magical potency.

A fire blazed near its base. Yellow-red tongues of flame leaped upward, wreathed with spirals of blue-gray smoke. Between the fire and the rock, a stout wooden stake eight feet tall had been driven into the ground.

The braves faced the rock, Bison Eyes grouped on the left, Dawn Hawks on the right. Both clans were strong, numerous, and well respected. Nearly evenly matched in numbers and fighting prowess, they were great rivals.

A stir went through the crowd. Something was happening.

A handful of shadowy figures stepped out from behind the rock, coming into view of those assembled in the hollow. They ranked themselves in a line behind the fire, forming up like a guard of honor in advance of their leader. Underlit by the flames' red glare, they could be seen and recognized.

Mighty warriors all, men of renown, they made up Red Hand's inner circle of trusted advisors and henchmen, his lieutenants.

Ten Scalps was a giant of a man, one of the strongest warriors in the Comanche nation. He'd taken ten scalps as a youth during his first raid. After that he stopped counting.

Sun Dog, his face wider than it was long, had dark eyes glinting like chips of black glass.

Little Bells, with twin strings of tiny silver bells plaited into his lion's mane of shoulder-length hair, stood tall.

Badger was short and squat, with tremendous upper body strength and oversized, pawlike hands.

Black Robe, clad in a garment he'd stripped from a Mexican priest he'd slain and scalped, was next. Part long coat, part cape, the tattered garment gave him a weird, batlike outline.

The cadre's appearance was greeted by the crowd with appreciative whoops, shrieks, and howls. The five stood motionless, faces impassive, arms folded across their chests. They held the pose for a long time, their stillness contrasting with the crowd's mounting excitement.

After a moment, a lone man emerged from behind the rock into the firelight. He wore a war bonnet and carried a lance.

The Bison Eyes clansmen vented loud, full-throated cries of welcome, for the newcomer was none other than their own great man, Red Hand. But Red Hand's entrance was almost as well received by the rival Dawn Hawks.

He was a man of power, a doer of great deeds. He had stature. He had stolen many horses, enslaved many captives, killed many foes. With skill and daring he had won much fame throughout the plains and deep into Mexico.

Circling around to the front of Arrowhead Rock, Red Hand scrambled up onto a ledge four feet above the ground. Facing the assembled, he showed himself to them. Roughly thirty years of age, he was in full, vigorous prime, broad-shouldered, deep-chested, and long-limbed. Thick coal-black hair, full and unbound, framed a long, sharp-featured face. His eyes were deepset, burning.

He was crowned with a splendid eagle-feather war bonnet whose train reached down his back. He wore a simple breechcloth and knee-length antelope skin boots. A hunting knife hung on his hip.

From fingertips to wrists, the backs of his hands were painted with greasy red coloring, markings that were stripes, wavy lines, crescent moons, and arrows. His right hand clenched the lance, holding it upright with its base resting atop the rocky ledge. Ten feet long, it was tipped with a wickedly sharp, barbed spear blade.

This was no Comanche war spear. He had taken it in Mexico the summer before from a mounted lancer, one of the legions of crack cavalry troops

sent by France's Emperor Napoleon III to protect
his ally Maximilian of Austria-Hungary.

Red Hand knew nothing of the crowned heads of
Europe nor of Napoleon III's mad dream of a New
World Empire that had prompted him to install a
Hapsburg royal on the throne of Mexico. Red Hand
knew killing, though, dodging the lancer's lunging
spear thrust, dragging him down off his fine horse,
and cutting his throat.

Word of this enviable weapon spread far and
wide among the Comanches. More than a prize,
the lance became a talisman of Red Hand's pres-
tige. It evoked no small interest, with many braves
pressing forward, craning for a better look.

Red Hand lifted the weapon, shaking it triumph-
antly in the air. It was met by a fresh round of appreciative whoops.

Notably lacking in enthusiasm, was Wahtonka, a
Dawn Hawks chief standing in the front rank of his
clan. He, too, was a great man, with many daring
deeds of blood to his credit. But he was fifty years
old, a generation older than Red Hand.

Of medium height, Wahtonka was lean and wiry—
all bone, sinews, and tendons. His hair, parted in
the middle of his scalp, was worn in two long, gray-
flecked braids. His face was deeply lined, his mouth
downturned, dour.

Red Hand's enthusiastic audience did nothing to
lighten his mood. Others were not so constrained
in their appreciation of the upstart, Wahtonka

noticed, including many of his own Dawn Hawks. Too many.

The young men were loud in their whooping and hollering, and a number of older, more established warriors also stamped and shouted for Red Hand.

Wahtonka cut a side glance at Laughing Bear standing beside him. Laughing Bear was of his generation, himself a mighty warrior, though with few deeds in recent years to his credit. He was Wahtonka's kinsman and most trusted ally.

Laughing Bear was heavyset, with sloping shoulders and a blocky torso, thick in the middle. His features were broad and lumpish. The gaze of his small round eyes was bleak. He looked as if he had not laughed in years. Red Hand's appearance this night had not struck forth in him any spirit of mirth. He shared Wahtonka's grave concerns about the growing Red Hand problem.

The hero of the hour basked for a moment in the gusty reception given him, before motioning for silence. The Comanches quieted down, though scattered shrieks and screams continued to rise from some of the more excitable types. The clamor subsided, though the crowd kept up a continual buzzing.

"Brothers! I went in search of a vision," Red Hand began, his voice big and booming. "I went in search of a vision—and I have found it!"

The warriors' cheers echoed across the nighted prairie.

Red Hand's face split in a wicked grin, showing

strong white teeth. "In the old times life was good. The game was thick. Birds filled the skies. The buffalo were many, covering the ground as far as the eye could see." He had a far-off look in his eyes, as if gazing through the distance of space and time in search of such onetime abundance.

He frowned, his gaze hardening, dark passions clouding his features. "Then came the white men," he said, voice thick, almost choking on the words.

The mood of the braves turned. Whoops and screeches faded, replaced by sullen, ominous mutterings accompanied by much solemn nodding of heads in agreement. Red Hand was voicing their universal complaint against the hated invaders who were destroying a cherished way of life.

"First were the Mexicans, with their high-handed ways," he said, thrusting his lance toward the south, the direction from which the initial trespassers hailed.

"They came in suits of iron, calling themselves 'conquerers.'" Red Hand sneered at the conquistadors who had emerged from Mexico some three hundred and fifty years earlier. It might have been yesterday, so fresh and strong was his hate.

"They rode—horses!" Red Hand's eyes bulged as he assumed an expression of pop-eyed amazement, his clowning provoking shouts and laughter. "We had never seen horses before. The horses were good!"

He paused, then punched the rest of it across. "We killed the men and took their horses! We burned the settlements and killed and killed until only cowards were left alive, and we sent them running back to Mexico!"

The braves spasmed with screaming delight, some shouting themselves hoarse.

Red Hand waited for a lull in the tumult, then continued. "From that day till now, they have never dared return to our hunting grounds. We could have wiped them off the face of the earth, chasing them into the Great Water, had we so desired. Aye, for we Comanche are a mighty folk, and a warlike one. But we were merciful. We took pity on the poor weak creatures and let them live, so they could keep on breeding fine horses for us to steal.

"One black day, out from where the sun rises, came the Texans."

Texans—the Comanches' generic term for Anglos, English-speaking whites.

"Texans! They, too, wanted to steal our land and enslave us. They had guns! The guns were good. So we killed the Texans and took their guns and killed more, whipping and burning until they wept like frightened children!

"Not all did we kill, for we Comanches are a merciful people. We let some live so we could take more guns and powder and bullets from them. Their horses are good to steal, too! And their women!

"But the Comanche is too tender hearted for his own good," he said, shaking his head as if in sorrow. "For a time, all was well. But no more. The Texans forget the lesson we taught them in blood and fire.

They come creeping back, pressing at our lands in ever-greater numbers. They will eat up the earth if they are not stopped.

"What to do, brothers, what to do? I prayed to the Great Spirit to send me an answer. And I dreamed a dream. The sky cracked open! The clouds parted, and an arm reached down between them—a mighty red arm, holding a burning spear. The Fire Lance!

"The hand darted the spear. It flew down to earth, striking the ground with a thunderclap. When the smoke cleared, I alone was left standing, for all around me the Texans lay fallen on the ground. Man, woman and child—dead! Dead all, from oldest to youngest, from greatest to most small. All dead. And this was not the least of wonders.

"Everywhere a white person had fallen, a buffalo rose up. Here, there, everywhere a buffalo! They filled the plains with a thundering herd, filling my heart with joy. So it was shown to me in a dream, as I tell it to you. But I tell you this. It was no dream, but a vision!"

Wild stirrings shot through the crowd, a storm of potential energy yearning to be released.

"A true vision!" Red Hand bellowed.

The braves chafed at the bit, straining to break loose, but Red Hand shouted down the rising tumult. "The Great Spirit has shown us the Way— kill the Texans! Take up the Fire Lance! Kill and burn until the last white has fled from these lands, never to be seen again! The buffalo will once more grow thick and fat! All will be well, as in the days of our fathers!"

Brandishing his lance, Red Hand shook it at the heavens. Pandemonium erupted, a near riot. The hollow basin became a howling bedlam as the wild crowd went wilder.

So great was the uproar that, in the tipis, the women and children marveled to hear it. Any outsider, red or white, hearing it crashing across the plains, would have taken fright.

Red Hand hopped down off the ledge that had served him as a platform and stepped back into the shadows, partly withdrawing from the scene while the disturbance played itself out. His henchmen followed.

Presently, order was restored, if not peace and quiet. The braves settled down, in their restless way.

Red Hand put his head together with his five-man cadre, giving orders.

Carrying out his command, Sun Dog and Little Bells moved around to the east side of Arrowhead Rock, where a lone tipi stood off by itself in the gloom beyond the firelight. Sun Dog lifted the front flap and went inside.

A moment later, a figure emerged headfirst through the opening as if violently flung outward, falling facedown in the dirt at Little Bells's feet.

Sun Dog reappeared. He and Little Bells bracketed a sorry figure, grabbing him by the arms and hauling him to his feet. The newcomer was a white man in cavalry blue. A Long Knife, one of the hated pony soldiers!

There was a collective intake of breath from the mob in the hollow, followed by ominous mutterings and growlings. As one, they pressed forward.

The captive wore a torn blue tunic and pants with a yellow strip down the sides. He was barefoot. His hands were tied in front of him by rawhide strips cutting deep into the flesh of his wrists. He sagged, legs folding at the knees. He would have fallen if Sun Dog and Little Bells hadn't been holding him up.

He was Butch Hardesty, a robber, rapist, and back-shooting murderer. He had a system. When the law got too hot on his trail, he would enlist in the army and disappear in the ranks, losing himself among blue-clad troopers and distant frontier posts. When the pursuit cooled off, he would steal a horse and rifle and go "over the hill," deserting to resume his outlaw career. He'd go about his business until the law started dogging him again, once more repeating the cycle.

In the last years of the War Between the States, he worked his way west across the country, finally winding up at lonesome Fort Pardee in north central Texas. He deserted again, and had the extreme bad luck to cross paths with some of Red Hand's scouts. He'd been doubly unfortunate in being taken alive.

He'd been beaten, starved, abused, and tortured near the extreme. But not all the way to destruction. Red Hand needed him alive. He had a use for him. Hardesty was taken north, to the conclave at Arrowhead Rock. Kept alive and on hand—for what?

Out of the tipi stepped a weird hybrid creature, man-shaped, with a monstrous shaggy horned head.

Coming into the light, the apparition was revealed to be an aged Comanche, pot-bellied and thin-shanked. He wore a brown woolly buffalo hide head-dress complete with horns. He was Medicine Hat, Red Hand's own shaman, herbalist, devil doctor, and sorcerer.

Half carrying and half dragging Hardesty, Sun Dog and Little Bells hustled him to the front of the rock. Medicine Hat shambled after them, mumbling to himself.

The cavalryman produced no small effect on the crowd. Like a magnifying lens focusing the sun's rays into a single burning beam, the trooper provided a focus for the braves' bloodlust and demonic energies.

Hardesty was brought to the stake and bound to it. Ropes made of braided buffalo hide strips lashed him to the pole with hands tied above his head. Too weak to stand on his own two feet, the ropes held him up.

When Comanches took an enemy alive, they tortured him, expecting no less should they be taken. Torture was an important element of the warrior society. How a man stood up to it showed what he was made of. It was entertaining, too—to those not on the receiving end.

Hardesty bore the marks of starvation and abuse. His face was mottled with purple-black bruises, features swollen, one blackened eye narrowed to a glinting slit. His mouth hung open. His shirt was ripped open down the middle, his bare torso having been sliced and gouged. Cactus thorns had been driven under his fingernails and toenails. Twigs had been tied between fingers and toes and set aflame. The soles of his feet had been skinned, then roasted.

Firelight caused shadows to crawl and slide across Hardesty's bound form. He seemed as much dead as alive.

Black Robe now went to work on him with a knife whose blade was heated red-hot. It brought Hardesty around, his bellows of pain booming in the basin.

Badger shot some arrows into Hardesty's arms and legs, careful to ensure that no wound was mortal.

Each new infliction was greeted with shouts by the braves. It was great sport.

Hardesty was scum and he knew it, but he played his string out to the end. His mouth worked, cursing his captors. "The joke's on you, ya ignorant savages. I ain't cavalry a'tall. I'm a deserter. I quit the army, you dumb sons of bitches, haw haw! How d'you like that? Ya heathen devils."

A few Comanches had a smattering of English, but were unable to make out his words. All liked his show of spirit, however.

"The gods are happiest when the sacrifice is strong," Red Hand said. "Make ready for the Fire Lance."

Medicine Hat muttered agreement with a toothless mouth, spittle wetting his pointed chin. Reaching into his bag of tricks, he pulled out a gourd. It was dried and hollowed out, with a long neck serving as a kind of spout. The end of the spout was sealed by a stopper. Pulling the plug, he closed on the captive.

Hardesty slumped against the ropes, head down, and chin resting on top of his chest. He looked up out of the tops of his eyes, his pain-wracked gaze registering little more than a mute flicker of animal awareness.

Red Hand moved forward, out of the shadows into the light. It could be seen that his face was freshly striped with black paint.

War paint! The sight of which sent an electric thrill surging through the throng.

Red Hand motioned Medicine Hat to proceed. The shaman's moccasined feet shuffled in the dust, doing a little ceremonial dance. Mouthing spells, prayers, and incantations, Medicine Hat neared Hardesty, then backed away, repeating the action several times.

He held the gourd over the captive's head and began pouring the vessel's contents on Hardesty's head, shoulders, chest, and belly, dousing him with a dark, foul-smelling liquid. Compounded of rendered animal fats, grease, and mineral oils, the stuff was used as a fire starter to quicken the lighting of campfires. It gurgled as it spewed from the spout.

Groans escaped Hardesty as his upper body was coated with the stuff. Medicine Hat poured until the gourd was empty. He stepped away from Hardesty, who looked as if he'd been drenched with glistening brown oil.

Red Hand moved forward, the center of all eyes.

The shaman was a great one for brewing up various potions, powders, and salves. Earlier, he had applied a special ointment to the spear blade of Red Hat's lance. The main ingredient of the mixture was a thick, sticky pine tar resin blended with vegetable and herbal oils. It coated the blade, showing as a gummy residue that dulled the brilliance of the steel's metallic shine.

Red Hand's movements took on a deliberate, ritualistic quality. Holding the lance in both hands, he raised it horizontally over his head and shook it at the heavens. Lowering it, he dipped the blade into the heart of the fire. A few beats passed before the slow-burning ointment flared up, wrapping the blade in blue flames.

Red Hand lifted the lance, tilting it skyward for all to see. The blade was a wedge of blue fire, burning with an eerie, mystic glow—a ghost light, a weird effect both impressive and unnerving.

Quivering with emotion, Red Hand's clear, strong voice rang out. "Lo! The Fire Lance!"

He touched the burning spear to Hardesty's

well-oiled chest. Blue fire sparked from the blade tip, leaping to the oily substance coating the captive's flesh. The fire-starting compound burst into bright hot flames, wrapping Hardesty in a skin of fire, turning him into a human torch.

He blazed with a hot yellow-red-orange light. The burning had a crackling sound, like flags being whipped by a high wind.

Hardesty writhed, screaming as he was burned alive. Fire cut through the ropes binding him to the stake. Before he could break free, he was speared by Red Hand, who skewered him in the middle.

Red Hand opened up Hardesty's belly, spilling his guts. He gave a final twist to the blade before withdrawing it. He faced the man of fire, lance leveled for another thrust if needed.

Hardesty collapsed, falling in a blazing heap. The fire spread to some nearby grass and brush, setting them alight.

At a sign from Red Hand, members of his five-man cadre rushed up with blankets, using them to beat out the fires. Streamers of blue-gray smoke rose up. The night was thick with the smell of burning flesh.

Red Hand thrust the blue-burning spear blade into a dirt mound. When it was surfaced, the mystic glow was extinguished, the blade glowing a dull red.

Chaos, near anarchy, reigned among the Comanches. The horde erupted in a frenzy, many breaking into spontaneous war dances.

Above all others was heard the voice of Red Hand. "Take up the Fire Lance! Kill the Texans!"

Much later, when all was quiet, Wahtonka and Laughing Bear stood off by themselves in a secluded place, putting their heads together. The horned moon was low in the west, the stars were paling, the eastern sky was lightening.

"What should we do?" Laughing Bear asked.

"What can we do? Go with Red Hand to make war on the whites." Wahtonka shrugged. "Any raid is better than none," he added, philosophically.

Laughing Bear grunted agreement. "Waugh! That is true."

"We shall see if the Great Spirit truly spoke to Red Hand, if his vision comes to pass," Wahtonka said. "If not—may his bones bleach in the sand!"

CHAPTER TWO

The town of Hangtree, county seat of Hangtree County, Texas, was known to most folks, except for a few town boosters and straitlaced respectable types, as Hangtown. So it was to Johnny Cross, a native son of the region.

Located in north central Texas, Hangtree County lay west of Palo Pinto County and east of the Llano Estacado, known as the Staked Plains, whose vast emptiness was bare of towns or settlements for hundreds of square miles. Hangtown squatted on the lip of that unbounded immensity.

The old Cross ranch lay some miles west of town, nestled at the foot of the eastern range of the Broken Hills, called the Breaks. Beyond the Breaks lay the beginnings of the Staked Plains.

Johnny, the last living member of the Cross family, had come back to Hangtree after the war. He lived at the ranch with his old buddy Luke Pettigrew, two not-so-ex-Rebels trying to make a go of it in the hard times of the year following the fall of the Confederacy. They were partners in a mustang venture. Hundreds of mustangs ran wild and free in the Breaks and Johnny and Luke sold whatever they could catch.

Growing up in Hangtree, Johnny and Luke were boyhood pals. When war came in 1861, both were quick to fight for the South, like most of the menfolk in the Lone Star state. Luke joined up with Hood's Texans, a hard-fighting outfit that had made its mark in most of the big battles of the war. In the last year of the conflict, a Yankee cannonball had taken off his left leg below the knee. A wooden leg took its place.

Johnny Cross had followed a different path. For good or ill, his star had led him to throw in with Quantrill's Raiders, legendary in its own way, though not with the bright, untarnished glory of Hood's fighting force. Johnny spent the next four years serving with that dark command, living mostly on horseback, fighting his way through the bloody guerrilla warfare of the border states.

A dead shot when he first joined Quantrill, he soon became a formidable pistol fighter and long rider, a cool-nerved killing machine. His comrades in arms included the likes of Bloody Bill Anderson, the Younger brothers, and Frank and Jesse James.

The bushwhackers' war in Kansas and Missouri was a murky, dirty business where the lines blurred between soldier and civilian, valor and savagery, and it was easy to lose one's way.

When Richmond fell and Dixie folded in '65, Quantrill and his men received no amnesty. They were wanted outlaws with a price on their heads. On the dodge, plying the gunman's trade, Johnny Cross worked his way back to Hangtree County, where he wasn't wanted for anything—yet.

A dangerous place, the county was one of the most violent locales on the frontier. Trouble came frequently and fast, and Johnny was in his element. He and Luke crossed trails and teamed up. A mysterious stranger named Sam Heller—a damned Yankee but a first-class fighting man—roped them into bucking a murderous outlaw gang.*

When the gunsmoke cleared, Johnny and Luke had come out of it with whole skins and a nice chunk of reward money.

Johnny and Luke saddled up and pointed their horses east along the Hangtree Trail, heading into town to blow off some steam after working hard during the week. Hangtown was a couple hours ride from the ranch, but then, Texas was big. Every place in Texas was a fair piece away from everywhere else.

They rode out in the morning, when it was still cool. Texas in late June got hot early and stayed that way long after sundown. The Hangtree Trail was a dirt road stretching east-west across the county. It had rained the night before, washing

*See *Savage Texas*, the first volume in the series.

things clean and wetting down the dust. The sky was cloudless blue, the grass and trees bright green.

Luke Pettigrew was long and lean. War wounds left him hollow-eyed, sunken-cheeked and gaunt. He was starting to fill out, but there was still something of a half-starved wolf about him. Tufts of gray-brown hair stuck out on the sides of his head under his hat, and the sharp tips of canine teeth showed over the edge of his lips.

He was mounted on a big bay horse, a rifle fixed to the right-hand side of the saddle and a crutch on the left. He was good with a rifle, fair with a pistol. A sawed-off shotgun hung in a holster on his right hip, for when the fighting got up close and personal.

Johnny Cross was of medium height, athletic, and compactly knit. He had black hair and hazel eyes that sometimes looked brown, sometimes yellow, depending on the light and his moods. He was clean shaven, something of a rarity when most men wore beards or mustaches.

When he'd been with Quantrill, he lived rough in the field, going weeks, months without a shave, haircut, or bath and wearing the same clothes night and day until they began coming apart, shredding off his body. These days, he set a high value on bathing, shaving, and clean clothes. His nature was fastidious, catlike even.

He wore a flat-crowned black hat, a dark broad-cloth jacket, and a gray button-down shirt. His black denim pants hung over his army-issue boots.

A pair of hip-holstered Colt .44s showed beneath his jacket. A lightweight pistol was tucked away in one of his jacket pockets, a carbine was tucked into his saddle scabbard, and a couple more pistols were stashed in his saddlebags.

Riding with Quantrill had taught him the value of having plenty of firepower where he could get to it fast. Returning to Hangtree had firmed up that belief.

Ahead lay a low ridge running north-south, cut at right angles by the Hangtree Trail. Hangtown lay just east of the rise.

North of the trail rose the Hanging Tree, a towering dead oak, silver-gray and lightning-blasted. It had broken limbs sticking out from its sides. At its foot, lay black, sticklike crosses, slanting wooden grave markers, and weedy mounds of Boot Hill, burial place of the poor, the lost, and the damned.

South of the trail, the rise was topped by a white-painted wooden church with a bell tower topped by an obelisk-shaped steeple. Nearby was the church-yard cemetery, neat and well kept.

Johnny and Luke crested the ridge. On the far side, the trail dipped and ran east into Hangtown. Once in town, the road became Trail Street, the main drag. It was paralleled on the north by Commerce Street, south by Mace Street.

At the east end of Trail Street stood the court-house and the jail, Hangtown's only stone buildings, built in the 1850s. The courthouse fronted east, a two-story brown sandstone structure with a clock tower. The jail fronted north, its long walls running north-south, a one-story brick building with iron bars on the windows. South central of town a jumble of adobe houses and wooden huts grouped around an oval plaza. Mextown.

Southwest of town was a grassy open field with a stream running through it. A wagon train was camped there, with more than two dozen wagons arranged in a circle. Horses and oxen were pastured nearby. Smoke rose from cooking fires. People moved to and fro, youngsters weaving in and out around them.

Johnny and Luke rode down the ridge into town. It was a little past ten o'clock in the morning.

Saturdays were usually busy in Hangtown. Ranchers and their families from all over the county came in to trade, barter, or buy. The fine late June weather had brought them out in big numbers. Wagons lined boardwalk sidewalks fronting the stores on both sides of Trail Street. Groups of kids ran up and down the street, playing tag.

Many cowboys and ranch hands worked only a half day on Saturday; they would start coming in after twelve noon. The week's wages burned a hole in their pockets, itching to be spent on whiskey, women, and gambling.

Johnny and Luke put their horses up at Hobson's Livery stables and corral, which was south of the jail. Once the horses were squared away, Johnny said, "Let's get some chow."

"Hell, let's get a drink," Luke said.

"Chow first. It's early yet."

Luke gave in with poor grace and they went into Mabel's Café. They sat at a table, ordered breakfast, and soon were digging into a big meal of steak and eggs, biscuits, and coffee.

Fortified, they exited the restaurant a few minutes later. Johnny reached into an inside breast pocket of his jacket for one of several long, thin cigars he kept there. He bit the end off, spat it out, and lit up. Luke used a penknife to cut a chaw off a plug of tobacco, stuck it in the side of his mouth, and commenced to work on it.

They moved on, north to Trail Street. With his crutch wedged under his left arm, Luke swung along with the facility that comes with much practice. Men with missing limbs were a commonplace throughout the land in the war's aftermath.

Johnny padded along at a nice easy pace so as not to get Luke winded. Besides, he was in no hurry. Turning left at Trail Street, they went west along its south side, nodding to acquaintances, saying hello in passing. Johnny smoked his cigar, trailing blue-gray smoke. Luke squirted tobacco juice from time to time.

Johnny liked to watch the passing parade, especially the pretty girls, the town misses, and ranchers' daughters. They were bright eyed, with well-scrubbed shining faces.

Their wayward sisters, denizens of the saloons and the houses, were mostly still abed, not yet astir. Johnny liked them well enough, too—perhaps too well. But they belonged to a half world of gamblers, barkeeps, whores, hardcases, and thrill seekers—sinners all. They were nightbirds who flew when the sun went down.

At ten-thirty in the morning, respectable folk held sway, crowding the wooden plank sidewalks fronting the stores. Luke flattened against a wall to dodge a gang of kids chasing each other, shouting back and forth. He and Johnny made their way west, sidestepping knots of people.

"Lot of strangers in town," Luke said.

"Must come from that wagon train, Major Adams's outfit," Johnny said.

The strangers were a rough-hewn lot, decent-seeming enough, but bearing the look of having done a lot of hard traveling with a long way yet to go. Some were staring, others shy, but all had the aspect of wayfarers. Pilgrims.

"Where're they going, Johnny?"

"West to Anvil Flats and then across the plains to the Santa Fe Trail, I reckon."

"And then?"

Johnny shrugged. "Denver, or the mines in Arizona or Nevada. California, maybe. Who knows?"

"Damn fools." Luke jetted some tobacco juice into the street. "I mean, the ones taking their families with them."

"Can't leave 'em behind," Johnny said reasonably.

"Well, maybe not. But they got a hard road ahead. Lucky to make it without losing their hair."

"Major Adams knows his business, they say."

"They say."

"His wagons have gotten through so far."

"Not all of them. Injins and outlaws, desert and mountains did for more'n a few."

"That ain't the Major's fault. They knew their chances when they set out," Johnny countered. "Anyhow, what've they got to go back to? Most of them are Southrons. All they own is their wagons and what's in them."

"They're lucky Billy Yank left them that much," Luke said.

They crossed the street to the Cattleman Hotel with its raised front porch and veranda. A half dozen wooden steps accessed it, with another such stairway leading down at the opposite end. Johnny and Luke went around it, walking in the street fronting the structure.

"Ever get a hankering to go wandering again, Johnny? See what's over the next hill, break new trails?"

"Not lately. I've been a rolling stone for a long time. I'd like to stay put for a while. You?"

"Can't say as I've got itchy feet, seeing as I only got one foot left to get a itch on. Hangtown ain't nothing special to me, now that the rest of us Petti-grews is either dead and gone or moved on. But it'll do for now."

"Why'd you ask, then?"

"Seeing them pilgrims got me to wondering, that's all."

Across the street was the Alamo Bar, a high-toned

watering hole. Farther west, on the next block, was Lockhart's Emporium, the biggest general store in the county.

A stout middle-aged matron with a couple kids clinging to her skirts stood outside the store. A lightweight, four-wheeled cart drawn by a single horse was pulled up alongside the boardwalk.

A store clerk laden with packages came out the front door. He was young and thin, with a book-keeper's green-shaded visor on his head. He wore a white bib apron over a long-sleeved striped shirt and pants. The bulky parcels wrapped in brown paper and tied with string were held in front of him against his chest, piled so high he couldn't see over them. He navigated by peeking around and to the side of them.

He was followed by a young woman. She held two bundles by the strings, one in each hand, arms at her sides. Masses of dark brown hair were pinned up at the top of her head. She had wide dark eyes, high cheekbones, and a well-formed, clean-lined face. In a yellow dress, she was slim, straight, and shapely.

She was worth looking at, and Johnny Cross did just that.

The store clerk and the young woman set the packages down in the back of the cart and went back into the store.

"Good-looking gal," Johnny stated. "Seems famil-iar, somehow."

"That's Fay—Fay Lockhart, hoss," Luke said, laughing. "Don't you recognize her?"

"She's filled out nicely since the last time I saw her. I'd have bet she would have been long gone from Hangtown. She always talked about how much she hated it here and couldn't wait to leave."

"She's been gone, and now she's back. Like you."

"And you!"

"No staying away from Hangtown, is there? Calls you home. Fay got married and moved away, but here she is, back at the same ol' stand."

"Married to who?" Johnny pressed.

"Some stranger, name of Devereaux. Cavalry officer. Way I heard it, they met while she was visiting kinfolk in Houston. He was on leave. They courted in a whirl and got hitched. He went back to join his troops and got killed a month or two later. Fay came back here to live with her folks."

Johnny thought that over. "Believe I'll go say hello to the widow."

"That'd be right sociable of you."

"I'm a sociable fellow, Luke."

"With a pretty girl, you are."

Johnny didn't deny it. "Coming?"

Luke shook his head. "She's your friend."

"Yours, too."

"I knew her to say hello to, back in the day. That's 'cause I was a friend of yours. Elsewise we moved in different circles. Them high-and-mighty Lockharts don't have no truck for us Pettigrews."

"For the Crosses, neither," Johnny said.

"You and her got along pretty good, I do recall."

Johnny tried to wave it away. "Kid stuff."

"She ain't no kid now," Luke said.

"I noticed."

Luke indicated some empty rocking chairs on the front porch of the Cattleman Hotel. "I'll set there for a while, take a load off."

"Them stairs ain't gonna be a problem?"

"I can handle 'em."

"I'll be along directly, then."

"Take your time. Tell Fay I said hello, for what it's worth. If she even remembers me. Regrets about her dead husband and all—you know."

"Sure." Johnny tossed the stub of his cigar into the street, where it landed with a splash of tiny orange-red embers. Crossing the street, he climbed the three low, wooden steps to the boardwalk. He took off his hat, running a hand through straight, longish black hair, pushing it back off his forehead and behind his ears. He put the hat back on, tilting it to a not-too-rakish angle.

Unconsciously squaring his shoulders, he took a deep breath and went into Lockhart's Emporium for the first time in over five years.

It was a big rectangular space, with a short wall fronting the street. Rows of shelves filled with goods lined both long walls. Beyond the door lay an open center aisle flanked by trestle tables, bins, and barrels filled with merchandise—everything imaginable. From black broadcloth jackets and gingham dresses to bolts of cloth, needles, and thread. Hardware, including plows, tools, harnesses, traces and saddles. Cracker barrels and casks of nails, sacks of beans and flour, rows of canned goods. Luxuries and necessities, it was filled with a world of stuff.

Owner Russ Lockhart, Fay's father, was absent from the premises. No doubt he was at the big table in a private dining room at the Cattleman Hotel, where his brother-in-law, town boss Wade Hutto, held court every Saturday morning, attended by Hangtown's gentry of bankers, merchants, and big ranchers. The Saturday morning meets were one of the few things that could entice Russ Lockhart out from behind the store's cash register.

The store was busy, crowded with customers. Johnny didn't have to look hard to find Fay. She just naturally stood out from the rest as she showed a bonnet to a townswoman. Her aunt Nell, a sour-faced old biddy, was helping out.

A watchful young woman who kept a wary eye on the clientele, Fay glanced up to see who had entered. She saw a handsome, well-dressed young man about her own age, a not-so-usual sight that made her look twice.

"Would you take care of this lady, Aunt Nell? I'll only be a moment." Not waiting for an answer, Fay put the bonnet down, scooting out from behind the counter and down the center aisle.

Nell started to squawk, choking it off as Fay kept moving toward the newcomer, her eyes shining, smiling warmly. "Johnny! Johnny Cross!"

"Howdy, Fay. Long time no see."

She reached out with both arms, taking his hands, squeezing them warmly. He couldn't help noticing a thin gold band circling the base of her ring finger. Wedding band.

Unsure how to respond, he was a bit awkward.

Fay leaned forward, kissing him lightly on the cheek. His skin tingled at the contact. Some free-falling strands of her hair brushed his face, smelling sweet. Intoxicating.

She stepped back, still holding his hands, looking him over. "It's so good to see you!"

She released him, hands falling to her sides. "I heard you were back. I was wondering when we'd run into each other. Why didn't you come to see me sooner?"

"I've been busy getting settled back at the ranch, fixing the old place up," he said.

"You've been busy, all right. Everybody's talking about how you cleaned up that awful outlaw gang. You're a hero, Johnny!"

"Don't believe everything you hear, Fay. These things are like fish stories, they get all puffed up in the telling. I just pitched in and helped out a little where I could, that's all."

"Don't be so modest. It was a wonderful thing you did. Not a man or woman was safe with those killers on the loose."

"Nice of you to say so, anyhow. I was sorry to hear about your loss, Fay. Your husband, that is. Real sorry."

Fay's face clouded, emotion flickering across it. Her blue eyes were shadowed and sorrowful, her mouth turned down at the corners. "Thank you, Johnny. Lamar—Captain Devereaux—was a gallant officer and a gentleman."

"I'm sure."

"You would have liked him."

Johnny wasn't so sure about that, but he nodded as if he was.

Fay said, "Who hasn't lost someone in the war? Your brother, Cal . . ."

Johnny shook his head. "No, Cal didn't make it."

"That's what I heard. Now it's my turn to say I'm sorry."

"Thanks."

Behind the counter, Aunt Nell snapped, "Fay! I could use some help here!"

"In a minute, Aunt Nell. I'm talking with an old friend."

Nell thrust her head forward, peering at the young man. "Johnny Cross! Land's sakes! I didn't recognize you. It's the first time I ever saw you in clean clothes."

"Nell!" Fay said sharply.

Johnny touched the tip of his hat brim to the older woman. "And a good morning to you, ma'am."

"Is it? We'll see," Nell said, her tone and expression indicating otherwise.

"So you're going to be staying in Hangtree?" Fay asked.

"For a while," Johnny answered.

"Good. I'm glad." Faye smiled, putting the full force of her considerable personal appeal behind it.

Johnny felt it all the way down to his toes as he became distantly aware of some kind of commotion brewing outside. It was like the buzzing of a nearby fly that hadn't quite yet begun to pestify.

Somebody shouted out in the street. People in the store started moving up front to see what it was all about.

A man outside was yelling, going on about something at some length and sounding distinctly unhappy.

Muffled by distance, Johnny couldn't make out the words. But he didn't care for the man's tone. Something about it, some raw, ragging note of derision, made the back of his neck start to get hot.

Fay frowned, glancing toward the storefront windows.

"What's all that commotion?" Nell said, sharp voiced with irritation.

"Some drunk, probably," a stiff-faced rancher put in.

"Hmph! And before noon, too! I declare I don't know what this town is coming to!" Nell exclaimed.

"He don't sound like no happy drunk," Johnny noted. He was just getting reacquainted with lovely Fay when a shot sounded.

"Uh-oh." *That's Hangtown for you,* he thought. *A fellow can't even strike up a chat with a pretty girl on Saturday morning without gunplay breaking out.*

Fay started toward the door. Nell thrust out a hand as if to arrest her progress. "Fay, don't—"

Others moved toward the storefront for a better look. Johnny, cat-quick, rushed up the center aisle, smoothly interposing himself between Fay and the open doorway. "You want to be careful when bullets are flying, Fay. Best wait here where it's safe. I'll go take a look."

She started to say something but he was already out the door. The disturbance was centered two streets east on Trail Street. Only the one shot had been fired. The shouting continued, however, with no letup. It was louder and more abusive than before.

Johnny started toward it, then glanced back to see what Fay was doing. She stood just inside the doorway looking out but not following.

Glancing right, Johnny saw Luke standing along the rail of the Cattleman's front porch, facing toward the ruckus. He breathed a silent prayer of thanks that Luke wasn't involved in the fracas. Trouble had a way of finding Luke, and vice versa.

Of course, Luke thought the same thing about Johnny. They were both right, but at least, they were both well out of the trouble this time.

The street ahead was emptying. Scrambling for the sidelines, some sheltered in doorways, alcoves, or behind abutments. Others, farther away, thinking themselves safe, stood out in the open, craning to see what the ruckus was all about.

Men came out of the hotel lobby and dining

room in a rush to see what was happening. They stood flattened behind upright pillars, crouched behind rocking chairs, peeking around corners. Staring oval faces clustered in the front entrance, others pressed against the windows.

Luke stood leaning for support against a porch column. Johnny pressed forward, boot heels scuffing on the plank boardwalk, until he crossed the street and climbed up on the porch. "Hey, Luke."

"You're just in time for the show."

Two men faced off in the square where a side-street met Trail Street. They were at opposite ends of the square, one at the northeast corner, the other at the southwest, facing each other across the diagonal.

A man standing near Luke peeked out from behind a white column. "Bliss Stafford's gunning for Damon Bolt! Called him out!"

"He must be crazy." Another man stood on one knee, peering between the bars of the porch rail.

"Crazy drunk," said a third.

"I seen it all," said the first speaker. "Damon was going to the barbershop when young Stafford ran out of the hotel and drew on him."

"He must've been inside laying for him," the second man said.

Damon Bolt was the owner of the Golden Spur, a saloon and gambling hall frequented by a fast, hot-blooded sporting crowd. A riverboat gambler from New Orleans, he'd come west after the war, settling in Hangtown.

Johnny knew him casually. He liked the man, what he'd seen of him. Liked the way he handled himself. Bliss Stafford was unknown to him. It was the first time he'd heard the name.

Bliss Stafford stood with his back to the hotel. Hatless, he showed a mop of yellow-gold curls. His expensive clothes were rumpled and wrinkled, as though he'd slept in them. He crouched with a smoking gun in his right hand, swaying, as though reeling under a wind only he could sense.

Opposite him stood Damon Bolt. His right hand rested near the butt of a holstered gun worn low on the right hip. He was tall and thin, almost gaunt, with a high pale forehead and deepset dark eyes. The hair on his head and his mustache were raven black.

He wore a brown morning coat, red cravat, tan waistcoat, and brown pants. His neat, small feet were encased in shiny brown boots. He seemed calm and self-possessed, oblivious of being under a drawn gun.

Bliss Stafford circled around to one side, angling for a better line of fire on Damon. His movements showed his face in three-quarter profile to those on the hotel's front porch.

He seemed younger than Johnny, and more immature. Handsome in an overripe way, his looks were spoiled by a sullen, sneering mouth. His face was flushed, his eyes were red.

Johnny nudged Luke. "Who's this here Stafford?" he asked, low-voiced.

"Stafford family came in last year," Luke said, speaking out of the side of his mouth. "Ranchers—a hard-nosed bunch. Bought up some prime land on the South Fork. Ramrod Ranch, they call it. Got more gun hands than cowhands riding for the brand. Bliss is the youngest, the baby of the family. A mean drunk and not much better sober."

"He must be a damned fool, calling out Damon Bolt," Johnny whispered.

The man standing by the white column turned and gave them a sharp look. "Walk soft, strangers. Bliss has killed his man and more. All the Staffords have. A bad outfit to buck."

"I'll take my chances," Johnny said. "But thanks for the advice," he added, seeing from the other's demeanor that he meant only to pass along a friendly warning.

Bliss Stafford drew himself up. "I'm calling you out, gambler!"

"I have no quarrel with you, Stafford," Damon Bolt said.

"I got a quarrel with you. You should never have got between me and Francine."

Damon frowned. "This is hardly the time or place to bandy words about a lady, sir."

"Things were fine between us until you horned in!" Bliss shouted.

"You are mistaken, sir. Miss Hayes has made it clear your attentions to her are unwelcome."

"You're a liar!"

Damon shook his head, seeming more in sorrow than in anger, almost pitying the young man.

Bliss's face, already florid, reddened further as he went on. "You're a fine one with all your fancy talk, making out like you're a real Southern gentleman. You ain't fooling nobody. Everybody in town knows what you are—a four-flushing tinhorn and whoremonger!"

Damon gave off a chill. "Have a care, sir. Say what you will about me, but I don't care to hear the ladies in my employ being abused."

"You don't, eh? What are you going to do about it?"

"You're the one with the gun. What are you going to do?"

"I'm going to kill you."

A man stood at the head of a press of spectators thronging the front entrance of the hotel. He pushed forward, starting across the porch. He wore a broad-brimmed hat, good clothes, and shiny boots. He was fiftyish, trim, with a handsome head of silver hair, a neatly trimmed mustache, and the beginnings of a double chin.

He was Wade Hutto, a powerful man in the town and the county. He descended the front stairs into the street, circling round into the intersection. Moving at a measured pace, he approached the face-off from the side, showing himself to both men yet careful not to get between them.

Johnny nudged Luke with an elbow. "Looks like the bull of the woods is sticking his horns in."

"Must be something in it for him. Ol' Wade don't stick his neck out for nothing," Luke said.

In the street, Hutto harumphed. "What the devil are you two playing at?"

"Ask Stafford. He threw down on me," Damon said.

"You got a gun—use it," Bliss Stafford spat out.

"Put that gun away, Bliss," Hutto said.

"Like hell! This is no business of yours, Hutto. Back off before you get hurt," Bliss warned.

"Everything that happens in Hangtree is my business, you young jackaknapes," Hutto said, coloring.

"You might throw some weight with these toothless townmen, but nobody tells Bliss Stafford what to do."

"Vince might see it different."

Some color came into Bliss's face. "Yeah, well, Pa ain't here now."

"A good thing for you he's not, otherwise he'd knock some sense into you," Hutto said. "I've got a lot of respect for Vince, too much to let you go off half-cocked and get yourself into bad trouble, Bliss."

"I kicked over the traces a long time ago. Now I do what I please. And it pleases me to give this tinhorn what he's got coming to him."

Hutto turned to Damon. "Maybe I can get a straight answer out of you, Bolt. What's this all about?"

Bliss Stafford spoke first. "It's about my girl, Francine. Damon's trying to keep me from her, keep us apart. That's why he's got to die."

Hutto looked grave, like a doctor giving a heedless patient bad news. "You're playing with fire, Bliss. Vince told you to forget about Francine Hayes."

"What does Pa know about it? He's old. I'm young! I got blood in my veins, hot blood, not ice water. Francine belongs to me. She's mine!" Bliss made a warning gesture with his free hand, dismissing Hutto. "I'm through talking. Slap leather, gambler!"

"Against a drawn gun?" Damon said lightly, the corners of his lips upturned in a mocking smile. "I think not."

Bliss Stafford thought that one over. From his deeply lined brow and fierce frown, it could be seen that thinking was hard work for him. Coming to a decision, he shoved his gun back in the holster. "There! Now we're even up. The odds good enough for you, now? There's nothing to stop you from reaching. Why don't you draw?"

"It's too nice a morning for killing," Damon said.

"Draw, damn you!"

Damon tsk-tsked in a tone of real or affected sadness. "You see how it is, Hutto? There's just no reasoning with the boy."

"Boy? Who you calling boy? You see a boy around here, kill him. Because I surely mean to kill you," Bliss cried.

"Don't do it, Bolt," Hutto said.

"You're my witness, Hutto. You and everyone else here. I gave him every out," Damon said.

Bliss Stafford shook with rage. "Enough talk! I count to three and then I'm coming up shooting!"

"You're making a big mistake, Bliss," Damon said.

"One!"

"Still time to back off and save yourself."

"Two!"

"Shoot and be damned, then."

"Three!" Bliss drew his gun, clearing the holster. A shot rang out.

Bliss jerked as a slug tore into his chest. The impact spun him around halfway, his leveled gun unfired.

Damon's gun was held hip-high, pointed at Bliss. A puff of gunsmoke hovered around the muzzle.

Bliss looked surprised. He crossed gazes with Hutto, whose face showed pity mingled with contempt, but no surprise. Bliss toppled, falling sideways into the dirt. A final trembling spasm marked the last of the life leaving him.

Hurrying west on Trail Street—too late!—came Sheriff Mack Barton and Deputy Clifton Smalls.

Damon stepped back. Turning, he covered the newcomers with his gun. The lawmen slowed to a halt.

Barton, in his mid-forties, had a face like the butt end of a smoked ham. A wide straight torso hung down from broad, sloping shoulders; his legs were short and bandy. He wore a dark hat, gray shirt, black string tie, and a thin black vest with a tin star pinned over the right breast.

A Colt .45 was holstered on the right hip of a well-worn gun belt. He'd stayed alive for a long time by not rushing into things blindly. He was not about to start.

Deputy Smalls was tall, thin, reedy. Storklike. His gun stayed holstered, too. He took his cue from his boss.

Wade Hutto hauled from his jacket pocket a handkerchief the size of a dinner napkin and mopped his face with it. He'd sweated plenty during the face-off. "Nice work, Sheriff. You managed to get here too late to stop it."

Few dared talk to Barton in that tone, including Hutto, except when he was rattled, as he was now.

"You got no call to speak to me like that, Wade," Barton said.

Hutto had put Barton in as sheriff. For most intents and purposes he was Hutto's man, but Barton had a stubborn maverick streak that showed itself when he was crowded—he was a real son of Texas. There was no sense in getting on his bad side anytime, but especially with a potential crisis brewing.

Hutto backed down. "You're right, of course, Sheriff. I spoke out of turn in the heat of the moment. Sorry."

"That's all right," Barton said gruffly.

"This is a hell of a mess!"

Damon eased his gun into the holster, hand loitering not too far from the gun butt.

"Might as well inspect the damage." Barton and Smalls edged around the body, Hutto joining them. Bliss Stafford lay twisted on the ground, upper body turned faceup. A dark red hole marked his left breast.

Barton glanced down at the body, making his quick, expert appraisal. "Dead."

"Deader'n hell," Smalls seconded, nodding.

Hutto turned to Damon. "You went and did it. You couldn't just wing him. Oh no. You had to kill him. Now it's Katie-bar-the-door! Oh, there'll be hell to pay when Vince hears of this. Why didn't you shoot the gun out of his hand, or just wound him?"

"Who do you think I am—Bill Hickock?" Damon retorted.

"You got him right through the heart. I call that pretty fair shooting!"

Damon shrugged.

Barton took off his hat, scratched his head. He heaved a great sigh. "What happened?"

"I was on my way to Lauter's Tonsorial Parlor for a shave and a haircut when Bliss came gunning for me. I wouldn't draw, but he fired on me anyhow," Damon said.

"What for did he have a mad on?—as if I didn't know," Barton said.

Damon was silent.

"Things finally came to a head over the Hayes gal," Hutto volunteered.

"Francine Hayes," Barton said.

"If that's her name, yes."

"Don't bull me, Wade. You know her name. We all do. Francine Hayes. Lord knows Bliss and Vince have been kicking up a ruckus about her lately.

Little slip of a gal got Bliss all tied up in knots so he couldn't think straight," Barton said. "Not that he was ever much of one for using his head."

"Bliss wanted Miss Hayes to run off and elope with him," Damon said. "Impossible, of course, even if she was willing—which she wasn't—Vince would never have stood for it. He even sent his son Clay around to buy her off. Francine was willing about that, but Bliss was having none of it. He threatened to kill his own brother if he tried to interfere. Francine held out, for which Bliss blamed me. He thought if I was out of the way he'd have a clear field."

Damon looked around at the various witnesses and rubberneckers hemming in the scene. "You all saw it. Bliss would have it this way. He left me no choice. I had to defend myself."

"Mebbe, but that won't cut no ice with Vince," Barton said.

"I can stand it."

"You only think you can," Hutto said.

Damon looked at him. Hutto was first to break eye contact, looking away.

"A clearcut case of self-defense, Sheriff. Everybody saw it," Damon said.

"How many will swear to it at the inquest, though?" Barton asked. The milling crowd shrank back, sheepish, none meeting the lawman's eyes. "Anybody?" Barton pressed.

"I will," Johnny Cross said, standing at the porch rail.

Barton stood with fists on hips, looking up at him. "Now why does that not surprise me?"

Johnny shrugged. He and the sheriff had a history, going back to Johnny's boyhood days when Barton was deputy.

"I reckon we still got the right of self-defense in this country. That Stafford fellow was on the prod, spoiling for a fight. Damon did what he had to do. I would've done the same, so would any man here. That's how I'll tell it in court," Johnny said.

"Me, too" Luke chimed in.

"Just a couple of public-spirited citizens, eh?"

"You know us, Sheriff. Always ready to help out the law," Johnny said.

Barton laughed out loud without humor at that one. "You only been back for a month or two so you might not be up to speed yet. What do you know about Vince Stafford and his Ramrod outfit?"

"Not a thing."

"A bad bunch to mess with."

"That supposed to make a difference to me?"

"Not you, you're too ornery." Barton turned to Luke. "You got no excuse, though. You've been back long enough to know the way of things."

"I ain't worried, Sheriff. I got you to protect me," Luke said, all innocent-faced.

"Yeah? Who's gonna protect me?"

"Deputy Smalls?" Johnny suggested.

"You boys don't give a good damn about nothing, do you? I like your nerve, if nothing else,"

Barton said. "It's your funeral. Don't say I didn't warn you."

"Duly noted," Johnny said cheerfully

Damon Bolt cleared his throat. "I'm free to go?"

"Free as air," Barton said. "If you're smart you'll keep going, a long way off from here."

"That's not my style, Sheriff."

"No, it wouldn't be. You'd rather stay and get killed."

"I'd rather stay," Damon conceded.

"We won't argue," the sheriff said.

"You know where to find me for the inquest."

"If you're still alive. Vince Stafford knows where to find you, too."

"I'll be waiting."

"He won't come alone."

"The undertaker can use the business. Things have been slow around here lately."

"Laugh while you can, Damon. It won't be so funny when the lid blows off this town."

"We'll see. We through here, Sheriff?"

"For now."

"I'll be on my way, then. I've got a date with the barber for a shave and a haircut," Damon said.

"Tell him to make the corpse presentable," Barton said sourly.

Damon nodded to Johnny and Luke. "Stop by the Spur later. I'll buy you a drink."

"It's a go," Johnny said. Luke nodded assent.

Damon went up the street to the barbershop and went inside.

"Decent fellow at that," Wade Hutto said, musing.

"Too bad he's got to die," Barton said.

Spectators gathered around the body of Bliss Stafford, gawking, buzzing. Deputy Smalls plucked at Barton's sleeve. "Somebody's got to tell Vince."

"You want to be the one to tell him his pup is dead?" Barton asked.

"No, thanks!"

"He'll find out soon enough," Wade Hutto said. "No doubt somebody's already on the way to the ranch to give him the word."

"Good news always travels fast," Barton said sarcastically.

"Careful, somebody might hear you," Hutto cautioned.

"At this point, who gives a damn?"

"I do," Hutto said. Gripping Barton's upper arm, he led him off to one side for a private chat.

"Somebody was bound to burn down Bliss Stafford sooner or later. He was a troublemaker and a damned nuisance," Barton said.

"Good riddance!" Hutto said heartily.

"Too bad it was the gambler. Some lone hand done it, some drifter, we could step back and wash our hands of it. But it ain't some nobody, it's Damon Bolt. He'll fight."

"He's got friends, too. Gun hawks. He'll make a mouthful for Vince at that. Hard to swallow."

"I hope he chokes on it," Barton said feelingly.

"Those Staffords have been getting too big for their britches. Trouble is, the town's in the way. Hangtown could get pretty badly torn up."

"No way to stop it. Blood will have blood. Vince won't rest till he's taken Damon's head."

"It's a damned shame, Mack. Say what you will about Bolt, he's a gentleman in his way. Vince makes a show of setting himself up as a rancher, but he's little better than an outlaw."

"He's a dog, a mangy cur. One with the taste of blood in his mouth," Barton said.

"Why not bring him to heel?" Johnny Cross asked.

Hutto and Barton started. Soft-footed Johnny had come up behind them without their knowing it.

"You shouldn't go around sneaking up on people. It's a bad habit," Barton said, with a show of reasonableness he was far from feeling.

"How much did you hear?" Hutto asked.

"Enough—and that's plenty. But I don't go telling tales out of school." Johnny got to the point. "Stafford's crowding you? Cut him down to size."

Hutto looked around to make sure nobody else was within earshot. Luke Pettigrew stood nearby, leaning on his crutch, grinning. But Luke was Johnny's sideman and knew how to keep his mouth shut, too.

"The Ramrod outfit is a rough bunch," Hutto said.

"No shortage of gunmen in Hangtown," Johnny said.

"But they've got no quarrel with Stafford."

"Pay 'em. They'll fight readily enough. There's enough hardcases in the Dog Star Saloon alone for a decent-sized war, and you can buy most of 'em for a couple bottles of redeye."

Hutto sniffed. "What's Damon Bolt to me, that I should start a range war with the Ramrod to save his neck?"

"Stafford's spread is on the south fork of the Liberty River. You're the biggest landowner on South Fork," Johnny said. "How long before he makes a move on you?"

"He wouldn't dare!"

"Why not?"

Hutto had no ready answer to that one.

"Why let him pick the time and place? Hit him now before he hits you," Johnny said, speaking the siren song of the Tempter.

Hutto was not easily swayed. "Your concern for my welfare is touching. What's in it for you?"

"I like Damon. He'll fight. Round up enough guns to hit Stafford where he's not expecting it and you can muss him up pretty good. The way to stop 'em is to bust him up before he gets started."

"We'd be taking a long chance," Hutto said, torn, fretful.

"It's your town," Johnny said, "but it won't be for long if you let someody hoorah it whenever he likes."

"I need time to think things out."

"Think fast. Move faster."

"Just itching for a fight, ain't you?" Barton said.

"Uh-huh," Johnny said. "That's what I do."